# Motor City Magic

## Donny Wilson

# Chapter 1

*They say stranger things have happened. But have they happened to you?*

**D**ark. Rich. Bold. Aromatic. There's nothing like the whir of a coffee grinder, the way it can cut through the high pitched laughter of the group of girls sitting at a cluster of oversized couches and soft chairs. My name is Nolan West. I own a coffee shop on the outskirts of Downtown Detroit called Detroit Bold. Detroit Bold sits at the edge of a bustling street, where the industrial remnants of the city's past meet the vibrant energy of its resurgence. The exterior is a blend of old brick and sleek glass, with large windows that let in plenty of natural light. The sign above the door is a striking combination of rustic wood and modern metal, with the shop's name etched in bold, stylish letters.

Stepping inside, you're greeted by a warm, inviting atmosphere that balances modern design with cozy, nostalgic touches. The walls are adorned with a mix of exposed brick and dark wood paneling, giving the space a timeless feel. Industrial-style pendant lights hang from the high ceiling, casting a soft glow over the polished concrete floor.

The counter, a long slab of polished walnut, is the heart of the shop. Behind it, the gleaming espresso machine and an array of grinders and coffee makers stand ready for action. Shelves lined with jars of beans, each labeled with their origin and roast date, add a touch of authenticity and a promise of quality.

To the left, a collection of mismatched yet harmonious furniture forms cozy seating areas. Plush couches in deep shades of burgundy and forest green, oversized armchairs with soft, worn leather, and sturdy wooden tables create a perfect blend of comfort and style. The walls are decorated with local art, rotating exhibits that give the shop a dynamic, ever-changing vibe.

The back wall features a chalkboard menu, artfully written with the day's offerings: everything from classic espresso drinks to unique house specials. A small stage in the corner hints at the occasional live music or poetry night, adding to the shop's eclectic charm.

The scent of freshly ground coffee beans mingles with hints of cinnamon, vanilla, and cocoa, creating an intoxicating aroma that makes you feel right at home. The sound of the grinder, the hiss of the steam wand, and the gentle murmur of conversations all blend into a comforting symphony that defines Detroit Bold.

From my vantage point behind the counter, I can see it all. The regulars who come in every morning, exchanging pleasantries and sharing snippets of their lives. The newcomers who pause, take in the ambiance, and then decide to stay a while, perhaps drawn in by the warmth of the space or the promise of a perfect cup of coffee.

This place is more than just a coffee shop. It's a haven, a community, a small piece of Detroit's beating heart. And it's mine. As for me, I'm a pretty average Joe of average height, average build, average education, and slightly above average business sense which caused me to dump everything I had into opening Detroit Bold—a coffee shop on the outskirts of Downtown Detroit. My love for all things coffee and six months abroad in Europe visiting every café I could find lead me here. Unlike some owners, I actually love to barista. My co-barista, Dawson, sat in the corner on the other side of the counter on a large down pillow. He's the most reliable employee I have and works for practically nothing but the odd scrap of food and belly rubs every quarter hour. Dawson is an enormous Canadian Golden Retriever whom I'm almost positive was a barista in a former life. While I don't let him drink coffee, he's wildly attracted to the smell. I put coffee grounds in my garden to deter animals and it ended up attracting Dawson who came sniffing around everyday before I gave in and adopted the fur ball.

Reaching behind a stack of old books, I retrieved a small cylinder of coffee beans. These weren't just any coffee beans. These were the finest beans from a small, family-owned farm in the highlands of Guatemala. Grown at an altitude that gave them a unique, complex flavor, the beans had been meticulously harvested by hand. The farm used traditional methods, ensuring each bean was picked at the peak of ripeness. They were then roasted to perfection—a medium-dark roast that brought out the beans' inherent chocolate and citrus notes without overpowering their natural sweetness. I had kept these beans hidden for a reason; they were my personal stash, a reminder of the time I had visited the farm and seen the passion and care that went into every aspect of their production. These beans were special, reserved for moments when I needed to reconnect with my love for coffee.

As I poured the beans into the grinder, the familiar aroma began to fill the air, rich and inviting. I stared intently at the coffee grinder almost as if I was looking through it. My stare became a scowl as the sound of the grinder seemed to suddenly shift.

I squinted and turned my ear towards the grinder. For a moment, I could swear music was coming from the device. It was subtle at first, a faint melody interwoven with the mechanical grinding noise. As I listened, the notes became clearer, coalescing into a hauntingly beautiful concerto that seemed to resonate deep within me. Each note was vivid, almost tangible, as if the music was being played directly into my soul.

The melody was mesmerizing, pulling me in, and I found myself swaying slightly to its rhythm. Just as I was about to fully lose myself in the music, sparks shot from the outlet, snapping me back to reality. The grinder's mechanical life came to a bitter end, leaving only the memory of the ethereal music lingering in my mind.

I stared at the now lifeless grinder, a mix of confusion and awe washing over me. What had just happened? I had never experienced anything like that before. Shaking my head, I tried to dismiss it as a figment of my imagination, but deep down, I knew there was something more to it.

"If I didn't know better, I'd say you're trying to burn this place down for the insurance money?" came a voice from the entranceway.

The voice belonged to Celeste. She was a short woman, but her presence filled the room. Her natural hair was styled in an enormous twist out, each curl seemingly defying gravity. Wisps of hair shot out wherever they saw fit, an unruly halo that was probably a health code violation. But she was so beautiful that I didn't care one bit. Her skin was a rich, deep chocolate, and her smile was a dazzling white crescent that contrasted beautifully against it. Her large, almond-shaped eyes were framed with thick lashes, and they seemed to twinkle with a mix of mischief and warmth as she looked at me. Her full lips were perpetually on the verge of a grin, and as she approached, the scent of coconut and shea butter wrapped around me like a comforting embrace.

"Earth to Nolan!" she exclaimed as she forced her way past me.

In my reverence, I hadn't realized I was still holding the coffee grinder's remains. Snapping out of my trance, I turned to face her.

"You know, if anything is going to burn this place down, it's going to be one of the million hair products you use."

"I only use natural products. You know that's why I work here, right? An endless free supply of coconut oil."

"Remind me to change your direct deposit to coconut oil. You know you're late, right? But since you're wearing yoga pants and a crop top, I'm definitely not complaining," I said, letting my eyes linger on her attire. Her form-fitting yoga pants and the cropped top showcased her toned physique, making her look effortlessly confident.

"Oh, I was here on time. I was just watching you destroy yet another coffee grinder," she replied, snatching the grinder cord out of the wall and beginning to stow it away.

"You didn't think to stop me?" I retorted.

As she bent over to toss the ruined grinder into a bin that served as a graveyard for my failed appliances, her shirt lifted slightly, revealing a hint of a tattoo I'd never noticed before. It trailed up her spine in crisp, dark lines, as if spelling out some secret word or phrase. As her shirt fell back into place, I looked up to see her catching my gaze with a knowing, crooked grin. My cheeks flushed with warmth, and I could feel my eyes widen.

"You're so cute when you're flustered. See something you like?" she teased, sauntering toward me.

I swallowed hard and looked down at her as she drew close. She stopped just short of walking directly into me, tilting her head up to meet my gaze. The golden light from the storefront window bathed her face, illuminating her features and making her eyes shine like hazel gems.

"What makes you think I'm flustered?" I challenged, maintaining my composure.

Before she could respond, the chime of the café door interrupted us. We both turned to see a tall, brooding man entering the shop. He was draped in a long, dark coat, his expression hidden beneath the shadow of his wide-brimmed hat. As he dusted off his jacket, I noticed his sharp, angular features and piercing gaze that seemed to take in every detail of the room. His presence was unsettling, a stark contrast to the warm, inviting atmosphere of the café.

Celeste was no longer standing in front of me; she had moved to pour a cup of coffee for the newcomer. The man's intense eyes followed her every move, making me feel a protective instinct rising within me. As Celeste approached him with the coffee, he nodded in acknowledgment, his expression inscrutable.

"To be continued," she said, glancing back at me with a smile before turning her attention to the customer.

I watched her walk away, her graceful movements mesmerizing. Shaking my head to clear my thoughts, I glanced back at the brooding man who so rudely interrupted a moment I'd been waiting for since the second Celeste came through my door several months ago. He was unpacking his satchel and rearranging things on the table. My stare became a glare.

"That's the guy who's been coming in here like twice a week for a couple of months, right?" I asked, my voice low enough to keep our conversation private.

"Fan?" she snapped back with a playful smirk.

"I know we have good coffee, but that's all he ever orders, and he just... gives me a strange vibe," I replied, still watching the man as he meticulously arranged his belongings.

"Well, I think he's cute," Celeste replied, tucking a curl behind her ear, a teasing smile playing on her lips. "And his order is coffee with cinnamon and sage," she shot back as she made her way to his table, throwing a glance over her shoulder.

"Coffee with cinnamon and sage?" I muttered to myself. "Sounds like a drink for a guy with a secret."

Celeste turned slightly, catching my eye as she walked. "Maybe he's just got good taste, unlike some people," she teased, her eyes sparkling with mischief.

I chuckled, trying to shake off the irritation. "Oh, come on, you're telling me you're not the least bit curious about what he's up to?"

"Maybe I am, maybe I'm not," she said, reaching the man's table. Her demeanor shifted effortlessly to friendly and professional as she greeted him, "Here's your coffee, with cinnamon and sage, just the way you like it."

The man nodded, a barely perceptible smile tugging at the corners of his mouth. "Thank you," he said in a deep, gravelly voice that resonated with quiet confidence. He glanced briefly in my direction, then back to Celeste, his gaze lingering on her a moment longer.

I watched their interaction, feeling a twinge of jealousy I tried to push aside. Just like that, our magic moment was cut short by Mr. Creepy Cinnamon and Sage.

Celeste returned to the counter, a teasing glint still in her eyes. "You should try talking to him sometime, you know. Might make a new friend," she said, leaning against the counter beside me.

"Yeah, maybe. But he seems more like the silent, brooding type. Not exactly my idea of a fun conversation," I replied, crossing my arms.

"Not everyone has to be as charming as you, Nolan," she quipped, nudging me with her shoulder.

"True, but if he keeps getting in the way of our banter, I might have to start charging him a jealousy tax," I joked, trying to regain my usual playful demeanor.

Celeste laughed, her eyes crinkling with amusement. "I'll make sure to add it to his tab next time," she said, her voice light and teasing.

I smiled back, grateful for her easy laughter and the way she could make even the most awkward moments feel natural. Still, the mystery man was a puzzle I couldn't quite solve, and I made a mental note to keep an eye on him, just in case he was more than just a fan of coffee and spices.

Celeste and I weren't always like this. Although I was madly in love with her from day one, I never crossed that line. We worked together. Hell, she worked for me. If that wasn't a surefire way to get canceled or slapped with a lawsuit, I didn't know what was. But as the days and weeks went by, it became clear that I wasn't the only one feeling the attraction. It all started with a little harmless flirting and graduated to moments like these. However, every time I had the chance to tell her how I felt, I pulled back.

At first, it was because she had just gotten out of a relationship two weeks into working here. The last thing I wanted to be was a rebound, and although she seemed heartbroken the day they broke up, she was entirely fine the next day. Come to think of it, she hasn't mentioned him once since then—which worked out in my favor. It let us get closer.

Celeste began working extra shifts, and we'd go shopping for the café together on the weekends. This was all when she had time. Not long after she began working here, she finally picked up the job she really moved to Detroit to acquire. She became the senior archivist at the Detroit Public Library. Celeste was so excited the day she got offered the job. She came into Detroit Bold on her day off just to tell me.

I'd never seen someone filled with more joy. She wrapped her arms around me and laid her head on my shoulder. I remember her warm breath on my skin as she screamed into my chest. I picked her up and spun her around, her legs knocking over an entire sack of coffee beans that we immediately slipped on. We went tumbling to the ground, her on top of me.

Coffee beans pressed into my arms and back while we lay there laughing like we were the only two people in the shop. Her laughter was infectious, lighting up her eyes and making me feel like the luckiest guy alive. That was the moment I knew it was entirely over for me. Celeste held a place in my heart that was deeper, richer, and bolder than even the most exotic cup of Joe.

As we lay there, catching our breath amidst the sea of scattered beans, Celeste leaned in closer, her eyes softening as she looked at me. "You know, you make a pretty good beanbag," she teased, a mischievous glint in her eye.

"Well, it's all part of the service," I replied, trying to keep my voice steady even as my heart raced. "Free bean massages for all our employees."

She chuckled, her fingers brushing against my cheek. "You're ridiculous, Nolan," she said, but her voice was warm and full of affection.

I wanted to tell her then how I felt, how much she meant to me. But instead, I just smiled and said, "Only for you."

We lay there for a moment longer, neither of us in a hurry to move. The world outside could wait. Here, amidst the aroma of freshly roasted beans and the warmth of her laughter, was exactly where I wanted to be.

As she finally got up, brushing beans from her clothes, she offered me a hand. "Come on, we better clean this up before someone sees and thinks we're nuts."

"Too late for that," I quipped, taking her hand and letting her pull me to my feet. "But I think they already knew."

We spent the rest of the day cleaning up, exchanging glances and smiles, each knowing there was something more between us but neither ready to say it out loud. Yet. But for now, those unspoken words hung in the air, a promise of something more.

# Chapter 2

*Out of the foil and into the grinder.*

E astern Market is a historic farmers' market not far from Downtown Detroit. It's been around for nearly two centuries and still holds the title of the largest farmers' market in the nation. I have vivid memories of summers here as a kid. My mother would bring me down to see my father on the weekends. He worked as a butcher, and he loved what he did. That was before he was gunned down in an alley after closing up one day.

Detroit is a beautiful place and gets a bad rap, which is unfortunately based on past truths. Yes, at one point, Detroit was the murder capital of the United States. However, it was never some lawless, dystopian wasteland the media made it out to be. Detroit is steeped in rich history, and Eastern Market is a big part of it.

The market itself is a vibrant mosaic of colors and sounds, where vendors hawk everything from fresh produce to artisanal goods. The air is thick with the scent of roasting coffee, grilling meats, and the earthy aroma of fresh flowers. Stalls are lined with baskets of ripe tomatoes, shiny bell peppers, and bundles of fragrant herbs. The market's red brick buildings stand as proud reminders of a bygone era, their walls echoing stories of the countless traders and shoppers who have passed through.

I come here to think, and of course, to get beans for my business. The success of any great café is in the beans, and my vendors have the good stuff! Celeste and I usually come to the market together when the new stock comes in, but she was at the library doing whatever archivists do. One of these days, I told myself, I'd finally visit the library and see Celeste in her element. It was only fair since she sees me in mine every week.

Today was particularly busy at the market. I weaved through a bustling crowd of families, artists, and hipsters all sharing the common goal of hunting for Detroit's best finds. Unfortunately, the only available parking was several blocks from where I picked up my stash. My muscles screamed at me as I lugged a huge sack of coffee beans over my shoulder and made my way back to the car.

Something in my periphery caught my eye. I looked over and saw the brooding man from the coffee shop. He was perusing a vendor who had a long table of books and tapestries. For as many months as he'd been coming into the shop, I'd never seen him at the market.

Curiosity got the better of me. I decided to walk over and see what else I could learn about this guy. Taking a deep breath, I readjusted the burdensome bag of beans on my shoulder. But as I approached, I looked up and the man was gone. More puzzling still, the book vendor had vanished as well. In their place was a table selling what looked like t-shirts and coasters.

The market may have been busy, but there's no way I could have lost him and the vendor in a crowd. I crossed to the place where he had been standing and approached the new vendor.

"Excuse me, do you sell books and tapestries?" I asked, hoping to get some clarity.

"No, but if you're looking for a coaster you've never seen before, you've come to the right place," the man replied, handing me a coaster to look at.

The coaster was made from what looked like an old vinyl record. Even before reading it, I recognized the coaster I was holding as Miles Davis' 1959 record, *Kind of Blue*. It was one I had in my extensive vinyl collection. I tapped the coaster against my palm and looked at the rest of the items for sale before addressing the vendor once more.

"The man that was here before me, what did he buy?" I asked, hoping for a lead.

"What man?" the vendor replied, his face blank.

I was definitely more than a little puzzled, but I bought the *Kind of Blue* coaster and bid the vendor farewell. Hoisting the beans on my back, I took one more look around the market and headed back to my car.

The encounter left me with an unsettling feeling. Either I was going crazy, or that man was more interesting than I had thought. As I walked away, I couldn't shake the feeling that something strange was afoot in the market, something that perhaps tied back to the mysterious man who frequented my coffee shop. The market, with all its history and secrets, had given me more than just coffee beans today—it had given me a mystery.

Back at the cafe, I finished hauling in the beans, wishing I had more than my barista Jalen to help me. Jalen could make a damn good cup of coffee, but he was thin as a rail and struggled to lift even the most modest hauls from the market. Beads of sweat covered Jalen's face as he leaned heavily on the counter. I clapped him on the shoulder in thanks.

"Jalen, why don't you hit the gym with me sometime?" I asked, grinning.

He reached under the counter and retrieved an energy drink of some sort. He chugged it before answering.

"Not everyone can be as jacked as you. You must have been hitting it pretty hard the last few months," he replied, giving me a nod of admiration.

I looked down at my polo, which was slightly damp from sweat, and noticed I was definitely filling it out more. On average, I run a few times a week, do calisthenics, and really just do basic strength training at the gym to stay in shape, but he was right—I had put on a bit more muscle than usual.

I made a silly show of flexing my bicep and answered, "It's all in the beans!"

"Yeah, okay," he replied sarcastically and went back to the corner behind the counter where he was sitting when I arrived.

I smiled and took a look around the shop. There were lots of regulars, a group of high schoolers giggling in the corner, and in the back at his normal table was the mystery man. He was writing feverishly in a journal of some sort, totally engrossed. His coffee cup looked untouched; it had to be cold by now. Jalen and I took at least 10 minutes bringing in supplies. Maybe I would go over and offer him a warm-up, see what I could find out.

As I took a step, I saw his hand hover over his mug. Ripples of some sort seemed to flow from his palm. Moments later, steam rose from the mug, and I could distinctly smell sage and a hint of cinnamon. My heart almost beat out of my chest. What just happened?! Did he just heat the cup with his hand?

I looked over at Jalen, whose nose was still in his book. No one else witnessed this. My throat felt dry, and my mind was beside itself. Was I imagining things? The encounter at the market had already left me on edge, and now this?

Before I could muster up the courage to confront him, he slapped his journal shut, securing it with a leather strap, rose, and hurried out the main entrance, passing me in a whiff of sage and so many questions.

As he brushed past me, I caught a glimpse of intricate tattoos on his forearms, symbols I couldn't recognize. My curiosity was piqued, and I felt an inexplicable urge to follow him, to understand what I had just witnessed.

But I stood frozen, torn between the rational part of my mind that told me to leave it alone and the curious part that wanted to dive headfirst into whatever mystery this man held. My eyes followed him as he disappeared into the street, leaving behind an aura of mystery and a lingering scent of sage.

Who was he? And what was he doing in my café? I shook my head, trying to clear my thoughts, and returned to the counter. But the questions kept swirling in my mind, intertwining with thoughts of Celeste and the strange occurrences that seemed to be happening more frequently.

Jalen looked up from his book and noticed my distracted state. "You good, boss?"

"Yeah, just thinking," I replied, trying to sound casual.

"Thinking about what?"

"Oh, just...coffee stuff," I said, waving my hand dismissively.

But as I resumed my duties, a part of me knew that this was more than just "coffee stuff." There was something happening beneath the surface of my seemingly ordinary life, and I couldn't shake the feeling that the mysterious man was somehow connected to it all.

# Chapter 3

*So you want to learn magic.*

Sunday afternoon was slow. While the cafe usually saw a steady stream of patrons coming and going as they made their way back to other areas of the city, today seemed to only bring in the odd customer every half hour or so. This, however, worked in my favor. The man I witnessed being a human stovetop had returned and was sitting at the same table in the back of the room. I stared at the man, wondering if I would witness another odd event. I was startled from my surveillance when Celeste jabbed me in the arm a lot harder than I thought was necessary.

"Hey! I called your name like three times. If I didn't know any better, I'd say it was you that has the crush on Mr. Cinnamon Sage," Celeste said, as she slid the man's order towards me. Her playful smile was infectious, but I couldn't help but feel a twinge of embarrassment.

I chuckled, trying to play it cool. "I'm just curious about him, that's all. You know how I get about regulars."

Celeste raised an eyebrow, clearly not buying it. "Curious enough to stare at him like he's about to sprout wings and fly away?"

"Hey, it's a slow day. Gotta keep myself entertained somehow."

She leaned in, her eyes twinkling with mischief. "Maybe he's a wizard or something, and you just caught him mid-spell."

I laughed, grateful for her ability to lighten the mood. "Yeah, maybe he's here to enchant the cafe and make the beans roast themselves."

"I'm taking off early for my after-hours shift at the library," she said, slipping into a more serious tone. "Are you okay? You've seemed distracted all afternoon."

"Me? Yeah! I'm good. Go! I'll close up. Thanks for today."

"Now I know something is up. Since when do you thank me for doing my job?"

"Get out of here! Try not to get coconut oil and Eco-styler on the rare books," I barbed, throwing a teasing smirk her way.

"That's more like it. See you tomorrow." She gave me a quick hug, her familiar scent lingering in the air as she left.

I watched Celeste walk out, her presence always a comforting constant in my life. But as soon as she was gone, the weight of my curiosity settled back in. The cafe felt emptier without her, a stark contrast to the puzzling presence of the man in the back.

I took a deep breath, steeling myself for what I hoped would be a casual interaction. I crossed to the front door, discreetly locking it and turning the open sign to closed. This was it—my chance to see what was really going on with this guy.

I headed back to the counter and started to pick up the man's coffee. I paused, looking down at the still-steaming mug, admiring the foam heart Celeste had crafted on top. I couldn't help but smile, thinking about her attention to detail and the warmth she brought to the cafe. But then I remembered the oddity of the man, and with a smirk, I plucked an ice cube from the cooler and plopped it into the coffee, watching as the design dissolved.

Satisfied, I stirred the coffee and removed my apron, draping it over the counter before making my way to the back of the cafe. As I approached, I took stock of what I could. The man was seated, but I could tell he was tall—several inches taller than my 6'0. He had a thick beard and a broad frame under the weathered jacket he donned. In his hands was a leather-bound book, the title of which had been worn off long ago and was no longer legible.

"Here's your coffee," I said, setting the mug on the table with a deliberate clink.

He looked up, his piercing eyes meeting mine, and for a moment, I felt a strange sense of familiarity, as if I had seen him before, not just in the cafe but somewhere deeper in my mind.

"Thank you," he said, his voice deep and resonant, almost like a song. There was an aura about him, a presence that seemed to fill the room.

"So, you come here often," I quipped, trying to ease the tension with humor. "Do you always order the same thing?"

He smiled faintly, a hint of amusement dancing in his eyes. "I'm a creature of habit, I suppose."

"What's with the book?" I asked, nodding towards the tome in his hands.

He glanced at it, then back at me. "Just something I've been working on. It's a bit of a passion project."

"A writer, huh? What's it about?"

He hesitated, a flicker of something—uncertainty, maybe?— crossing his face. "It's complicated," he finally said, a cryptic response that only fueled my curiosity further.

"Well, if you ever need a second opinion, I'm a pretty decent critic," I offered, trying to keep the conversation light while probing for more.

He chuckled softly, a sound that was surprisingly warm. "I'll keep that in mind."

As I stood there, an awkward silence stretched between us. I felt like I was on the edge of something profound, a mystery waiting to unfold, but unsure of how to reach out and grasp it.

"Anyway, enjoy your coffee," I said, stepping back. "Let me know if you need anything else."

"Thank you," he said again, his gaze lingering on me for a moment longer before returning to his book.

I retreated to the counter, my mind a whirlwind of thoughts and possibilities. "I bet Celeste would love to get her hands on that," I thought as I glanced back at the man. Being too eager and too interested is the best way to get found out, and yet I began shifting things around on the counter, all the while keeping a close eye on the man.

A couple of minutes ticked by, and I was about to give up hope when the man finally reached out for the mug. Instead of grabbing it by the handle, he placed his hand over the mug, almost grasping it. The air around his hand began to shimmer and ripple as if I was staring directly into an oven. But there was more. There seemed to be a faint glow surrounding his fingertips. My heart began to hammer in my chest, and I could feel the blood rushing in my veins. What had I just witnessed? Steam rose from the mug as the man brought it to his lips.

"Holy shit!" The words escaped my mouth before I could stop myself. I made a beeline for the table and planted myself across from the man, grinning like a madman.

"You just heated that up with your hand!" I blurted, my voice a mixture of disbelief and exhilaration.

He looked at me with a knowing smirk, his eyes twinkling with an amused glint. "You don't seem particularly surprised."

I leaned forward, resting my elbows on the table as I tried to wrap my mind around what I'd just seen. "I'm more surprised you're not waving your hands and wiping my memory."

"The thing is, I have wiped your memory. It just doesn't seem to stick. This is the third time we've had this conversation."

"Or you're just shit at magic? Or am I some powerful chosen one who can't be enthralled by your sorcery?" I joked, though a part of me hoped there was truth in it.

"Well, I don't know about chosen, but you do have the touch," he replied, his voice rich with an enigmatic quality that only deepened my curiosity.

"You mean like that 80's song from Transformers?" I quipped, trying to keep the mood light, though my heart was pounding with a mixture of fear and exhilaration.

"Yes, like the song from Transformers. But if you start singing it, I'm going to make you forget that song altogether."

"Touchy! So?" I stared at him intently as the question hung in the air.

"So what?" he replied.

We were quiet for a long time while we stared at each other. My heart raced, and I noticed my hands shaking before I started again.

"So, aren't you going to have the talk with me? Let's skip over the part where you try and convince me I'm crazy and just tell me the truth. Magic is real, and if magic is real, all the other supernatural stuff like werewolves, genies, and the Loch Ness monster must be real too. Gimme the spiel."

"No. I'm not going to have the talk with you. You are going to let me finish my coffee in peace, and tomorrow I'm going to find another café that can serve me hot coffee."

"Or, or you can teach me just that one tiny trick you use to keep your coffee warm, and I'll never bother you again."

"Magic is like riding a bike. You'll want to go faster, farther, but there's no safety gear for magic. You won't just scrape your knee. You'll be dead."

"That was ominous, and oddly close to 'the talk' you said you wouldn't have with me."

The temperature in the room seemed to rise several degrees, and the hair on my arms stood up. The man's eyes glowed bright orange for just an instant, and then he began to smile broadly. He gestured for me to sit down.

He snapped his fingers and turned his palm towards the ceiling. A ball of light hovered just above his skin, casting an ethereal glow that danced across the walls. Beads of sweat formed on my forehead as the ball began to burn hotter and brighter. I was acutely aware of the smell of sage, cinnamon, and burnt sugar. The man closed his hand, and the brilliant globe winked out of existence, taking every trace of heat with it.

"Is that something anyone can learn? Teach me!" I exclaimed, feeling an almost desperate yearning to understand and wield this strange power.

The man looked at me quizzically and shook his head.

"Why would I teach a stranger magic? A pushy, dare I say underhanded stranger?" he replied, his tone teasing yet firm.

"Free coffee for life!" I offered, half-joking, half-serious.

"You've got a deal!" the man replied sardonically. He scooped up his book, rose to his feet, and headed towards the door.

"Wait!" I rose and shouted after him. "What do you want? Name your price."

The man stopped at the door and glanced back, his hand resting lightly on the handle. For a moment, I thought he might leave without another word, but with a sigh, he turned and strode back to the table, each step deliberate and measured. He moved like someone accustomed to being in control, his posture unyielding, his presence filling the room in an unsettling way.

He sat down across from me, still clutching the weathered leather-bound book he'd carried in, cradling it almost like a child. He leaned back in the chair, the legs creaking slightly under his weight, and fixed me with a long, steady stare. His eyes were dark, bottomless pools of something I couldn't quite place—was it curiosity? Amusement? Or something far more calculating? Whatever it was, it pinned me to the spot, like I was a specimen under a microscope.

The air between us seemed to thicken, growing almost tangible. I shifted uncomfortably, resisting the urge to fidget. He didn't blink, didn't move, just stared. It wasn't the kind of look that came from idle observation—it was like he was sifting through me, piece by piece, pulling apart my essence to see what made me tick.

When his eyes met mine, something clicked inside me, a sensation so visceral and immediate it was like stepping off a ledge without realizing it. It wasn't just his gaze; it was the weight behind it, an intensity that pressed against my chest, my mind, my very being. There was something ancient in his eyes, a depth that felt both foreign and eerily familiar, like a half-forgotten melody from a dream.

My thoughts spiraled as I tried to place the feeling. It was as though he wasn't merely looking at me but through me, past the surface, into the recesses of who I was—or who I thought I was. It wasn't invasive, not exactly, but it was disarming, like someone rifling through a box of your memories without asking permission.

The room seemed to blur at the edges, narrowing to just the two of us. I opened my mouth to speak, to break the suffocating silence, but nothing came out. My mind searched frantically for an anchor to steady me, a name for this overwhelming sensation, but it eluded me. Just as I felt on the cusp of grasping it, the man spoke, his voice low and steady, each word cutting through the fog like a razor:

"You're not quite what I expected."

His tone was neutral, but there was an undercurrent of something I couldn't quite pin down. Respect? Disappointment? Amusement?

"Well," I managed to choke out, my voice coming out hoarser than I intended, "I get that a lot."

His lips twitched into a faint, almost imperceptible smile, one that didn't quite reach his eyes. "I imagine you do."

"You have the gift, my friend. Most people would have missed what I did entirely. They wouldn't have felt it, and they definitely would not have been able to see it." He rose, walked closer and stood face to face with me.

"Why do you want to learn magic?" he asked.

The weight of his question hung in the air, pressing down on me as I stared back at him. Why did I want to learn magic? The man's tone was neutral, but something about the way he asked made the moment feel monumental, like I was standing on the edge of a precipice, and the wrong answer might send me tumbling into an abyss.

I took a breath, letting the familiar smells of the shop ground me. The rich scent of coffee beans and the faint sweetness of vanilla wafted in the air, mingling with the soft hum of the espresso machine cooling down after a long day. The room felt smaller than usual, the dim light casting long shadows that danced across the walls. This wasn't just another question. This was the question, one that demanded more of me than I was sure I could give.

His gaze bore into mine, unyielding and expectant. It wasn't intimidating, exactly, but there was a weight to it, as though he could see every thought, every hesitation, every buried secret. His eyes seemed to demand honesty, and yet I couldn't help but feel like he already knew what I was going to say.

"Why do you want to learn magic?" he repeated, his voice softer this time but no less piercing.

Why? I asked myself again, the word echoing in my mind. Before this moment, the answer had seemed so simple. Curiosity, fascination—maybe even boredom. But now, faced with the reality of it all, those reasons felt paper-thin. There was something deeper, something gnawing at the edges of my consciousness. It was as though this encounter had stirred something within me that I hadn't known was there, something primal and ancient.

"Because...because I have to," I said finally, my voice barely more than a whisper. "Something is drawing me toward it. It's like...it's like I've been missing a piece of myself, and I didn't even know it until now. When you used magic, I felt something—something I can't explain. It wasn't just awe or wonder; it was like I'd found something I was supposed to have all along. Like I was connected to it."

I fell into the seat behind me, the weight of my own words stealing the strength from my legs. My chest felt tight, and my head buzzed with the enormity of the revelation. Was I really saying this? That magic wasn't just some curiosity for me, but something intrinsic? Something essential?

The man's lips curved into the faintest smile, the kind that made you feel like you'd passed some unspoken test. He sat down across from me, his movements deliberate and smooth. Reaching for the coffee mug, he placed it in the center of the table between us.

"You pull this coffee mug toward yourself," he said, his voice calm but carrying an unmistakable challenge. "And I'll teach you magic. My price is simple: you let me use this coffee shop however I see fit. A place to recharge, to unwind. It won't interfere with your day-to-day. But first, the test."

I stared at the mug, my thoughts racing. A sly smile tugged at my lips as an idea formed. If magic was about creativity, then I could find a way to cheat the system. Without hesitation, I darted my hand toward the mug, ready to pull it across the table.

But I never reached it.

My arm froze mid-motion, every muscle locked in place as though I'd been encased in cement. Panic surged as I tried to move, but my body refused to obey. I was stuck, helpless, with my hand hovering uselessly above the table.

"Rule number one," the man said, his tone carrying a sharp edge of amusement. "Don't try to outsmart me. This isn't one of your silly young adult novels or one of your outlandish comic books. If you want to move the mug, you'll do it the right way—with magic."

He released his hold on me, and I staggered back in my chair, rubbing my arm as sensation returned. My face burned with embarrassment, but the fire in his eyes told me there was no room for shame here. I had to do it his way, or not at all.

I gasped, trying to steady my breathing. "You're gonna have to teach me that one," I said through ragged breaths, attempting humor to mask my unease.

He simply arched an eyebrow, his expression cool and unreadable. "Let's see if you're teachable first."

I stared at the mug like it held the secrets of the universe. In a way, maybe it did. The shop was beyond quiet, save for the faint hum of the espresso machine cooling down behind me. The rich aroma of coffee lingered in the air, grounding me in this surreal moment. The dim lighting cast long shadows across the room, and the faint creak of my chair felt deafening in the silence.

"How the hell am I supposed to move this thing?" I muttered to myself. My thoughts raced. How could I possibly manipulate something with my mind when I'd just learned magic was real five minutes ago? I leaned forward, resting my hands on the table. My fingers flexed against the worn wood as I closed my eyes and repeated a mantra in my head.

"Magic is real. Magic is real. Magic is real."

I opened my eyes and focused on the mug. Nothing happened. The room remained still, save for the man's quiet, almost predatory gaze. My jaw clenched, frustration bubbling to the surface. I flexed my fingers against the worn wood of the table, the grooves and scratches a testament to years of service and countless conversations. This was my space, my sanctuary. Now, it felt like a battleground.

The mug sat there, resolute and mocking. I could feel the man's gaze burning into me, equal parts amusement and expectation.

Frustration clawed at me, but I wouldn't let doubt creep in after everything I had witnessed in such a short period of time.

Focus, Nolan. This was your chance, your moment to prove you weren't just some coffee-slinging nobody. I straightened in my chair and fixed my gaze on the mug. It was so unassuming, just a vessel for coffee, yet it felt like a key to something so much bigger.

The air around me shifted subtly, like the room itself was holding its breath. The comforting aroma of coffee became sharper, more electric, tingling at the edge of my awareness. I focused on the mug, trying to recall the moment he'd heated it with his hands. There had been a spark, a ripple in the atmosphere that felt alive. I chased that memory, reaching for that same sensation.

Warmth blossomed in my chest, spreading down my arm to my fingertips. It was faint at first, like the flicker of a match, but it grew stronger, surging with a pulse that matched my heartbeat. I extended my hand toward the mug, and for a moment, it felt like the world narrowed to just the two of us—the mug and me.

The mug trembled.

A soft scraping sound broke the silence as it slid across the table, spilling warm coffee across the back of my hand. Its heat grounded me in the reality of what I'd just done.

I stared, wide-eyed, my breath catching in my throat. "Holy—"

"You're a wizard, Harry," the man quipped in a mockingly gruff voice, breaking the tension with a well-timed pop culture reference.

I couldn't help but chuckle at his delivery. "Thought you said those books were silly," I replied, raising an eyebrow.

"Everybody gets one," he shrugged with a smirk. Then his expression shifted, becoming more serious. "You asked me my price. Detroit is very old, filled with more history and mystery than you could possibly imagine. There are more places in this city that hold much more magic than you'll ever see me do. I'm surprised this is the first time you're encountering it. I am in town in search of something that lies beneath the Eastern Market. It's old, it's valuable, and it will require your help to obtain. You help me obtain it, and I'll teach you all I know about magic."

"Valuable like I will no longer need to buy lottery tickets valuable?" I replied, my mind racing at the possibilities. I had visions of extravagant vacations and endless luxuries.

"Valuable to me. You shouldn't be buying lottery tickets anyway," he replied with a hint of admonishment. "Help me with my research, give me a place to work, and when the time comes, help me acquire the artifact."

I hesitated, the weight of his words settling over me like a fresh cold brew. There was something in his voice—a reverence, almost a nerdy enthusiasm for the mystery of it all—that was contagious. Despite my better judgment, I felt the pull, the thrill of the unknown beckoning.

"You've got yourself a deal," I said with a smile, feeling both excitement and trepidation.

"My name is Alan Tempris. You can call me Tempris," he said as he extended his hand, his eyes never leaving mine.

I took his hand and gave him a firm shake. "Nolan," I replied. His grip tightened to an almost crushing level, and he leaned forward, his voice dropping to a low, serious tone.

"Rule number two, tell no one about me or the arrangement we have. Magic is not a toy and trust is not a given. Understand?" he said, his words carrying an unspoken weight.

I could feel my palm heating up, and I knew at that moment he was using the same kind of magic he'd just used to warm his drink. The heat intensified, and I could feel my palm begin to blister. I've never been one to back down from a fight or a challenge, so I began to squeeze, giving as well as I was getting. Just as the heat became unbearable, Tempris smiled, and I felt a cold rush of energy flow into my hand as he released it. I turned my palm upward and, to my astonishment, it was fine. The skin was slightly red from the pressure of the handshake, but there were no blisters, burns, or signs that he'd attempted to melt my arm.

"I'll teach you that one too," Tempris said with a taunting grin, his eyes gleaming with amusement.

"What's with all the secrecy and the menacing magical handshake?" I replied, still flexing my fingers, trying to shake off the lingering sensation.

"I need you to know magic is not a toy. You are about to learn about a whole world of things that you couldn't possibly imagine. Magic isn't out in the open for a very good reason, and you need to understand that. Knowledge is power, and it is also very dangerous. Tell me you understand," Tempris said as his gaze bore into my soul, his words carrying the weight of years of wisdom and experience.

I let a moment pass to fully take in Tempris' words. He was right. From the moment I saw him create a ball of light in his hand, I knew this was not just something much bigger than my understanding—it was bigger than me. The air seemed to thrum with the possibilities of what lay ahead, and for a moment, I was overwhelmed by the magnitude of what I was getting into.

"I understand," I said, meeting his gaze, feeling the gravity of the situation settle over me like a cloak.

"Good! First things first, we will need a place to train. There's a lot to learn, and you'll want to practice in private."

"I've got just the place!" I said, my mind wandering to the dirty, unused cellar beneath our feet.

As we both stood, a thought struck me, and I turned to Tempris with a curious look. "Hey, you said earlier you wiped my memory. Did you actually do it, or were you just messing with me? I mean, should I be worried about forgetting where I parked my car or suddenly wondering why I have a coffee shop?" I asked, feigning concern.

Tempris chuckled, a deep, rumbling sound that seemed to fill the room. "Relax, Nolan. I'm a magician, not a monster. I only dabble in mind-wiping on Tuesdays," he replied with a wink. "You're safe... for now."

"Good to know," I said, laughing. "Guess I'll avoid making any deals with you on Mondays then."

"Smart man," Tempris grinned, following behind me. "Now, let's see if you can remember how to find this training spot of yours."

Visions of ancient secrets and untapped power filled my thoughts as I considered the journey that lay ahead. Magic was real, and I was about to dive headfirst into its mysteries. Whatever lay beneath the Eastern Market, I was determined to uncover it, and with Tempris as my guide, I felt ready to embrace the unknown.

# Chapter 4

*Teachable moment.*

The cellar beneath the café was dark and musty, the air thick with the scents of mold, old coffee, and stale air. It was the kind of place that seemed to swallow light and sound, a hidden nook in the bustling world above. The space had gone mostly unused, except for the few times I stored excess coffee on the battered shelves that lined the stone walls. Cobwebs clung to the corners, and a thin layer of dust coated everything. This was the first time anyone besides Celeste and I had been down here since Detroit Bold opened.

Tempris surveyed the room with a critical eye, shrugging off his jacket and draping it over one of the shelves. He knelt and placed his hand on the cold stone floor, and suddenly, a soft blue light sprang forth from several symbols that appeared as if summoned from another realm. The glow bathed the cellar in an ethereal light, casting long shadows that danced across the walls. I could feel a thrumming power emanating from the runes, an ancient energy that seemed to vibrate through the air.

"These runes and sigils will keep this area safe from any permanent damage we may cause," Tempris explained, his voice calm and reassuring. "From here on out, you could shout bloody murder down here and not a soul would hear you."

"Good to know," I said, my voice dripping with sarcasm. "Reassuring to hear that our little secret magic club has a soundproof cellar. Just like every well-adjusted hobby."

I looked down at the strange alphabet glowing beneath me, a complex web of lines and curves that shimmered with power. "Am I going to have to learn this?" I asked, gesturing at the runes. "Because I can tell you right now, my handwriting isn't great, and as much as I like to travel, foreign languages aren't my magic school specialty."

Tempris chuckled, rubbing his temple as if he were dealing with a particularly slow student. "'Magic school,'" he echoed with amusement. "You can call it whatever you like. There's no school for little magic users like you see on TV—not one that matters, anyway."

I opened my mouth to ask more questions, my curiosity bubbling over like a shaken soda, but Tempris held up a hand, cutting me off with a knowing smile. "Patience, Nolan. All will be revealed in time. For now, just know that these runes will do their job. And as for learning them, let's just say you'll pick up what you need to know as we go along. Think of it as... on-the-job training."

I couldn't help but chuckle at the notion of learning magic in the same way one might learn to fix a leaky faucet. As the blue light continued to pulse gently from the floor, I felt a sense of anticipation mixed with trepidation. The air in the cellar felt charged with possibility, and I couldn't shake the feeling that I was standing on the brink of something extraordinary and possibly dangerous.

"Alright, Professor Tempris," I said, offering a mock salute. "Let's see what kind of magic I can stir up without blowing up the joint."

Tempris grinned, a mischievous gleam in his eyes. "That's the spirit. Now, let's get started. We have a lot to cover, and the clock is ticking."

"Let's get the basics out of the way," Tempris began, his voice steady and measured as he launched into what felt like a well-rehearsed lecture. "The world of magic is vast. Unless you have the gift, it's easy to mistake magic for the mundane."

He swept his arm through the air in front of me, and for a fleeting moment, I caught a glimpse of something—a vague shimmer that vanished as quickly as it had appeared. It was like a ripple in the fabric of reality, barely perceptible but undeniably there.

"Magic exists on a different visible spectrum than we're used to," he continued. "This Veil masks most magic from the mundane eye. Where someone with the gift might see someone wink out of existence in a flash of light, an ordinary person may just notice someone is no longer standing there."

I leaned forward, intrigued by the concept. "The Veil?" I asked, wanting to know more. "Is it like a force field or something?"

Tempris smiled, clearly pleased by my curiosity. "The Veil is more like a natural law," he explained, "a barrier that exists between the magical and mundane worlds. Just as gravity or electromagnetism are fundamental forces of nature, so too is the Veil. It's what keeps the two worlds separate yet intertwined, allowing them to coexist without interfering with one another."

As he spoke, Tempris created another orb of light, this one larger and more brilliant than the last. The orb hovered above his palm, casting ominous shadows across his face and illuminating the cellar with an ethereal glow. It was mesmerizing, the kind of light that seemed to draw you in and hold you captive.

"I could hold this in front of someone," Tempris said, gesturing to the orb, "and they might notice it's a bit warmer than usual, but they wouldn't see it unless I wanted them to. It's that simple." He twirled his hand, and the orb vanished, leaving only the afterimage burned into my retinas.

I nodded, trying to wrap my head around the concept. "So, the Veil is like a filter?" I ventured. "It decides what we can and can't see?"

"Precisely," Tempris replied. "The Veil is like a filter that screens out magic from those who aren't attuned to it. For those with the gift, it's a matter of focusing past the Veil to see the truth beneath the surface. But for everyone else, magic remains hidden in plain sight."

I mulled this over, fascinated by the idea that there was a whole world hidden just beyond the reach of most people. "It's like a secret society," I mused aloud, "existing right under our noses."

"Exactly," Tempris said with a nod. "And just like any secret society, there are rules and hierarchies, traditions and customs. But more importantly, there are responsibilities. With knowledge comes power, and with power comes the duty to use it wisely."

I leaned back against the stone wall, absorbing everything he was telling me. It was a lot to take in, but I felt an electric thrill at the prospect of uncovering these secrets and learning to wield magic myself.

"So, how do I see past the Veil?" I asked, eager to get started. "Is there a spell or something?"

Tempris chuckled, shaking his head. "No spell required," he said. "It's more about attuning your senses and expanding your awareness. You've already seen glimpses of it, even if you didn't realize it. That's why you noticed the shimmer and the warmth of the orb."

I nodded, recalling the faint shimmer I'd seen earlier and the heat from the orb. "So I just need to pay closer attention?"

"Precisely," Tempris replied. "Pay attention to the details, the things that don't quite fit. Trust your instincts, and let your curiosity guide you. With time and practice, you'll learn to see past the Veil and tap into the world of magic that lies beyond."

"What about people who don't know they have the gift but witness these amazing things and have no one to help show them?" I asked, my curiosity piqued. It was a genuine question, one that tugged at a deep-seated empathy I hadn't fully acknowledged until now.

"Those are the unfortunate few who sometimes end up in insane asylums or living their days on the streets spouting what, to most of us, sounds like nonsense," Tempris replied, his tone turning somber. "However, most of the time, our subconscious suppresses what we can't understand. Our brains have a way of tricking us into seeing the ordinary even when we know there is more."

His words struck a chord with me, sending a ripple of unease through my thoughts. I had always considered myself perceptive, but now I wondered how much I had missed, how many magical moments I had dismissed as mundane. What if I had been one of those people, lost and confused, with no one to guide me?

The thought lingered as Tempris continued, his voice commanding my attention. "First thing! You will listen to me at all times. Magic is not inherently dangerous. However, depending on the wielder and your affinity, it could be deadly."

"What do you mean by my affinity?" I asked, intrigued by this new term.

"Your aptitude, your leaning, your knack," Tempris explained. "We've already determined you can use magic; we just have to determine what kind. This isn't Harry Potter, where everyone can just learn everything. Everyone can, of course, do the basics, which we call Universal Magic. These are simple magical manipulations that anyone with magical ability can grasp, like minor telekinesis or light manipulation. But beyond that, there is always an affinity towards one, or on the rare occasion, two things. Now it's time for you to learn yours and just how magic works."

As he spoke, Tempris stepped out of the circle and motioned for me to step inside. I hesitated for a moment, taking a deep breath to steady myself before moving forward. The circle was an intricate tapestry of glowing runes and symbols, each one pulsating with a faint blue light.

I walked forward and stood roughly in the center of the glowing marks. Immediately, I could smell ozone, and the hairs on the back of my neck stood up. The sensation was electric, like static in the air before a storm. But there was something else too—a strange sense of familiarity, as if I had done this before, in another life or another time.

"You'll get used to that feeling after stepping into the wards a few more times," Tempris said, noticing the discomfort on my face. "The wards I placed here will keep all magic used inside of the circle from spilling out and harming anything or anyone."

I nodded, still trying to process the myriad of emotions swirling within me. There was fear, yes, but also a profound excitement. I was standing on the threshold of a world I had only dreamed of, and I was eager to take the plunge.

I started to speak, to voice my concerns, but Tempris continued, his eyes fixed on mine with an intensity that silenced any doubts I had.

"Your affinity will reveal itself in time," he said, his voice a mix of reassurance and authority. "Trust the process. Magic is as much about self-discovery as it is about power. You'll find your way."

"Alright, Professor Tempris," I said, offering a mock salute. "Let's see what kind of magic I can stir up without blowing up the joint."

Tempris grinned, a mischievous gleam in his eyes. "That's the spirit. Now, let's get started. We have a lot to cover, and the clock is ticking."

Tempris walked around the circle of runes with a deliberate, measured pace, each footfall echoing softly in the dark cellar. His presence filled the room with an aura of calm confidence, as if he had performed this same lesson countless times before.

"Do you ever hear a song although there's no music playing? Smell something familiar for no apparent reason? Have an itch you just can't scratch?" he asked, his voice echoing in the stillness. "These can be signs of magic. Grasping the concept, applying the concept, and doing it efficiently are nearly impossible for most people."

I watched him with a mix of fascination and skepticism, leaning against the cold stone wall. "It doesn't seem that hard," I said, trying to inject some humor into the moment. "I did just move a cup like twenty minutes ago." I flashed a self-satisfied smile, but Tempris was unfazed.

"It's true, you have a gift, but what you accomplished was barely the basics," he replied, pausing in his stride to look at me intently. "You have to understand the concept of magic. Let's try something. Open your mind and slow your thoughts."

He stopped pacing and stood still, the faint orange glow in his eyes flickering like a candle flame. I felt a tingle of anticipation, but nothing seemed to happen. Maybe I wasn't focusing enough, I thought. I took a deep breath, closing my eyes and trying to push away the clutter in my mind. I concentrated on the memory of the first time I witnessed Tempris perform magic—the scent of sage, something sickeningly sweet, and there was something else.

"A note," I whispered, almost afraid to break the silence. "I hear a music note. C?"

"Very good, Nolan," Tempris said, nodding approvingly. "Now, even if you heard the correct note, how do you describe it? What sound does it really make? This is where your mind needs to take you. Look at the broken shelf on the wall. Imagine rubbing your fingertips across it. What does it feel like? How would you describe the color red to a blind person?"

I paused, furrowing my brow in thought. "It's uh...red," I admitted, my voice trailing off as I realized the difficulty of the task.

"Exactly. When you begin to understand the workings of magic, it creates new synaptic pathways, new connections in your brain. Your mind finds ways to explain the new, the unexplainable." His words were accompanied by a renewed glow in his eyes, an intensity that seemed to ignite the air around us.

The cellar felt alive with energy, a pulsing current that was just beyond the edge of my perception. It was as if the world had been draped in an invisible veil, and I was being invited to peek behind it. I took another deep breath, pushing aside my doubts, and tried to dive deeper into the sensations swirling around me.

"Focus your thoughts," Tempris instructed, his voice a steady guide. "This time, find your way through to what you really know is there."

I concentrated on the note I'd heard, letting it resonate in my mind. The sound was pure and clear, vibrating through my very being. I reached out with my senses, trying to grasp the intangible, the unseen threads of magic that I could feel weaving through the air. The sensation was electrifying, as if I was standing on the brink of something vast and unknown.

Suddenly, I felt a shift, a subtle change in the atmosphere. The world seemed to tilt ever so slightly, and I sensed something—a presence, a force—that had been lurking just out of sight. It was exhilarating and terrifying all at once, like stepping onto a tightrope stretched across an abyss.

"Do you feel it?" Tempris asked, his eyes locked onto mine, searching for understanding.

"I think I do," I replied, my voice barely above a whisper. "It's like... there's a whole other layer to everything."

"Precisely. Magic is not just about bending reality. It's about perceiving the reality that already exists but remains hidden to most," Tempris said, his voice filled with an enthusiasm that matched my own growing excitement.

Closing my eyes, I reached out with my thoughts, trying to find that elusive sensation I had felt before. For a moment, there was nothing but darkness and silence, and I worried that I was getting nowhere. Seconds ticked by, each one stretching into eternity, as my focus began to drift. I could feel doubt creeping in, whispering that perhaps I wasn't cut out for this.

Then, just like that, it happened again—a flicker, a spark, a whisper of something just beyond my grasp. What was it? A sound in the distance? A chime? No, it was heat! A wave of warmth washed over me, enveloping my body like a comforting embrace. It was more than just a physical sensation; it was a presence, something alive and vibrant. My body relaxed, yet I felt as though I was flexing a muscle I never knew I had.

And there was something else. Coffee! The unmistakable aroma filled my senses, complex and bold, with the richness of a dark roast. It was a scent I knew well, almost like putting on an old glove. But there was one problem: there was no coffee in the basement, none at all.

I opened my eyes, and to my astonishment, my entire body was engulfed in flames. Bright orange and red danced across my skin, flickering like a living entity. Panic surged through me as I frantically shook my arms and patted them down, trying desperately to extinguish the fire. The flames clung stubbornly to my body, but I noticed something strange—they weren't burning me.

Confusion mixed with terror as I realized my shirt was indeed starting to catch fire, and instinct took over. I dropped to the ground, rolling frantically across the cold stone floor. But instead of smothering the flames, the heat intensified, roaring to life around me. I tried to scream, but when I opened my mouth to inhale, fire filled my lungs.

The sensation was both excruciating and surreal. My chest burned as if a forge had been lit within, and my throat felt raw and scorched. I coughed, and the sound that emerged was not a scream, but a WHOOSH!—a release of energy that reverberated through the room.

Dizziness threatened to overwhelm me, and I was entirely consumed by fear. My mind raced, imagining Celeste finding the shop reduced to a smoldering crater with nothing but my charred remains left behind. I had always feared a foolish death, but immolation by magic was a new and terrifying twist.

And then, it was over.

I opened my eyes, expecting to see the blackened remains of my own body, but instead, I found myself staring at the ceiling. My lungs filled with air, sweet and cool, and my flesh was intact. Aside from a few singes on my shirt, there was no evidence that I had been consumed by fire.

The basement was silent except for the echo of clapping that bounced off the stone walls. I turned my head to see Tempris standing there, a bemused expression on his face.

"I guess we found your affinity," he said with a sly grin, stepping into the circle and looking me over. "Not bad for your first try, though I'd recommend working on your fire control."

I sat up, still shaking from the experience, a mix of relief and disbelief flooding through me. "Affinity?" I asked, my voice hoarse but alive with curiosity.

"Yes, your natural alignment with a particular element or type of magic," Tempris explained, crouching down beside me. "Yours appears to be fire. It can be unpredictable and powerful, much like yourself, I imagine."

I chuckled weakly, the humor and mystery of the situation not lost on me. "Unpredictable, sure. Powerful? I think I nearly barbecued myself. How am I not dead?" I asked, the seriousness of my question cutting through the laughter.

Tempris shook his head with a knowing smile. "Not to say it can't be done, but you can't harm yourself with your own magic. Your magic is unique down to every cell in your body. What's more, you can control, absorb, and use what equates to Magic Atoms."

"Magic Atoms?" I repeated, intrigued.

"Yes, Magic Atoms, or 'MAs,'" he said, waving a hand dismissively, as if the explanation was too simple. "They're everywhere, attaching themselves to those who can use magic. It's a sloppy science lesson on magic, but I'm no teacher."

I nodded, trying to wrap my mind around the concept. "So these MAs are the reason I can use magic?" I asked.

"Not as such," Tempris replied, tilting his head thoughtfully. "They are more the reason magic exists and is able to be wielded. Think of them as the building blocks of magic, the smallest particles that make up the fabric of magical reality."

I looked at my hands as if I could somehow see something as small as an atom. The thought was mind-boggling, yet oddly exciting. Something occurred to me as I gazed at my unblemished skin.

"Can I run out of magic?" I asked, a note of concern creeping into my voice.

"No," Tempris said with a chuckle. "Magic is an infinite resource for those who know how to tap into it. But more on that shortly."

He backed out of the warded circle, crossing his arms as he leaned against the stone wall. The basement seemed somehow more alive now, charged with an energy I hadn't noticed before.

"Now, do it again," Tempris instructed, his voice firm but encouraging. "And this time, try not to set yourself on fire!"

I took a deep breath, feeling a mixture of excitement and apprehension. Closing my eyes, I focused on the sensation of magic, that warmth, and the smell of coffee. The memory of the fire still lingered, a reminder of both the power and the danger of what I was attempting.

Reaching out with my mind, I concentrated on the Magic Atoms, imagining them swirling around me like a living mist. I could almost feel them, tiny particles humming with potential, waiting to be called upon. I focused on harnessing them, drawing them toward me without the chaos of before.

Slowly, I opened my eyes, expecting to see flames. Instead, a gentle glow surrounded my hands, a shimmering aura that flickered like candlelight. The warmth was there, comforting and steady, without the overwhelming heat.

Tempris nodded approvingly, his expression one of pride and satisfaction. "There you go, Nolan. That's more like it. Now, remember this feeling, this control. It's the first step in mastering your magic."

I couldn't help but smile, the joy of success mingling with the thrill of discovery. The mystery of magic still loomed large, but for the first time, I felt like I had a grasp on it—a tenuous, fragile hold, but a hold nonetheless. I wasn't sure what I expected when I asked to learn magic, but conjuring fire wasn't even on my list, let alone near the top. I mean, fire? Sure, it might be useful for relighting a pilot light or dealing with a particularly stubborn candle during a power outage, but the idea of wielding something so inherently dangerous made my palms sweat. Tempris had assured me this was just the first step, though his assurance felt more like a dare.

I stared at the tiny flame flickering in my palm. It was mesmerizing, alive in a way that no science class or backyard bonfire could ever explain. The heat was real, but the fire didn't burn me—it felt warm, like holding sunlight in my hand. "Cool," I muttered, trying to suppress a grin. And then it hit me: I was holding fire. Real, magical fire. What if it didn't stay small? What if I sneezed and turned the whole coffee shop into a smoldering pile of ash?

Tempris smirked, leaning against the wall like he had all the time in the world. "Relax," he said, as though he could sense the internal panic brewing behind my wide-eyed stare. "It's not going to explode unless you want it to."

"Not exactly reassuring," I muttered, carefully closing my fingers to snuff out the flame. The heat dissipated, and I flexed my hand, half-expecting to see scorch marks. Nothing. My skin was as smooth as ever—well, except for the faint coffee stains I could never seem to scrub off.

"First step's the hardest," Tempris said, his tone shifting to something almost encouraging. "Now you know you can do it. The rest is about control, focus, and not setting yourself on fire."

"Thanks for the vote of confidence," I replied, rolling my eyes. "And here I thought this would be as easy as waving a wand and saying, 'Alohomora.'"

Tempris chuckled, a low, rumbling sound that seemed to vibrate through the room. "Wands are training wheels, kid. You've got raw potential. Harnessing it without a crutch is what separates the real mages from the dabblers."

I leaned back against the dusty wall, the weight of his words settling over me. "So what's next? Do I get to summon a dragon or something?" I joked, though part of me half-hoped he'd say yes.

"Not unless you're ready to lose a limb," he deadpanned, his smirk returning. "For now, let's stick to not burning down the place. Baby steps."

Putting one foot in front of the other had always seemed like such a simple concept, but with magic now in the mix, it felt like walking a tightrope over an active volcano. One wrong move, and the consequences could be catastrophic. But the thrill of it—the sheer possibility—was addictive.

I took stock, breathing deeply for what felt like the first time in an eternity. The cellar was dimly lit, a single bulb swaying overhead casting long shadows against the exposed brick walls. The air was cool and damp, smelling faintly of coffee grounds, earth, and the faint tang of old iron pipes. It should have been comforting—after all, this was part of my shop—but now it felt like a secret world hidden beneath the mundane one I'd lived in until today.

I continued to let the familiar smells of roasted coffee and damp stone ground me. The rows of old barrels and the antique espresso machine in the corner suddenly felt like relics from another life—a simpler, safer life that I was willingly stepping away from.

"So," I said, breaking the silence, "what's next? Or are we just going to stand here until one of us dies of old age?"

Tempris tilted his head, his dark eyes gleaming with something unreadable. "Next step is learning what not to do. And trust me, Nolan, that list is a hell of a lot longer than you think."

Great. A crash course in magical don'ts. My confidence wavered, but the flicker of flame in my memory was impossible to ignore. If this was just the beginning, what else was I capable of?

"I'm up for the challenge," I said, trying to sound more certain than I felt.

Tempris pushed off the wall, his movements smooth and deliberate. "Good. You're going to need that attitude. Magic isn't for the faint of heart."

As he turned to examine the shelves, I caught myself wondering—not for the first time—what I'd gotten myself into. But there was no turning back now. Whatever lay ahead, I was ready to face it. Probably.

The memory of the flame felt like both a promise and a warning. One foot in front of the other. Baby steps. Even if those steps could one day lead me straight into the fire.

# Chapter 5

*Show me your moves.*

I t took everything I had to keep my head upright as I stood in the cellar. Several days had passed since Tempris took me on as his impromptu student. I stretched my limbs and knew I'd been mentally, emotionally, and physically pushed to the limit. An open mind was one thing I prided myself on having, but what was this new and insane world I forced my way into?

"Don't lose focus," Tempris shouted, shaking me from my introspection.

I shot him a nod and returned to the exercise I'd been doing for the past two hours. After several attempts at calling forth fire with varying success, I was finally able to conjure a ball of fire in my hand. Tempris had me working on changing the size of the flaming globe over and over. I still had very little understanding of what was fueling my magic, but I knew in some way it was taking a toll.

"That fireball is cute, but make it hot. Your fear is holding you back. The number one killer of focus—and magic—is fear. Trust in your power and in yourself. You cannot burn yourself," Tempris explained.

He was right. I was afraid. My mind replayed the moment my body was engulfed in flames over and over again. I couldn't recall a single moment in my life that was more terrifying. The dark, feral, instinctual part of my subconscious knew fire was dangerous and that the pain of my flesh being ignited would be immense. However, Tempris was right. I'd been on fire, and there was no pain. There was shock, yes, and so much fear—but no pain. He said my magic was my own, down to a cellular level.

I saw Tempris smile, and I could feel my own grin begin to grow on my face. I focused. I focused with everything I had. The red-orange ball of fire grew hotter, brighter, and more intense. Waves of heat rippled in the air, and sweat poured from my brow, more from concentration than anything else. The flame began to burn blue, then a brilliant white.

"Hot enough for you?" I managed through gritted teeth, my voice strained against the fireball roaring in my palm.

Tempris didn't even flinch. No witty comeback, no sly grin—just that same damn impassive stare, like he was watching a mildly interesting documentary. And then it hit me. Or rather, it hit me, flipped me, and body-slammed me into a world of pain.

My fingers started to tingle, and before I could fully process that, they went completely numb. Then my brain decided to host the Olympics without informing the rest of my body. Waves of vertigo hit me like a sledgehammer, the world spinning violently out of sync. Cold numbness raced through my skull, followed by a thousand fiery needles prickling every corner of my mind. The fireball fizzled out, but the circus inside my head only got louder. I clutched my temples and realized—somewhat belatedly—that I was on my knees.

"When did I get down here?" I muttered, though it sounded more like a wheeze.

My breathing became shallow and frantic as I collapsed fully onto the cold stone floor. Long, deep breaths didn't help; in fact, they seemed to amplify the insane carnival of pain. Spikes, razors, and shattered glass all collided in my skull, each more insistent than the last.

Through the haze, Tempris stepped forward, his boots scraping softly against the floor. He crouched beside me, his face annoyingly calm as he examined my writhing, gasping form like a bug pinned under glass.

"I'm going to need you to stop thinking," he said, his tone flat and maddeningly unaffected.

"Stop—stop thinking?" I rasped, my voice breaking under the strain. Was he crazy? The only thing I could do right now was *think*. Think about the pain, think about what I'd done wrong, think about choking the life out of this smug bastard the second I got back on my feet.

"Yes. Stop thinking," he repeated, as though he were instructing a toddler. "Right now, your brain is overrun with magical energy. Imagine your neurons are packed tighter than rush hour on the Lodge. They've blocked the natural flow of magic your body needs to function. In essence, your brain is asleep—though it feels more like it's being stabbed with tiny, flaming pitchforks."

"No kidding!" I barked, though the sound came out more like a strangled groan.

"Unfortunately, you can't walk this one off," he continued, undeterred. "The only way to fix this is to clear your mind. Completely. And before you ask—no, you can't *think* about clearing your mind. You just have to *do it*."

"Do it, he says," I muttered, clutching my head as another wave of searing cold swept through me. "Sure. Let me just flip my brain's off switch. No problem."

As the pain deepened, I cycled through every thought in my arsenal, each one more useless than the last. I thought about how none of this would have happened if I'd just served Tempris his coffee and sent him on his way. I thought about what it might feel like to punch him square in the jaw, preferably after using magic to make my fist a sledgehammer. None of these helped.

Then I thought about Celeste—the time she booked a yoga instructor to use the multipurpose room in the back of the café. She'd dragged me into the class, insisting it would be "good for my soul." I'd spent the whole hour trying not to pass out from the stench of patchouli and wondering how a yogi could smell like old cheese. But there was a moment—a brief, fleeting moment—where I'd found peace. My breathing had slowed, my mind had cleared, and for just a second, everything felt still.

I latched onto that memory like a lifeline. Focus. Breathe. Don't think. Just...breathe.

Then my mind betrayed me. I started thinking about Celeste—her skin, her laugh, the way her eyes lit up when she teased me. And the pain returned, sharper than ever. I felt myself slipping, the darkness at the edges of my vision threatening to swallow me whole.

And that's when it clicked. The darkness. The silence. I didn't fight it this time. I grasped it, let it wash over me, and for once, my brain shut up. Slowly, excruciatingly, the prickling sensation began to fade. The vertigo eased, and the cold receded, leaving me gasping and trembling on the floor.

"Why didn't you warn me?" I rasped, my voice barely audible over my labored breaths.

Tempris leaned back on his heels, his expression as unreadable as ever. "I felt now was as good a time as any to test the upper limits of your ability."

I glared at him as I struggled to my feet, my legs shaking like a newborn giraffe. "You're a real piece of work, you know that?"

"Flattery will get you nowhere," he replied with a smirk.

As I steadied myself against the wall, I made a mental note: never, under any circumstances, try to impress Tempris again. Not unless I had a death wish—or an aspirin the size of a Buick. Something felt strange. My ears were ringing, and the smell of coffee bloomed in my nose once more.

"You should know the limits of your magic," Tempris continued, his voice calm and steady. "But you must also learn to push past them safely. Magic is not just a tool; it's an extension of yourself. It can be your greatest ally or your worst enemy, depending on how you wield it."

Despite the lingering pain, a sense of accomplishment washed over me. I had tasted the raw power of magic, felt its boundaries, and survived. It was exhilarating and terrifying all at once. However, the smell of coffee I experience when I use my magic continued to intensify.

"I feel weird," I said, getting to my feet and flexing my joints. The sensation was unsettling, like an orchestra tuning up in my bones, each note slightly off.

"You are going to feel a bit odd for a little while. You will be exhausted and sore tomorrow, but it will pass. Overuse of magic won't kill you, but it will force you to pass out if you can't get it under control," Tempris said, stepping closer to me. His words were reassuring, yet there was an undertone of seriousness that suggested I had crossed a line I didn't fully understand.

"No, I mean, I feel really weird," I pleaded, trying to convey the growing dissonance in my body. It was as if my entire being was caught between two realities, neither of which felt entirely solid.

Suddenly, my vision turned blue, and it felt like my bones were vibrating at mach speed. The smell of coffee and ozone tickled my nostrils. My senses were overwhelmed, a cacophony of stimuli clashing in my mind. Then, without warning, arcs of lightning forked from my fingertips. It was as if my body had become a conduit for some untamed force, desperate to escape.

Bolts of lightning shot out in every direction, lancing off the walls of the warded barrier. Tempris lifted his hand, and another kind of barrier protected him from whatever was happening to me. The sight was both terrifying and absurdly comical, like a scene from a poorly written superhero film. My body spasmed, and before I knew it, I lost consciousness, collapsing into the comforting embrace of darkness.

I awoke to find Tempris sitting by my side. I had vague memories of him trying to speak to me, his warm hands rubbing my temples, and his dark eyes boring into mine with more concern than I'd seen from him thus far. It was oddly comforting to know he had been there, grounding me in my moment of chaos.

"There you are. You had me worried for a moment. But just a moment," Tempris said as he sat back on his haunches. His relief was palpable, a gentle wave washing over the tension in the room.

"I am not a teacher. I have never taught anyone. You had me worried that I had made a mistake and that I let something happen to you. I thought I killed you," he confessed, a rare vulnerability in his voice.

"Aw, Alan, I didn't know you cared." I smirked, trying to lighten the mood despite my pounding headache.

"More than you know," he replied softly, his words carrying a weight that surprised me.

This was the first time I'd ever seen Tempris seem unsure of himself. He looked sad, frustrated, and there was a distant look in his eyes as if he was grappling with some internal conflict. It was a side of him I hadn't expected, and it added a new layer to the enigmatic figure who had barged into my life.

"Hey, how about we have coffee?" I suggested as I rose to my feet, eager to return to something familiar and comforting. "Really, I feel fine, and you look like you could use a little caffeine." I made my way toward the stairs, and Tempris smiled, following behind me.

Moments later, Tempris was sitting at the counter, and I was doing what I do best. My hands blurred from the bag of beans to the grinder to the portafilter basket on the espresso machine. The motions were automatic, a well-rehearsed dance that required no conscious thought. I tamped down the grounds until they were packed and smooth, the scent of freshly ground coffee filling the air with its rich, comforting aroma. I could feel Tempris' eyes on me, watching with an intensity that was both unsettling and reassuring.

As the espresso machine hissed and sputtered, I found solace in the routine, in the familiarity of creating something tangible and real. The world of magic was strange and unpredictable, but here, in the simple act of making coffee, I found my anchor.

"You know, this is one kind of magic I'll always understand," I said, taking a deep breath of the fragrant steam rising from the espresso machine. The rich aroma of roasted beans mixed with the familiar scent of the café, wrapping around me like a comforting embrace.

Tempris chuckled, with a nod. "Magic comes in many forms, Nolan. You just have to find the one that speaks to you. What made you want to learn all of this?" Tempris asked, gesturing at the array of coffee accoutrements with genuine curiosity.

"This? This is nothing. I'd say it's like learning anything else, but as we just saw, that's far from the truth. I'm not going to pass out from making an Americano," I replied, flashing a grin. The process of making coffee was second nature to me—a dance of movements and smells that required no conscious thought.

Tempris laughed before speaking. "There is art and technique with what you do, just like with magic. The more you learn, the more you'll understand," he said, his eyes filled with a mixture of admiration and intrigue.

I turned and placed two demitasse cups and a plate of assorted biscotti on the counter before him. The cups were small, elegant, and filled with a rich, dark brew. Tempris gave the cups a quizzical look.

"You already know how I take my coffee, and I never order espresso," he said, almost turning his nose up at the small steaming mugs. His expression was one of cautious skepticism, like a cat encountering a cucumber for the first time.

"Smell that," I said simply, gesturing toward the cup. The aroma was inviting, complex, and layered with unexpected notes.

Tempris brought one of the cups to his nose and inhaled deeply. "Sage with just the barest hint of cinnamon!" he exclaimed, his eyes widening in surprise.

"I infused, roasted, and ground my own blend as kind of a thank you for taking me on as a student. It's definitely not the flavor profile I go for, but I think I know why you drink it," I said and brought one of the cups to my lips, curious about the concoction I had created.

A smirk crossed Tempris' mouth, which he tried to hide behind the cup. "That obvious?" he said before snapping a small biscotti in half, the sound crisp and satisfying.

"Your magic. Your magic smells like sage. Not like the regular sage you'd burn or put in food, but it's definitely...sagey," I replied, savoring the unique blend I had crafted.

"You would be correct," he said in response, acknowledging the connection with a nod.

"At first, I thought using magic was messing with my senses, but I realized the magic was making that scent," I continued, the realization dawning on me as I pieced together the sensory puzzle.

"Consider the fragrance your magic gives off as kind of a signature. People can have similar signatures, but no one's is ever exactly the same. The smell and intensity can also sometimes differ depending on your emotions, and before you ask—yes, the scent of your magic can be shaped based on what you've surrounded yourself with—how you live your life. Your magic smelling like coffee is probably because it's a comforting, familiar smell, one that resonates with who you are at your core," Tempris explained, his words weaving a tapestry of understanding that wrapped around my mind.

"So that's why you like sage in your coffee? To mask your use of magic?" I asked, piecing together the practical implications of his preferences.

"At first. Then it just became a habit, and I liked the taste. However, many mages do practice using the scent of their magic in their everyday lives, when they can. I knew a magician whose magic smelled like gunpowder and another who smelled like old cheese—although he just had bad hygiene," he finished, adding humor to his explanation with a wry smile.

"Should I mask my magic?" I asked curiously, wondering if I needed to adopt similar practices.

"You needn't bother. You're around coffee enough that no one will notice, and in the magical community, it's really no big deal," Tempris answered, dismissing my concerns with a casual wave.

I hesitated for a moment, then asked, "So, what kind of magic do you use? I've never actually asked."

Tempris paused, his expression momentarily unreadable. "My magic is...a bit more universal," he replied vaguely, shifting his gaze to the steaming cup before him. "It's not as easily categorized as others."

Before I could press him for more details, he quickly added, "It allows me to adapt to various situations, which is why I'm often traveling."

His tone suggested that he was keen to move on from the subject, so I let it slide. There was warmth and sincerity in his eyes, a rare glimpse of the man behind the enigmatic façade.

"Thank you for this, Nolan. I travel a lot, and I'm usually never in a place long enough to make friends. This…this is nice. Not—not that I'm saying we are friends or anything, I just—" Tempris stumbled over his words, his usual confidence faltering as he tried to articulate his feelings.

I raised my cup to his and cut him off mid-sentence because I could see he was beginning to ramble. For the first time, I felt like he was uncomfortable, unsure of how to navigate the unfamiliar terrain of camaraderie.

"To friendship," I said and clinked our cups together, the sound resonating in the quiet café.

Tempris just stared at me with a surprised look on his face, clearly taken aback. We both smiled and sipped our coffee. I wrinkled my nose at the taste, the sage lingering on my tongue like a curious guest overstaying their welcome.

"Sage? This is gross," I said, stirring some sweetener into my mug to mask the herbal assault on my taste buds.

Tempris let out a chuckle and continued enjoying his odd coffee preference, clearly accustomed to the flavors that seemed so foreign to me. In that moment, amid the laughter and the warmth of the café, I felt a bond forming, one built on mutual respect, shared experiences, and the magic that connected us in unexpected ways.

The soft clink of a mug on the table stirred me from my swirling thoughts. Tempris leaned back in his chair, tapping the rim of his now-empty cup with one finger before his gaze settled on me. There was something in his eyes—something calculating, but also amused.

"There's still a little daylight left. How about one more lesson? It's an important one. Come on." He stood, grabbing his jacket from the chair beside him in one smooth motion, like a man who already knew I wouldn't refuse.

I blinked, caught off guard. "Field trip?" I asked, standing up and gathering our mugs.

Tempris didn't answer right away. Instead, he gave me one of his signature smirks—the kind that always seemed to imply he knew something you didn't—and strolled toward the door, his steps leisurely but purposeful.

I quickly rinsed out the mugs, placing them behind the counter, then slipped into my jacket. The familiar smell of coffee grounds mingled with the crisp scent of approaching evening as I followed him outside.

Up until now, all our lessons had been in the café's cellar—a cozy, secretive space filled with the scent of roasted beans, wood, and the faint hum of magic I was still getting used to. But stepping outside? That was new. And if there was one thing I'd learned about Tempris, it was that "new" usually meant "trouble."

# Chapter 6

*Eye opening.*

F all had wrapped Detroit in its familiar, unpredictable embrace. The scent of wet leaves mingled with the faint metallic tang of the city, and the streets seemed to shimmer under the warm glow of a sun that couldn't quite decide whether to stick around or retreat behind thick, grey clouds. The breeze was cool and crisp, tugging at the edges of my jacket until I shrugged it off, mirroring Tempris. Typical Michigan weather—fifty degrees one day, seventy-five the next. It kept you on your toes, much like the city itself.

We walked mostly in silence, the rhythmic click of our footsteps echoing off buildings that had seen generations come and go. Detroit's pulse beat steadily beneath us—alive, stubborn, and resilient. The streets were quieter today, the usual bustle of Eastern Market replaced with the slow trickle of locals out for a stroll and vendors packing up their remaining wares. I stretched my arms and rolled my shoulders, feeling the ache of muscles neglected in favor of training my magic muscle. My usual gym routine had taken a back seat, and while my mind felt sharper, my limbs were itching for movement.

Tempris led us down Gratiot Avenue before veering off onto Randolph Street. We passed familiar landmarks—old brick facades, art installations, and murals that told stories of the city's history and its people. He stopped abruptly at Cadillac Square, right in the middle of the intersection, and turned to face me. His eyes sparkled with that particular glint that told me he was about to drop some obscure historical knowledge.

"Look around," he said, sweeping his hand in a broad gesture. "175 years ago, this was Eastern Market. Of course, it wasn't called that back then. It was the heart of Detroit's original farmer's market, where traders sold hay, wood, and other essentials."

I frowned, taking in the bustling square around us. "Here? Hard to imagine. Now it's just a place where people grab coffee and wait for their rideshares."

Tempris smirked. "That's Detroit for you. It's always changing, always evolving. The city sheds its skin, but its bones—its magic—stay the same. Every cobblestone, every brick holds a story."

I let out a low whistle, feeling a pang of embarrassment. Born and raised here, and yet somehow, Tempris—a visitor—seemed to know more about my hometown than I did. "Guess I should brush up on my local history, huh?"

"Never too late," he replied with a grin, and we continued walking toward Campus Martius.

The square was alive with the energy of the season. Trees stood proudly, their leaves a riot of reds, oranges, and golds. Families milled about, kids chasing each other around the central fountain, their laughter mingling with the distant sound of a street performer playing jazz on a saxophone. The scent of roasted chestnuts from a nearby cart mixed with the aroma of freshly brewed coffee, creating a comforting, familiar warmth.

Tempris chose a bench near the center of the square, the fountain's gentle spray casting a fine mist that caught the fading sunlight. We sat, the quiet hum of the city settling around us like a blanket.

"Look around you, Nolan," he said, his voice soft but commanding. "Remember what I told you—magic lives on a different spectrum than what most human eyes can perceive. There are places, like this one, where it becomes easier to see. Times of day when it reveals itself if you know what to look for."

I scanned the area, taking in the ordinary beauty of Detroit in the fall. The sunset bathed the buildings in a warm, amber glow, and the light danced across windows like liquid gold. Leaves swirled in the breeze, whispering secrets as they tumbled to the ground. It was beautiful in its own right, but I wasn't seeing anything particularly magical.

Tempris was watching me, that ever-present smirk tugging at the corner of his mouth. "Now that you've taken in the mundane, I need you to focus. Feel for it. Remember what it felt like the first time you conjured magic. That tingle in your fingertips, the way the world seemed to shift just slightly out of sync."

I closed my eyes, taking a deep breath. The air smelled of damp earth and city grit, a strange but comforting combination. I reached inside myself, letting that familiar spark of magic flare to life. My heart rate picked up, and I felt the warmth spread through my chest, down my arms, into my fingertips.

When I opened my eyes, the world was different.

A shimmer of gold danced through the air, like tiny fireflies flitting from tree to tree. The fountain sparkled with an ethereal light, each droplet of water holding a prism of color. Magic clung to everything —people, buildings, even the cobblestones beneath my feet. It was like seeing the world through a kaleidoscope, patterns and hues shifting with every movement.

"It's beautiful," I breathed, the words slipping out before I could stop them.

Tempris leaned back, crossing his arms. "Isn't it? That's what I wanted you to see. Magic isn't just fireballs and lightning bolts. It's life itself. It's woven into the fabric of this city, into every story, every breath. Most people live their lives never knowing it's there. Never knowing that the extraordinary is right beside them."

I tore my gaze away from the dazzling display, my heart heavy with a sudden melancholy. "It's kind of sad, isn't it? That so many people go their whole lives without ever seeing this?"

Tempris's expression softened. "Perhaps. But not everyone is meant to see it. Magic chooses its vessels carefully. You asked why everyone can't use it—it's the same reason not everyone can be an artist or a mathematician. Some people are born with a connection to it, a spark that can't be taught."

His words hung in the air, heavy with meaning. I let the magic fade from my vision, the colors and light dissolving into the ordinary world once more. The sunset was gone, replaced by the cool, shadowed hues of twilight.

"I guess I've won some kind of cosmic lottery, huh?" I said with a wry grin.

"You've been given a gift," Tempris corrected. "It's up to you to decide what to do with it."

We sat in silence for a moment, the weight of his words settling over me like a second jacket. As the streetlights flickered on and the city transformed into its nighttime self, I couldn't help but feel like I was standing on the edge of something vast and unknowable.

"Alright," I said, standing and stretching. "How about we practice some more?"

Tempris chuckled, rising to his feet. "Eager, aren't we? Good. You're going to need that enthusiasm. This journey is only just beginning."

As we made our way back to the café, the lights of downtown Detroit casting long shadows across the pavement, I couldn't shake the feeling that my life was about to change in ways I couldn't yet comprehend.

"Hey," I said, breaking the silence as we walked. "You really think magic is hiding in places like this? Campus Martius, Eastern Market?"

Tempris gave me a sidelong glance, his eyes gleaming with that familiar mix of mystery and amusement. "Oh, Nolan. Magic isn't hiding. It's always been here. You just needed to know where to look."

I tried focusing my vision on the magical spectrum again. This time it was much more difficult, like trying to tune a radio dial that kept slipping between static and a distant, beautiful song. The shimmer I had seen earlier wasn't nearly as vivid, and my concentration wavered with each step forcing me to focus more intently. But every now and then, a glint of gold would catch my eye —a flicker on a lamppost, a twinkle on a storefront window, or a shimmer that danced along the the ever chilling breeze.

We walked past a street musician I remember seeing quite often. He was strumming his guitar. His notes drifted into the air, and for a brief moment, I caught a glimpse of something extraordinary: magic clung to him, swirling around like glittery, faint smoke from a fire. It clung to his hands, coiling around his fingers, and drifted upwards, like it was being carried by his music.

Was he aware of it? Did he know he was weaving magic into the very air? Or was it just... part of him?

I glanced at Tempris. While he did have more magic clinging to him than the average passerby, it wasn't as overwhelming as I'd expected. Maybe he wasn't the magical powerhouse I thought. He did say he had research in his blood.

Then I remembered: *What about me?*

Was I walking through the streets of Detroit with a glowing aura that shouted, "Hey! This guy just learned magic five minutes ago!" I made a mental note to find a mirror and take a good long look at myself when I got back to the café. The idea of seeing magic clinging to me like a second skin made my heart pound with excitement—and more than a little bit of dread.

Has all of this always been around me?

The thought tugged at me like a loose thread on a sweater. Had I really gone my whole life not noticing the magic woven into the city I loved? Was this why certain places always felt a little... different? The old brick alleyways, the forgotten murals, the way some buildings seemed to hum with a life of their own. It wasn't just history—it was magic.

We turned a corner, and I nearly stumbled into Tempris, who had stopped abruptly. He was staring at a statue near Campus Martius, his expression distant.

"You ever think about how much of Detroit was built on top of things we'll never know about? Things I'm hoping to lean about," he said, almost to himself. "Layers and layers of history. Some of it we remember, most of it we forget. And magic—real magic—gets buried along with it."

"That's kind of poetic for someone who just let my fry my brain with a fireball," I quipped, rubbing my temple for effect.

Tempris snorted. "Poetry and pyrotechnics aren't mutually exclusive."

I chuckled, despite the lingering memory of overusing magic. The man was an enigma—a strange mix of brooding scholar and sarcastic showman. He had a way of making the mysterious seem mundane, and the mundane seem magical.

We passed a group of tourists snapping photos in front of the Soldiers' and Sailors' Monument. I glanced at the statue, and for a split second, I thought I saw one of the stone figures *move*.

I blinked. Was that...? No, it had to be a trick of the light. Right?

Tempris caught my look and grinned. "Seeing things already?"

"Maybe. Or maybe Detroit just hits different when you've got magic in your eyes."

He nodded, his gaze scanning the square like he was reading a map only he could see. "Magic is old. It's older than this city. Older than any of us. And it doesn't disappear—it hides. It waits."

We walked in silence for a moment, his words hanging in the air like an unspoken challenge. *It hides. It waits.*

As we neared the edge of Campus Martius, a streetlight flickered, casting long shadows over the cobblestones. For a brief moment, I thought I saw those same golden shimmers dancing along the cracks in the pavement, winding their way through the city like veins of light.

"I'm starting to think this whole thing is going to be a lot more complicated than I thought," I muttered.

Tempris shot me a sideways glance. "Good. That means you're paying attention."

We stopped at a crosswalk, waiting for the light to change. The evening air was crisp, carrying the scent of roasted nuts from a nearby cart and the faint tang of the river in the distance.

As I stood there, I felt it again—that pull. The sense that I had stepped into a world that had always been right in front of me, waiting for me to see it. A world full of secrets, shadows, and stories just waiting to be uncovered.

The light changed, and we started walking again.

"You're hooked, aren't you?" Tempris asked, a smirk tugging at the corner of his mouth.

"Yeah," I admitted, a grin spreading across my face. "Yeah, I think I am."

As we walked back toward the café, I glanced over my shoulder one last time. The city shimmered in the fading light, alive with magic.

And I was ready to see it all.

# Chapter 7

*Time to go shopping.*

The next day felt like a thousand years had passed. I had aches in places I didn't know could ache, and a headache that felt as if my brain was trying to leave my skull. It was as though my body was staging a full-scale revolt against me. Every joint, every muscle, and every thought seemed to pulsate with a relentless, throbbing intensity. Tempris had told me I would need to take it easy because my body was still getting used to magic, but I had no idea he was this serious. It was like waking up with the worst hangover imaginable, minus the night of wild revelry to justify it.

I would have stayed in bed, wrapped in the cocoon of my sheets, if I had not promised Celeste we'd go to the Eastern Market together. The thought of disappointing her pulled me out of my stupor, though every fiber of my being protested. There was something about her that made it hard to let her down, even when my own body was doing its best to betray me.

I looked down at my watch through large aviator sunglasses, which did little to shield my eyes from the harsh light of day, as Celeste strolled up. Her presence was like a breath of fresh air, and I found myself smiling despite the pain.

"For someone so responsible, you sure are late all the time," I chided, trying to sound teasing rather than exhausted.

Celeste rolled her eyes playfully. "Sorry, I had another splitting headache this morning. I really don't know what's wrong with me. Have you been cutting our supply with cheap grounds?" she replied, a grin playing on her lips.

"Ha, ha, no! You've been getting headaches a lot lately. You should really get that checked out," I replied, my concern genuine despite the banter.

"If my benevolent employer would opt for health care benefits for his employees, I would! Even still, I'm sure I look a hell of a lot better than you do right now. Long night? Nose stuck in a book again?" she said, her voice tinged with both amusement and concern as she looked at me, her eyes searching my face.

"Something like that," I replied, turning away slightly to hide the fatigue etched into my features. I didn't want her to see how deep the weariness ran, how much my newfound magical endeavors had taken out of me.

Celeste chuckled softly, linking her arm with mine. "Let's get some mimosas in you! A little hair of the dog!" she suggested, her enthusiasm infectious.

The idea of mimosas was tempting, a welcome distraction from the pounding in my head and the soreness in my muscles. As we walked toward the market, I couldn't help but be grateful for Celeste's presence. Her energy was a balm to my frayed nerves, her laughter a counterpoint to the dull roar in my skull.

Despite the pain, I found myself enjoying her company more than ever. There was an ease to our interactions, a rhythm to our banter that felt both familiar and exhilarating. We moved through the bustling stalls of the Eastern Market, the vibrant colors and mingling scents providing a sensory overload that somehow seemed to ease the tension in my head.

Celeste was a whirlwind of curiosity, pulling me from vendor to vendor, her excitement palpable. Her headaches seemed to dissipate in the face of the market's lively chaos, and I wondered what could be causing them. My own exhaustion seemed to melt away, replaced by a sense of belonging and connection.

"So, what's really going on with you?" Celeste asked as we paused at a stall selling fresh flowers, her eyes fixed on a particularly bright bouquet.

"Just...life stuff," I said, keeping my answer deliberately vague. "You know how it is."

She looked at me, her eyes sharp and perceptive. "Nolan, you're not fooling me. You've been acting different lately."

"I could say the same about you," I retorted, trying to deflect the conversation away from my own mysteries. "Those headaches can't be fun."

She sighed, brushing a strand of hair from her face. "Yeah, they're not great. But I'm more worried about you. You know you can tell me anything, right?"

Her sincerity caught me off guard, and for a moment, I considered spilling everything—the magic, the headaches, the enigmatic Tempris. But I held back, unsure of how to explain it all without sounding insane.

Instead, I smiled and said, "I know, Celeste. And I appreciate it."

We found our way to a quaint diner-style restaurant and took a seat on the patio, where the sun was shining just enough to keep the morning chill at bay. Celeste immediately ordered drinks, and I couldn't help but wonder if mimosas were the best remedy for my magical headache. But I wasn't about to argue with Celeste's enthusiasm.

As we settled in, I watched her apply a generous amount of lip gloss, and it glistened in the light like a promise. She took a long sip from her glass, leaving a faint mark on the rim.

"Why do you do that?" I asked, curiosity getting the better of me.

"Do what?" she replied, her brow furrowed in confusion.

"Whenever we're out for drinks, you always reapply whatever it is you're wearing that day before you take a sip. It just rubs off on the glass. Seems like a waste," I explained, genuinely baffled by the ritual.

"Well, aren't we paying awful close attention to little ol' me? If I didn't know any better, I'd say you had a crush," Celeste said with a teasing smirk, her eyes dancing with mischief.

"I, uh, well, you see, it's just odd. That's all," I stammered, feeling my face heat up under her gaze.

She laughed, a sound like tinkling bells, and leaned back in her chair. "I know. It does seem kind of backward. My mom always wears fancy lipstick, and anytime she takes a sip of something, she leaves huge marks on the rim. This gloss isn't expensive, but it reminds me of her," Celeste said, her gaze drifting into the distance as she spoke.

"Are you two close?" I asked, my tone careful, not wanting to intrude on a tender memory.

"We are. I love my mom. I love my dad, too. My parents are still together. I kind of grew up all over. Never really had one place to call home," she said, her voice carrying the weight of nostalgia.

"Military brat?" I asked with a smirk, trying to lighten the mood.

"You could say that. My father always wanted me to follow in his footsteps, but I wanted to forge my own path. How about you and your folks?" she asked, turning the conversation back to me.

"I wish I could tell you I had some tragic backstory as to how I lost most of my family. I was grown by the time I lost both of them. I lost my mom and dad to a stroke and heart attack in the same year. Despite what most people like to believe, it's not always because of poor diet and lack of exercise. Sometimes it's simply genetics and the cruel wheel of fate," I told her, watching as her eyes began to mist.

"I'm really sorry. I couldn't imagine a world without my parents," she replied softly. Her hand reached for a napkin, and she dabbed at her eyes, her empathy reaching out to me like a gentle caress.

"I had them for a long time, I feel lucky," I paused before continuing. "I also feel lucky I have people in my life who kind of fill those places in my heart," I said, meeting her eyes with sincerity.

Celeste stared straight through me, and I could tell she knew she had my heart—hook, line, and sinker. The corners of her mouth turned up in her signature smug smile, and she began to play with the rim of her mug, her fingers smearing and destroying the perfect print from her lips.

"This was nice. We should do this more often. Talk, like really— talk. There aren't too many people I trust and even fewer I feel comfortable sharing with," Celeste said, her voice soft but sure.

"I agree. It's weird. It has been a long time since I talked about my parents, but you definitely make me open up. You're a safe space, Celeste," I admitted, feeling a warmth spread through me that had nothing to do with the alcohol.

Celeste flashed a brilliant smile, and for a moment, she almost couldn't meet my eyes, but then she held my gaze, her expression open and sincere. Her presence felt like a balm to the ache in my head and the uncertainty in my heart.

As we sipped our drinks and talked about everything and nothing, the world outside the patio faded away, leaving just the two of us in our own little bubble of connection. The laughter and conversation of other diners became a distant hum, the clinking of glasses and cutlery a gentle symphony that underscored our conversation. I realized then that this moment, this feeling, was magic in its own right—a kind of magic I was more than happy to embrace.

"You're a safe space too," she said as she leaned a little closer to the table.

As we lingered at our patio table, savoring the last of our drinks, I felt a sudden urge to prolong the moment. "Want to grab dinner later?" I asked, hoping for a positive response.

Celeste paused, an unexpected hesitation in her expression. "I actually have plans," she said, finally unable to meet my eyes.

"Let me guess, a hot date?" I said jokingly, trying to mask my disappointment.

"It actually is a date," she replied plainly.

My heart sank, and flashes of the future I'd imagined for us disappeared in a puff of smoke. I felt my breath catch in my lungs, the joy of the morning replaced with doubt and apprehension. I only hoped the turmoil I was feeling didn't show on my face. Seconds ticked by as I forced myself to say something.

"Oh, yeah? Who's the lucky guy?" I blurted out a little too loudly, my hand already reaching for my wallet to pay the bill, as if escaping the moment would ease the sting.

"Well, it's not a date-date," she clarified, a slight blush creeping up her cheeks. "He's a bit of a celebrity podcaster. He took notice of some of my comments and asked if we could meet."

"A celebrity podcaster, huh?" I said, more curious than I wanted to admit. "What's the podcast?"

"Oh, no! I'm not telling you so you can go stalking him and putting me in an awkward situation," Celeste said, applying more lip gloss with an exaggerated flourish.

"Maybe I just want him to come do a show from Detroit Bold! Podcasters could always use more sponsors!" I shot back, trying to keep the tone light despite my gnawing jealousy.

Celeste stood and took a final sip from her glass, throwing her purse over her shoulder with a playful twirl. "How about you let me work on that, then? Let's get shopping, come on," she said, spinning on her heel with a mischievous grin.

After brunch, we spent the afternoon wandering through the market, perusing the various shops and kiosks. I was soon laden with armfuls of bags as Celeste made it her mission to buy something from every vendor she encountered.

"It was supposed to be brunch and a little shopping. I didn't know you planned on buying a month's worth of produce and enough incense to start your own store," I grumbled good-naturedly, struggling to keep my balance under the weight of her purchases.

"I'm going in one more shop, then I'm done. I promise," she replied, strapping a bag of avocados to my arm before darting off again.

As the afternoon wore on, exhaustion began to catch up with me, my magic headache throbbing persistently at my temples. I spotted an empty bench and gratefully sank onto it, placing the bags beside me. The children playing nearby were laughing, their faces sticky with powdered sugar from a tray of beignets. I leaned back and closed my eyes, hoping to catch a bit of rest.

Drifting on the edge of sleep, thoughts of fire leaped into my mind. I could almost feel the heat on my skin, the image of black flames flickering in my vision. Though the heat was intense, it drew me in, and I reached out, wanting to touch the blaze. Just as my fingertips were about to make contact, the children's laughter startled me awake.

I wiped sweat from my brow, aware I must have looked a little crazed. The kids were now pointing at a man in colorful rags, who was putting on a puppet show. The puppet, a stunningly accurate miniature of the man himself, performed acrobatic flips and dances. Despite my best efforts, I couldn't see the strings guiding it.

After a few more tricks, the puppet took a bow and vanished into the man's pocket. Applause erupted from the small crowd gathered around, the children giggling with delight. The ragged performer collected his belongings and, with the creaking movements of an old man, rose to his feet.

As he turned to leave, he caught my eye and gave me a mirthful wink. In his eyes, I saw a familiar glowing energy that seemed to trail behind him as he disappeared into the alley. Was that magic? My curiosity flared, and I stood, following him to the alley.

The alley stretched on for blocks, but the man was nowhere in sight. I ventured deeper, a strange tugging sensation at the edge of my awareness. I reached out with my hand, and it began to grow cold, as if sensing something beyond my understanding.

"Nolan! Nolan!"

Celeste's voice jolted me back to reality. I turned to see her scowling, her arms full of the bags I'd left behind. In my haste to follow the ragged man, I'd made the rookie mistake of leaving someone else's belongings unattended in Detroit. Her gaze burned with frustration as I approached.

"I'm sorry! I thought I saw...something," I said hastily, taking every oversized bag from her arms with an apologetic grin.

Her expression softened slightly as she glanced past me into the alley, her curiosity piqued. She gave me and the alley a double take before her scowl returned.

"Just for that, we're going to three more shops!" she declared, a mischievous glint in her eyes.

She looped her arm through mine, careful not to disturb the delicate balance of the bags, and led me onward. My heartbeat quickened and I felt my skin prickle. The warmth of her body against mine felt nice. I hoped the fact that she was going on a date and I had a less than spectacular reaction to it wouldn't strain things between us. This was going to be a long day. As we waited for a car to pass, I took one last glance over my shoulder, my mind racing with questions. I'd have to ask Tempris about what I'd just experienced. For the second time in as many days, I started to second-guess this journey down the rabbit hole.

# Chapter 8

*Steeped in mystery.*

The next few days were a blur of confusion and anticipation. My encounter with the ragged man in the alley had ignited a wildfire of questions, and I was determined to get answers. Finally, the day arrived for my training session with Tempris. I had spent the break compiling a mental list of things I wanted to know, and I wasn't going to let this opportunity slip away.

As the session began, I bombarded Tempris with questions. I could sense his patience wearing thin, but the curiosity gnawed at me relentlessly.

"The feeling you experienced in the alley was a gateway," Tempris explained, his voice measured but tinged with frustration. "There are countless points throughout the world where the veil between the mundane world and the magical world is much thinner. In those areas, it is possible to pass between them."

He held up his hands and interlaced his fingers, illustrating his point.

"Ordinarily, it would take years of practice or at least familiarity with both planes to cross between them. What you experienced seems to be another level to this gift of yours. Forget everything you know about physics, quantum mechanics, even the theory of relativity. The mundane and magical worlds occupy the same space.

No, it isn't some mirror world of this one, and I don't even want you to mention the word 'multiverse'. Imagine, if you will, the magical world exists in pocket dimensions of this one."

His words hung in the air, a revelation that made my head spin. The idea that two worlds could coexist in the same space, separated by a mere veil, was both thrilling and terrifying. I tried to wrap my mind around it, but the more I thought, the more questions arose.

"Can you teach me how to find and pass through these gateways?" I asked, eager to explore this newfound potential.

Tempris rubbed at a week's worth of scruff on his chin and stared at me with a mixture of impatience and contemplation before rising and scooping up his jacket.

"I'm here to teach you magic. I'm not here to teach you about the entire magical world," he replied, his tone firm yet not unkind.

The separation between the mundane and magical worlds was complex and enigmatic. Although they occupied the same space, they operated under different rules and principles. The mundane world was bound by the laws of nature and physics, while the magical world existed beyond those limitations, a realm where the impossible became possible.

Despite their differences, the two worlds were intertwined in subtle and profound ways. The gateways that linked them were hidden in plain sight, accessible only to those with the knowledge and skill to perceive them. It was a delicate balance, a coexistence that required both worlds to maintain their distinct identities while allowing for occasional interaction.

I could see Tempris's frustration building, and I realized I was pushing too hard. He had already shared more than I'd expected, and I needed to be patient. The answers would come in time, but I had to earn them.

"I get it, I do. I just feel like I'm stumbling around in the dark here," I admitted, trying to temper my eagerness with understanding.

Tempris softened slightly, recognizing the sincerity in my voice. "You're not alone, Nolan. Navigating the magical world is a lifelong journey. Even the most seasoned practitioners are still learning. Take it one step at a time, and you'll find your way."

I decided to pry a little more, hoping to get some additional insight into the mysterious Veil that separated the two worlds.

"Okay, so I get that the mundane and magical worlds are connected by these gateways, but what's the Veil exactly?" I asked, hoping Tempris wouldn't shut down the conversation.

He let out a sigh, but I could tell he was relenting a little. "The Veil is a kind of barrier, Nolan. It's not a physical thing you can touch or see. It's an ancient force that separates our world from the magical one. It's been around for as long as anyone can remember, and it's there for a reason."

"For centuries, people have tried to understand the Veil. Some have attempted to harness its power, thinking it could be the key to unlimited magical energy or knowledge. But the truth is, the smart ones—the truly wise mages and scholars—they leave it alone. The Veil exists to protect both worlds, keeping them balanced. Tampering with it can have disastrous consequences."

I leaned in, fascinated by the idea. "But what if someone could control it? I mean, think about the possibilities!"

Tempris shook his head, a stern look crossing his face. "That kind of thinking is what gets people into trouble. Many have tried to control the Veil, and those who have ended up regretting it. Some lost their minds, others vanished without a trace, and a few unleashed chaos that affected both worlds. The Veil isn't something to be trifled with. It's a force of nature, beyond human comprehension."

The weight of his words hung in the air. It was clear this was serious business, far beyond the whimsical idea of waving a wand or casting simple spells.

"Okay, so the Veil separates the mundane and magical worlds, but what exactly is at stake if they were to collide?" I asked, eager for more clarity.

Tempris sighed, clearly recognizing my determination. "The Veil is more than just a barrier; it's a stabilizing force. Both worlds occupy the same space, but in different layers of reality. Magic exists in both the mundane and magical realms, not just as a force you can access, but as a fundamental part of existence in both worlds."

I raised an eyebrow, trying to wrap my head around the concept. "So, if these worlds were to collide or merge, what could happen?"

"Imagine it this way," Tempris said, his tone serious. "Both worlds are like parallel tracks running side by side. They coexist and interact subtly, but if they were to merge or collide, it could cause unknown and potentially catastrophic harm. The balance that the Veil maintains is crucial for both worlds' stability. Disrupting it could cause magical anomalies, distortions in reality, or even physical harm. Magic could become chaotic, uncontrollable, and even dangerous."

I pondered this, trying to picture the chaotic possibilities. "So, it's not just about keeping the worlds separate; it's about preventing total chaos?"

"Precisely," Tempris said, nodding in agreement. "The Veil acts as a safeguard, ensuring that neither world's magic overwhelms or disrupts the other. It's not just a matter of keeping things tidy; it's about preserving the very fabric of reality itself."

I took a moment to let this sink in. "So, tampering with the Veil or trying to breach it could be incredibly dangerous."

"Absolutely," Tempris said, his expression softening. "Even the most skilled practitioners know better than to meddle with forces they don't fully understand. The Veil exists for a reason. It's there to protect both worlds from the potential fallout of their interaction. It's a delicate balance that keeps everything running smoothly."

I nodded, feeling a newfound respect for the complexity of the magical world. "Alright, I get it. I'll be careful."

As the training session wound down, Tempris leaned against a nearby table, his expression more serious than usual. I couldn't help but notice the gravity in his eyes, a stark contrast to his usually nonchalant demeanor.

"Nolan," he began, his voice taking on a no-nonsense tone, "we need to have a serious talk."

I straightened up, feeling a mixture of apprehension and curiosity. "What's up?"

"You've been learning at an unprecedented rate," Tempris said, crossing his arms. "In the past two weeks, we've discovered that you can wield all four core elements—earth, air, fire, and water—along with strong universal and kinetic magic. This is unheard of."

I tried to hide my surprise with a grin. "Well, I guess I'm just a magical prodigy then."

"Hardly," Tempris shot back with a raised eyebrow. "It's not just about having potential; it's about responsibility. You need to be even more careful now. This kind of power can be extremely dangerous if not handled properly. I'm not a teacher. I'm just showing you what you're capable of. The real learning happens with practice and vigilance."

I nodded, feeling the weight of his words. "Okay, I get it. But how is it even possible that I can do all this? Isn't this kind of magic, like, a once-in-a-lifetime thing?"

Tempris scratched his head, looking momentarily flustered. "Honestly? I don't know. Magic doesn't usually work this way. It's like finding a unicorn in a haystack of unicorns. I've seen rare cases before, but this... This is off the charts. You've got to remember that magic is deeply personal and complex. Sometimes it just manifests in ways we can't predict."

"Great," I said, half-jokingly, "so I'm like a magical experiment gone rogue. Fantastic."

Tempris smirked, clearly entertained by my self-deprecating humor. "In a sense. But remember, with all this power, you've got to be cautious. The Veil isn't the only thing keeping things in check. Your own control is just as important."

"I'll do my best," I promised, though I couldn't shake the feeling of being in over my head.

Tempris checked his watch and straightened his jacket. "I've got to cut today's session short. I finally have a lead on that artifact I've been researching. It's taken a while, but I think I'm getting closer."

I looked at him, a mix of disappointment and curiosity in my eyes. "So, you're ditching me for an artifact?"

Tempris raised an eyebrow, his face breaking into a smirk. "Not just any artifact. It's crucial for understanding more about the magic world. Besides, you're probably better off without me hovering over you constantly."

I couldn't help but chuckle. "Thanks for the vote of confidence. What's the artifact anyway? Something shiny and ancient?"

"Something like that," Tempris said with a mysterious glint in his eye. "Despite what you might think, I'm not all that powerful as far as magic users go," he admitted, almost as if confessing a deep, personal truth. "And I don't seek to be. I'm not interested in throwing fireballs the size of boulders or bending reality to my will. I merely seek knowledge and understanding."

I raised an eyebrow, sensing there was more beneath the surface of his words. "So, you're like a magical scholar? That's why you're always chasing after ancient artifacts and forgotten spells?"

Tempris sighed, running a hand through his hair. "I'm not interested in power for power's sake, Nolan. I'm interested in understanding, in keeping the balance. That's why I'm here with you, teaching you—well, showing you what I can. But that's all I'm here to do."

"Just showing me what you can, huh?" I said, my tone half-joking, half-suspicious. "So what are you not showing me?"

He shot me a look that was half amusement, half exasperation. "Let's just say there are some things you're not ready to know. And some things I'm not ready to teach."

I frowned, not entirely satisfied with that answer. "So, how can I do all this magic, then? The four core elements, universal magic, kinetic magic—how is that even possible?"

Tempris didn't answer right away. He looked at me, his eyes narrowing slightly as if weighing his response. Finally, he shrugged. "I don't have a good answer for you, Nolan. Some people are born with gifts, and some... some have a little more than others. You're unique, that's for sure. But why? That's something you'll have to figure out."

The room fell into a contemplative silence, both of us caught in our own thoughts. I had a thousand more questions, but I could tell Tempris wasn't going to give me the answers I wanted—not yet, anyway.

Tempris glanced at his watch, then back at me. "I'm going to have to cut this short. I've got another lead I need to follow up on."

I could see the tension in his posture, the way his eyes flickered with something I couldn't quite place—something more than just his usual quest for knowledge. "Another lead on what?"

"Just some unfinished business," he replied, too quickly. He pulled on his jacket and headed for the door, clearly eager to leave. "Stay out of trouble while I'm gone, Nolan. And keep practicing. You've got a lot of potential, but that also means you've got a lot of responsibility."

I watched him go, a sense of unease settling over me. There was something he wasn't telling me, something important. And whatever it was, I had a feeling it was connected to the strange, powerful world I was only beginning to glimpse. But for now, I was left with more questions than answers—and a nagging suspicion that whatever Tempris was really up to, it was more dangerous than he was letting on.

# Chapter 9

*Closing time.*

T he Business was slow at the café, and the last few stragglers
finally made their way to the door as the evening deepened. I
went through the familiar motions of closing down, wiping
down counters, flipping chairs onto tables, and locking up the
register. As I finished up, I found myself lingering at the cellar door,
the place where I'd spent so many hours training with Tempris. With
him gone for a few days, I figured it was the perfect time to get some
much-needed R&R. I could already imagine myself at home, ordering
a pizza, curling up on the couch, and diving into a new streaming
series. So much had happened so quickly I really had not spent much
time to myself—or with Celeste, for that matter.

The thought of Celeste made me wince a little, like a bruise I
couldn't help but poke at. I know I'd been avoiding her, dodging her
texts, making lame excuses to cancel plans. Our weekend trip to
Eastern Market had been the last straw. We were supposed to spend
a whole Saturday wandering through stalls of fresh produce, quirky
knick-knacks, and overpriced artisanal candles—our kind of day. But
I bailed, claiming I was too swamped with work, when in reality, I just
couldn't stand the thought of seeing her after what I'd heard.

She went on a date with another guy! I mean, sure, Celeste wasn't
my girlfriend, and technically, we'd never actually expressed our

feelings to each other. But come on, our flirting and innuendos had ramped up past the point of no return. Everyone in our circle knew we were one awkwardly timed confession away from being a thing. Or so I thought. The fact that she'd gone out with someone else felt like a sucker punch I didn't see coming.

Was I being a total coward about it? Absolutely. Here I was, brave enough to dabble in magic, to summon fire and manipulate elements, but when it came to telling the woman I was head over heels for how I felt, I was utterly spineless. I could handle a magical mentor with the patience of a ticking time bomb, but one conversation with Celeste about my feelings? Nope. That was clearly beyond my skill set.

But as I stood there, keys in hand, staring at the cellar door that had become so symbolic of this new chapter in my life, I knew something had to give. Next time I saw her, I would tell her. I'd look her in the eyes and say, "Celeste, I like you. No, scratch that, I think about you all the time, and it's driving me nuts. So, what do you say we stop dancing around this and actually go on a date? A real one, with, you know, intentionality." Okay, maybe I wouldn't say it exactly like that, but the sentiment would be the same. It was time to stop running away and start facing things head-on.

Resolve resolving, I twirled my keys into my pocket and headed for the side street where I usually parked. The universe, however, had other plans for me tonight.

It was only as I approached the street that I noticed something off: all the streetlights on my side of the road were out, casting the pathway to my car in harsh, eerie shadows. As a native Detroiter, I wasn't one to be easily spooked by a dark street corner, but I also knew better than to be careless. I barely made it two steps away from the café when I heard footsteps scuffling behind me.

Out of the gloom, three men emerged, their clothes a mix of urban athleisure and factory workwear. The lead guy stood out, his scuffed Timberland boots crunching against the pavement, a navy blue puffy jacket clinging to his broad frame, and a neck tattoo that crept up to cover half his face. As a rule, I try not to judge people by appearances, but these three weren't exactly exuding friendly vibes.

They were heading straight for me, and I knew better than to assume it was a coincidence.

My first instinct was to turn back and re-enter the café, but I knew it was too late for that. Crossing the street seemed like a safer bet, maybe they'd lose interest if they thought I wasn't an easy target. But as I moved toward the curb, I spotted a fourth man stepping out from between two parked cars on the opposite side of the street, cutting off my escape route. My options were dwindling fast.

I'm decent in a fight. I've taken enough mixed martial arts classes to hold my own, but this was real life, not a controlled environment. Then there was my magic—sure, I could probably toast these guys, but the thought of actually killing someone turned my stomach. I had to talk my way out of this.

I turned to face them as they came within ten feet. "Sup, guys?" I blurted out, hoping to sound casual, though I knew how absurd I must have looked.

The lead man sneered. "You closed up for the night? We wanted some Frappés."

"That particular drink comes from McDonald's. I'm pretty sure they're still open, and they're not far," I said, pointing vaguely in the direction of Midtown, trying to keep my tone light.

But their body language told me everything I needed to know. They were fanning out in front of me, clearly more interested in something other than a sugary frozen drink. Two of them had their hands shoved deep in their pockets, and I couldn't help but worry about what they might be hiding. My gaze flicked from one to the other, mentally preparing myself for what might come next.

"How about you give us a ride over there? You goin' to your car? Give us your keys, we'll drive!" the lead man said, his tone dripping with false friendliness.

"Sure," I replied, fishing in my pocket for my keys. The instant distraction was all I needed to strike first.

I delivered a side kick to the guy on my left. The kick landed awkwardly, but it was enough to send him sprawling backward over the curb. Without hesitation, I turned and head-butted the second man before he could pull his hands out of his pockets. My forehead connected with his cheekbone, and he staggered back, clutching his face.

The other two rushed me, shoving me back until I was pinned against the café's brick wall. They threw a flurry of poorly aimed punches, most of which I managed to block, though a few landed painfully. I caught one of their swings and retaliated with a vicious uppercut that sent the man reeling. My hand throbbed from the impact, and I noticed the group starting to regroup, their eyes filled with a dangerous resolve.

The odds of fighting my way out of this were shrinking fast. I took a deep breath, channeling the fire magic into my hands. Flames licked at my palms, ready to unleash, but the image of their faces seared by my magic made me hesitate. I wasn't a killer. I wasn't even a real fighter. My concentration wavered, and in that split second, a fist collided with my jaw, sending me crashing to the ground.

Real-life fights aren't like in the movies. That one solid hit knocked me senseless. My vision blurred as they continued to beat down on me. A boot slammed into my ankle, and I heard the sickening snap of bone. Pain shot through my leg, and I could barely focus through the haze of agony and blows. Blood filled my mouth, and I spat it onto the gritty pavement. Their mocking laughter grated in my ears, stirring something primal inside me.

There I was, getting the shit kicked out of me all because I was too principled to cook these guys. No more. No way were they getting another hit in.

I pressed my palm to the ground, and a plume of fire erupted around me. The flames vanished as quickly as they had appeared, but the effect was immediate. The men recoiled in shock, one of them even yelping as he fell on his backside. I pushed myself up, wincing in pain as I took in the scene. The man who'd fallen was frantically trying to extinguish his pant leg, which had caught fire. His screams echoed in the night as the smell of burning flesh filled the air, making my stomach turn.

The sight of white bone poking through seared flesh snapped me back to reality. The smell was awful—sickly sweet and just wrong. All thoughts of using my magic to finish them off fled from my mind. My vision swam, whether from the pain or the horror of what I'd done, I wasn't sure. But then I saw the lead man pull a gun from his jacket, leveling it at me. Panic surged through me as I struggled to summon more fire, but my hands trembled uncontrollably.

Through the blur, I noticed another figure approaching from the shadows. Just great—another one. As if things weren't bad enough, I was about to be outnumbered four to one. I tried to focus, tried to muster up the strength for one last burst of magic, but it was too late. The man's finger slipped into the trigger guard, and the world slowed to a crawl. It was now or never. There was a flash and I felt my consciousness slip away.

# Chapter 10

*Ouch.*

I woke up in my own bed. The realization hit me like a double shot of espresso. The last thing I remembered was the gun pointed at me, the slow-motion descent into oblivion, and the certainty that I wasn't walking away from that fight. But here I was in my bed. My room. I was safe surrounded by the familiar posters, comforting smells and covered with my favorite blanket. I was groggy and a bit disoriented so I began flexing my muscles and wiggling my toes to make sure everything was still in working order. Surprisingly, I felt more or less intact. My ankle throbbed like I'd gone ten rounds with a steel-toed boot, but hey, I was alive. I couldn't quite piece together how I got home, though. I had these hazy memories of a brawl and then...nothing.

As I swung my legs off the bed and attempted to stand, a sharp pain shot up my ankle, and I winced, clutching the bedpost for support. The fight! It all came rushing back—the muggers, the gun, and that flash of fire. I was sure they'd shot me. Yet here I was, in one piece, albeit sore and bruised.

Then, the rich, inviting aroma of coffee wafted into my room. A part of me thought, maybe I accidentally discovered some new spell that summons coffee directly to bed. If so, I'm keeping it in regular rotation. But then the clinking of a spoon against a mug made me realize there was someone else here. My door creaked open, and in walked Tempris, looking as calm and collected as ever, holding a steaming mug of coffee.

"Good morning, Sleeping Beauty," Tempris said, handing me the mug with a smirk that was both annoying and oddly comforting. He glanced around my room, his nose wrinkling as he made a beeline for the armchair in the corner. With a look of distaste, he lifted a pile of clothes from the chair, dropping them unceremoniously on the floor before taking a seat.

"You were the guy," I blurted out, the words slipping out before I could think them through. "The one who showed up after that dude pulled a gun. I guess I have you to thank for waking up this morning."

Tempris leaned back, his expression softening just a bit. "Need I remind you, you're not invincible," he said, his tone teetering between concern and exasperation.

I glanced down at the various bruises mottling my skin and gingerly touched my throbbing ankle. "Yeah, no kidding," I muttered. The thought of hobbling around the café with a limp made me grimace, not to mention trying to explain my injuries to anyone who might ask.

As if reading my mind, Tempris spoke up. "The bruises will fade by tomorrow. The ankle will take a couple of days, but you should be able to walk by the time you go back to the café on Monday," he assured me. "Thanks to your increased use of magic, your Magic Atoms—or MAs, as I call them—are working overtime to repair the damage. They act as a blueprint for your body, helping to return everything to its normal state."

I raised an eyebrow, trying to wrap my head around this new tidbit of magical science. "So, magic isn't just about tossing fireballs or making things float? It's like a built-in healthcare plan?"

Tempris chuckled, but there was a seriousness in his eyes. "In a way, yes. But it's not foolproof. You can still get sick or injured, but your MAs will help accelerate the healing process. The more you use magic, the quicker your body adapts and repairs itself. However, this doesn't apply to non-magic users. Their MAs work differently and can't be manipulated in the same way."

I nodded, though a part of me wanted to press further—could magic be used to heal others, maybe even cure diseases? But before I could ask, Tempris shut it down with a firm, "Don't get any ideas, Nolan. Magic has its limits, and so do you."

I sighed, sipping the coffee. "So, I just lay low all weekend and hope nobody demands to see my face?"

"Yes, all of your hot dates will have to be canceled," Tempris replied, his smirk returning.

His words triggered a memory, one I'd been trying to avoid. Celeste. She was working at the café all weekend, which meant no chance of casually dropping by to say hello or seeing that smile of hers that had a way of making the world feel right. I'd been avoiding her, ever since she mentioned that date with another guy. I hadn't even told her about the magic, about the double life I was now leading. How could I? How could she ever understand?

Tempris watched me with a raised eyebrow, clearly noticing the change in my expression. I forced a smile. "Hey, thanks for the coffee. You didn't have to, you know?".

He shrugged, a small smile playing on his lips. "It's just coffee, Nolan. Don't read too much into it."

"Yeah, well, I know how much of a coffee snob you are. It's a big deal," I teased, trying to lighten the mood.

Tempris chuckled, leaning back in the chair. "It's good coffee, by the way. I'm not as much of a snob as you think."

"Sure could've fooled me. With your posh accent, immaculate clothes, and that leather-bound journal you carry around like it's the Holy Grail, I figured you were the type to only drink artisanal, fair-trade, single-origin brews."

Tempris pulled the journal from his jacket pocket and tapped it on his knee. "Every good magic user keeps a journal. Mine just happens to be vintage and handcrafted. There's a difference."

"Oh, bully! Bully!" I said, mimicking a British accent and raising my pinky as I took another sip of coffee. "So, what's in there anyway? You haven't exactly been forthcoming with the spell books and potion recipes."

"Research, Nolan. Research. Contained within are years of study, magical theories, successes, failures—everything I've learned and discovered. And before you ask, no, you can't read it. It's sealed with a blood ward, and only I can open it. Don't let curiosity get the better of you."

I raised my hands in mock surrender. "Got it, Merlin. Hands off the bougie magic journal. Check."

"Nolan, I'm serious. The ward is strong, and you're still a novice. If you try to open it, you could get hurt."

"Hey, message received. No touching the magic journal. And the same goes for you—don't mess with my espresso machine. It's expensive, dangerous, and if you break it, you'll be doing dishes for the rest of your life."

Tempris rolled his eyes, but a smile tugged at the corners of his mouth. We sat in comfortable silence for a while, finishing our coffee, the events of the previous night hanging between us like a heavy cloud.

I couldn't shake the feeling that I was still in way over my head. Magic, fights with muggers, hidden worlds—this was all so far beyond anything I'd ever imagined for my life. What was I even doing with this power? Where was it all leading?

As if sensing my spiraling thoughts, Tempris stood and walked over to the bed. He took the empty mug from my hands and placed it on the nightstand before leaning over me and placing a hand on my chest. I felt an immediate rush of warmth spread through me, calming my racing mind.

"Rest, Nolan," Tempris said, his voice gentle. "You've been through a lot. Let your body heal. Everything else can wait."

I nodded, my eyes growing heavy as the warmth from his hand seeped into me. Tempris had saved my life, and despite his aloof demeanor, I could tell he cared—maybe more than he'd ever admit. I felt safe, for the first time in a long time, as sleep began to pull me under.

We sat there in silence finishing our coffee. Every moment that passed brought my thoughts closer to the realization that I was a fish out of water and still barely knew what this power was. What did I want it for? Could I stop now that I started? As if he could sense my thoughts spiraling, Tempris stood and walked to the side of my bed. He took the empty mug from my hands and placed it on my nightstand. He leant over me and placed a hand on my chest. I tried to ignore the awkward intimacy of this man putting his full palm on my exposed pecks but he leaned even closer and I grew even more uncomfortable. We locked eyes and his iris' glinted in the bars of light making their way through my closed blinds. I felt warm. Tempris' hand glowed faintly and I felt a rush of power flow through me. I grew tired and began to drift off. The last thing I remember was Tempris rising from in front of me and finally feeling safe before sleep took me.

# Chapter 11

*The Green Eyed Monster.*

**W**ork was uneventful the following week when I returned. Celeste and I barely exchanged words. Whether it was because I was subconsciously keeping my distance while my injuries healed or avoiding the awkwardness of asking how her date went, I wasn't sure. Regardless, our usual playful banter had been reduced to polite exchanges. Thursday came around, and I finally decided I couldn't take it anymore—I had to break the silence.

The café was particularly slow that afternoon. It was just the two of us, catching up on random tasks. I noticed Celeste was planning to leave early; she had on her yoga gear—black leggings and a cropped hoodie—and her hair was pulled up into a messy bun. She looked beautiful. She was restocking one of the upper shelves behind the counter, stretching up on her tiptoes. I watched her for a moment, a smirk forming on my face as I realized she was stubbornly trying to reach a cabinet that was far out of her reach.

At five-foot-two, Celeste had no business trying to reach that high shelf without help. The hoodie rode up as she stretched, revealing a sliver of smooth skin just above the waistband of her leggings. The fabric of her yoga pants clung to her curves, accentuating every line as she reached. I couldn't help but admire the view, but I also knew she was moments away from knocking something over. So, I rounded the counter and came up behind her, my eyes still fixed on her lower half.

"Sugar," I said, standing close behind her.

Celeste dropped down from her toes and spun around, startled. Her eyes widened when she saw how close I was, and I could see the rapid rise and fall of her chest.

In my hands, I held a sack of refined beet sugar from the Michigan Sugar Company in Bay City. "You, uh, you forgot one," I said, holding it out to her, trying to sound casual.

Her eyes flicked to the bag, and she let out a small laugh, the tension easing from her face. "Thanks. I don't know why you buy this stuff," she replied, taking the sack from me, her fingers brushing against mine for a brief moment that sent a tingle up my arm.

"You know better than I do that vegans love weird stuff," I teased, using my foot to slide over the step stool she'd been ignoring.

"They don't like weird stuff. They like healthy stuff. And for the record, I was only vegan for a week," she shot back, stepping onto the stool and turning away from me. Her tone was light, but I caught the playful edge in her voice. "That's about as long as you dated that vegan, right? What was her name? River? Flower? Chrysanthemum or something?"

I felt the heat rising to my cheeks and busied myself by handing her the remaining sacks of sugar. "Valley. Her name was Valley," I muttered.

Her shoulders began to shake as she chuckled uncontrollably, the sound of her laughter filling the small space between us. I couldn't help but smile despite the embarrassment.

"Well, you still haven't told me your fella's name. He's a podcaster, and you're an academic, right? I bet it's something pretentious like Chadwick or Arthur. Arthur Perryfeather Crumpington of the New England Crumpingtons," I said, adopting an overly posh accent that I knew would get a rise out of her.

Her body stiffened, and she shoved another sack into the cupboard with more force than necessary. "Well, you'd be wrong," she replied curtly. "And he's not my 'fella.' 'Fella'—what are you, an 80-

year-old man? It was one date, and while I found him interesting, he wasn't my type."

She reached back for another sack of sugar, but there wasn't one left. Because of this, her balance faltered, and she started to tumble backward. I instinctively moved forward, catching her in my arms. She landed against my chest, and for a moment, time seemed to stretch out. Her head rested against me, and I could feel the warmth of her skin through my shirt. I inhaled deeply, her scent washing over me—coconut oil, shea butter, and something sweet I couldn't quite place. It was intoxicating.

She craned her neck to look up at me, her hazel eyes searching mine. We stood like that, caught in a moment neither of us seemed in a hurry to break. Her breath was warm against my neck, and I could feel the steady thrum of her heartbeat.

"So, what is your type?" I asked softly, my voice barely above a whisper.

Celeste's eyes softened, and a playful glint sparked within them. She brought her hands to my face, her palms cool against my skin, and pulled me closer. Our lips were just a breath apart, and I could feel her warmth radiating between us. Her lips grazed mine for an instant, a tantalizing tease, before she spoke, her voice low and teasing. "Guys who don't get jealous and avoid me for days because I go on one date."

She pushed me away, playfully but with enough force to break the tension. She crossed her arms, her expression a mix of amusement and something more serious. I could tell she wasn't just messing around—this was important to her.

"Celeste, I'm a big, dumb, jealous idiot who couldn't keep his cool at the thought of you going out with someone else," I admitted, rubbing the back of my neck. "I'm sorry. You're my friend, one of my best friends, really. I don't want anything to come between us—especially not my thoughtless behavior. Do you forgive me?"

Celeste stared at me for a long moment, her gaze piercing. I held my breath, waiting for her response. Finally, she shook her head, a small smile playing at her lips. "No, I don't forgive you. But I will—if you help me move a piano this weekend and a bunch of other stuff from storage."

"You've got a deal, but aren't you supposed to hire piano movers for something that delicate?" I asked, a grin tugging at my lips.

"Are you going to pay me piano mover money?" she shot back.

I turned and glanced out at the nearly empty café. A lone woman sat in the corner, reading a novel with a shirtless, muscular man on the cover. She was nursing the same frozen coffee she'd bought when she arrived.

"Yeah, let me help you move that piano!" I replied with a chuckle.

I expected her to be more excited about securing my assistance, but when I looked back at her, she seemed hesitant, almost nervous.

"What's wrong?" I asked, my brows knitting together in concern.

Celeste rubbed her hands together, an anxious gesture I'd seen before. "I got a new job," she said finally. "You're looking at the new head archivist of the Detroit Public Library!"

"Celeste! That's fantastic!" I exclaimed, pulling her into a tight hug. "Come on, get excited! That's something you've been working toward for so long!"

She leaned back, her eyes still unsure. "It means I won't be here as much. I'm not leaving you entirely—that's for certain! It's mostly during the week, but some weekends too. And I get to use the space for research and documentation."

I could hear the worry in her voice, so I hugged her tighter. "Hey, it's alright. I want to see your dreams come true. I'll be here, the café will be here. Don't let anything take away from the excitement of this opportunity. Especially if it means you can pay for a piano mover now," I added with a chuckle.

"You already promised, and you'd be surprised how little a head archivist makes! Thank you, Nolan," she said, pulling back and looking up at me, her eyes softening. "I was nervous about telling you because I know this place will fall apart without me. And you—you might fall apart without me."

"You're probably right," I admitted with a grin. "But your piano will fall apart with me. So there's that."

Celeste rolled her eyes and playfully swatted my arm, a laugh escaping her lips.

"You know, this will be the first time I've ever been to your place, right? There better not be a single piece of anything that says 'Live, Laugh, Love' on it," I teased, leaning against the counter with a grin.

Celeste rolled her eyes, a smile tugging at her lips. "I'm far more capable of decorating than some people. At least I pick things that actually match," she replied, gesturing around my café with a mockingly disapproving look.

I followed her gaze, pretending to take offense. "Hey! I'm worldly, and I like the world to see that. Besides, I got rid of the ugly stuff."

"Most of it," she countered, sticking her tongue out at me, her eyes sparkling with mischief.

I chuckled, savoring the moment. I had missed this—this effortless, playful banter with Celeste. It was like slipping back into a well-worn, favorite jacket. Comfortable, familiar, and somehow always just right. Avoiding her these past few days was probably the dumbest thing I could've done. I'd forgotten how easy it was to solve your problems by just talking about them, and how being around her could make everything feel a little lighter. A big part of me wanted to just spill the beans about my recent dive into the world of magic.

I knew it was probably a bad idea. Tempris had been very clear: keep it secret, keep it safe. But how could I not tell Celeste? She was the person I told everything to. We'd shared secrets that would make most people blush or run for the hills. And now, I was ruining this beautiful dynamic by hiding this huge new part of my life from her. Would she think I was losing my mind? Or would she lean in, eyes wide with fascination, wanting to know more? The thought of her reaction had been eating away at me, a gnawing urge to just let it all out.

"Earth to Nolan! Where did you go?" Celeste's voice snapped me back to reality. She was waving a hand in front of my face, her brows raised in amusement.

I blinked, coming out of my thoughts. "Oh, what?"

"I know you don't want to help me move a piano, but you don't have to look like you're planning your escape route." She laughed, her smile wide and genuine. "Six AM Saturday, got it? The truck will be dropping it off. We just have to get it in the service elevator. Don't worry, I've already measured, and it has wheels!"

"Six AM?" I repeated, groaning dramatically. "Are you trying to kill me, or is this part of some cruel and unusual punishment? Care to crack the whip any more while you're giving orders?"

"Oh, you haven't seen anything yet," she shot back with a wicked grin. "Just wait till we start moving all the other stuff. You'll be begging for mercy."

I couldn't help but laugh. "Why do I feel like you're planning to turn this into some kind of boot camp? What's next? Obstacle courses in the hallway?"

Celeste's grin widened, and she wiggled her eyebrows playfully. "Now there's an idea. Maybe I'll make you carry the piano up the stairs, see what those muscles are really made of." She reached out and gave my arm a playful squeeze, her touch lingering just a little too long to be casual.

I flexed instinctively, flashing a cocky grin. "You mean these guns? Please. I could bench-press that piano without breaking a sweat."

She burst out laughing, and I felt a flutter in my chest—something between excitement and nerves. I hadn't realized how much I'd missed making her laugh like that. And I hadn't realized how much I'd missed her touch. It was easy to get lost in these moments with Celeste, to forget about the complications, the secrets, the magic.

"You're ridiculous," she said, still laughing. "But seriously, Nolan, I'm glad we're okay. I was worried that things were getting weird between us."

I wanted to tell her then—about everything. The magic, the training with Tempris, the way my world had changed in ways I was still coming to grips with. But I hesitated. I wanted her to see me the way she always had: Nolan, the guy who made her laugh, who teased her, who she could always count on. I didn't want to become some weirdo in her eyes.

"You know me," I said instead, my voice softening. "I'm always up for a challenge, especially if it involves you. Even if it means getting up at the crack of dawn to move a piano."

"Good," she said, her smile returning, but there was something softer in her eyes now. "Because I'd hate to lose my best friend over something silly."

"Same here," I replied, meaning it more than I could express. I'd already been close to losing her once by being distant. I didn't want to risk it again, even if it meant keeping my secret a little longer.

For a moment, we stood there, just looking at each other, the noise of the café fading into the background. I could see the curiosity in her eyes, the questions she wasn't asking. Part of me wondered if she could sense that there was more I wasn't saying. And part of me was almost desperate to bridge the gap between what she thought she knew and what was actually going on.

But then she broke the silence with a sly grin. "Okay, hotshot. If you're so worldly, how about you help me choose a new rug for my living room after we move the piano? I'm thinking something Persian, maybe vintage. And if you suggest anything like that awful geometric thing you have here, I swear—"

"Hey!" I interrupted, feigning indignation. "That geometric thing is a conversation starter."

"Yeah," she said with a wink, "a conversation that starts with, 'Why the hell did you buy that?'"

We both burst out laughing, the tension from before easing into something lighter, more familiar. And for now, that was enough. Even as I wrestled with the urge to tell her everything, I realized that maybe it was okay to take things slow, to let this new chapter between us unfold naturally—piano moving, terrible rugs, and all.

# Chapter 12

*Beans.*

Detroit Bold was a little quieter, a little less lively and a lot more lonely the next couple of weeks. Celeste started showing up less and less, but I was proud of her. She set out to do something and she really did it. I stood in the spot Celeste usually occupied while she was here. The worn wood of the vintage flooring felt uneven beneath my feet. I wonder how many people walked these floors before I owned this place. Their jobs, adventures and journeys written into the old Oak. Or was it pine? I knew very little about carpentry but it did make me think of everything I've learned about magic up until now. I could do some pretty amazing things, but I knew for sure it was just the tip of the iceberg. What was I even learning this for? I wasn't going to go on the road doing shows, or join some underground magic missile league. I couldn't even tell anyone about it. So what WAS I doing this for? Someone was calling my name.

"Nolan. Nolan?" The voice questioned.

It was Toby. He was one of my long time regulars and a recent Wayne State University graduate. He loved coffee almost as much as I did and every time he would come in he'd ask if we'd gotten anything new. He was olive skinned with long dark hair that met his shoulders and a beard that just wouldn't fill in. It just so happened he was looking for work and when Celeste dropped the bombshell that she wouldn't be here as much, it was perfect timing. He'd been working at the cafe for a week and it was working out seamlessly. Now he was rattling a container in front of me.

"I was asking if we had any more of the special blend you got in from Mackinac," Toby asked with urgency and a concerned look on his face.

I looked around at the empty cafe then turned to him. "We don't have any customers. What's the emergency?"

Toby looked sheepish and simply said "I like this one a lot."

I laughed and turned to a cupboard behind me. The old hinges creaked melodically as the doors opened. This cabinet was one of the only things I kept from the original building. I reached in and pulled out a canister of coffee. Toby reached for it and I pulled it closer to my chest keeping it just out of reach from his grasping fingers.

"Aht, aht, aht! You use limited edition beans, you find limited edition beans! Look for something new while we're slow," I said and handed him the container.

Toby opened the lid and inhaled the dark coffee beans. I could see his shoulders relax and the tension leave his body. "When they say 'beans, beans, they're good for the heart,' this is what they are really referencing." He spun and headed to the grinder with a bounce in his step. I chuckled and felt relieved I was able to fill Celeste's spot with someone with a passion for the craft. Speaking of craft, I figured it was time to get in a little training. Tempris would be by in an hour so maybe I should get warmed up. I headed to the cellar.

# Chapter 13

*One man and a truck.*

S ure, I grumbled about it, but it wasn't hard for Celeste to convince me to help her move some large items she acquired into her new apartment. For one, I love being with her. Every nerve ending in my body seems to come alive when I'm around her, and ever since she started working at the library, I hardly see her at the café anymore. Which reminds me—I really need to hire some more help.

This was the first time I'd visited Celeste's home. So, before I arrived, I stopped by one of the florists at Eastern Market and got a bouquet of flowers. My knowledge of floriculture is severely lacking, so I asked Mable Jean what kind of flowers I should buy, and she gave me the third degree.

Mable Jean has been selling all kinds of things at Eastern Market for as long as I can remember. My parents used to take me there when I was a kid. We'd always visit Rocky Peanut Company for some snacks, and my mom would make it a point to say hi to Mable. She was already well into her sixties when I was about four feet tall, and I can't even imagine how old she is now. But that doesn't slow her down one bit. She's as spry and full of energy as anyone I know, moving around her stall with a grace and speed that would put people half her age to shame.

Mable Jean is a small, sturdy woman with skin the color of rich, dark chocolate that has weathered the years like a well-loved book—creased but still vibrant. Her eyes are sharp and quick, like a sparrow's, constantly darting around her stall, taking in every detail, every customer, every flower petal. She wears her silver-gray hair in long, thin braids that reach past her shoulders, often tied back with a colorful scarf that changes depending on the season or her mood. Today, it's a bright yellow with little sunflowers on it. She's dressed in layers—earthy tones and practical fabrics that speak of years of labor in the soil and sun, yet there's an elegance to her, a sense of pride in her appearance. She always has a smile ready, a big, wide grin that crinkles the corners of her eyes even more, and when she laughs, it's deep and warm, like the rumble of distant thunder.

"Will you just tell me what kind of flowers to get Celeste?" I asked with mock exasperation, leaning on the wooden counter of her stall.

Mable Jean looked up from where she was trimming a bunch of fresh eucalyptus, her eyes narrowing playfully. "What kind of flowers, what kind of flowers... what kind of question is that?" she said, shaking her head as if she couldn't believe the foolishness she was hearing. "Have you told her how you feel about her?" She leaned forward in her chair, resting her hands on her well-worn cane, the one her son hand-carved for her birthday a few years back.

"How do you know how I feel about her?" I asked, a little taken aback.

She gave me a look like I'd just asked why the sky was blue. "As simple as a rose blooms in the spring is how simple and emotionally uncomplicated you are, Nolan. I've known you since you were a little boy who would cry when he got pricked by a thorn. I think I know when your heart is in bloom," she replied, her voice lilting with that poetic cadence she often used.

I let out a small, embarrassed laugh. "Uh, I guess. But yes, I do like Celeste, and no, I haven't told her. I'll let the flowers and manual labor do the trick," I replied, shrugging a little.

Mable Jean shook her head, chuckling softly. "Boy, you're going to need more than manual labor if you want to win a girl like Celeste.

She's a smart one. Won't be fooled by a strong back and a pretty face."

She stood up with surprising agility and started gathering materials from around her stall—ribbons, delicate stems, and vibrant flowers, some of which I'd never seen before. I watched her move, her hands steady and practiced as she snipped, twisted, and tied. She had a kind of rhythm to her work, like she was dancing in place. I couldn't help but wonder what it would be like to live a life like hers—simple but deeply fulfilling. She loves this market, loves what she does, loves her family. Seven kids, sixteen grandchildren, and she still finds time to grow flowers, herbs, and God knows what else.

Meanwhile, I love my café, sure, but I don't know if that's where my future lies—especially given the strange circumstances I've found myself in lately. Could I be like Mable Jean, doing one thing for decades and still finding joy in it every single day? The thought lingered in my mind as she continued crafting the bouquet.

When Mable Jean finished, she crossed over to me, holding out a beautiful bouquet wrapped in soft burlap and tied with a deep blue ribbon. "Here you go," she said, her voice gentle. "For a new home, for a new beginning, and for a love that's still finding its way."

She pointed to each flower, her voice becoming almost reverent. "These are yellow tulips—for hope and cheerfulness, something bright to welcome her to a new place. White hyacinths for loveliness, 'cause I know that girl is as lovely inside as she is out. And these..." She touched the pale pink roses at the center. "For admiration and friendship. But they've got a hint of blush to them, just a whisper of something more."

I felt my cheeks warm a bit, nodding along as she spoke. "You think she'll like them?"

Mable Jean's eyes softened, and she patted my hand. "She'll love them, Nolan. Not because of what they are, but because of what they mean coming from you. You just need to figure out if you want to keep giving her friendship flowers, or if you're ready to give her something else."

I stared at the bouquet in my hands, my mind spinning with thoughts of Celeste. "Thanks, Mable Jean," I said, my voice a little quieter than before.

She smiled that big, wide smile of hers, a chuckle rumbling from her throat. "Go on, now. Don't keep that girl waiting. And Nolan—" she added as I turned to leave, "be good to her. She's got a heart as big as all outdoors, and she cares for you more than you know. Don't be a fool and let that slip away."

I nodded, giving her a small wave as I headed off, the bouquet feeling heavier in my hands, filled with meaning and maybe—just maybe—a little bit of magic of its own.

As I arrived in Midtown, I took in the sight of Celeste's building along Woodward. The exterior had that classic brickwork you'd expect from an old Detroit structure, but it gleamed like it had just gotten a fresh coat of polish. Gentrification at its finest. I spotted Celeste beside a large moving van, deep in conversation with a guy in a Detroit Pistons T-shirt who looked about as interested in moving the piano as I was in auditioning for a reality show. From the look on her face, I could tell she was trying to charm him into doing the heavy lifting for us. I stayed back, not wanting to interrupt her little negotiation dance.

"Look, I would *fasho* move this piano if it was on the first floor, but I'm not equipped to do it, and it's just me today," the guy was saying, his voice a mix of fatigue and resignation.

"Can't you call someone? I gave you a big tip already, and look at me, I can't get this upstairs," Celeste replied, her voice turning sugary sweet as she batted her eyelashes. She was laying it on thick, and I had to bite back a grin.

"Like I said, I barely got it off this truck. I can't get it upstairs by myself, know what I'm sayin'," he said, already starting to close the back of the truck. Clearly, her charms were wearing thin.

Celeste caught sight of me and her face lit up like she'd just found a twenty in an old jacket pocket. "Well, if it's help you need, I've got help! Nolan, come here!" She waved me over. "Nolan can help you. He's big and strong, just like you, and there's another $50 in it for you," she said, flashing that winning smile and patting my pockets like I was some sort of human ATM.

I tried to dodge her hand, but I was caught off guard, one hand holding a bouquet of flowers and the other gripping my oversized coffee tumbler. She slid her hand into my pocket like a pickpocket-in-training, and for a brief second, our eyes met. I could feel a flush creeping up my neck, but she just grinned mischievously as she pulled out my wallet and extracted a fifty-dollar bill. The mover—a black guy in his late twenties with a thick beard—chuckled at the scene, shaking his head.

"Damn, man. She got you good, but we got this, bro, come on," he said, slipping on a pair of work gloves.

Celeste took the flowers from me, her smile softening as she inhaled their scent. She then snatched my coffee and took a long sip, her eyes meeting mine over the rim of the tumbler before she turned and sashayed into the building. The mover and I watched her go, her hips swaying like she owned the world. He turned to me with a knowing smirk.

"That you? That better be you," he said, his voice half-joking, half-serious.

"Something like that," I muttered, feeling my cheeks heat up. And with that, we got to work.

Moving a piano is a lot like trying to push a boulder uphill with a spoon—an exercise in pure futility. Jonathan, the mover, leaned against the loading ramp, his shirt sticking to his back with sweat despite the cool autumn breeze. He had a muscular build and a no-nonsense demeanor, but even he looked like he'd had enough. "Man, why you ain't just hire a real piano moving company?" he panted, wiping his brow.

I dropped my over-shirt which was little more than a sweat rag at this point, and plopped down on the edge of the ramp, wondering the same damn thing. My thoughts briefly flitted to the idea of using magic. Tempris and I had both learned that my control wasn't the best, and Celeste's precious piano would probably end up in splinters if I tried something that reckless. Besides, I wasn't about to reveal my magic in front of a stranger. Jonathan might not need that kind of trauma in his life.

As I sat there, trying to remember every detail of Tempris's lessons, I felt it—something like the hum of electricity beneath my skin. It was eerily similar to the sensation when my lightning magic first sparked, but different. I glanced over at Jonathan, who was busy scrolling through his phone, probably looking up better job options. I began to hear blood rushing in my ears, like the ocean during a storm, drowning out everything else. For a second, I could hear nothing but this roaring noise, yet within it was a strange clarity.

I flexed my fingers and stared at my hands, a tingling sensation creeping across my skin, and then—just like that—it was gone. What the hell was that? I racked my brain for something Tempris had once said. "Nolan, you have to find the light in the dark, the unexplainable moment becoming clear." Right, like that was easy to grasp.

I took a deep breath and tried to focus on the noise again. My mind sifted through the chaos, every sound bending and blending, but amidst it, there was something—a sliver of silence. I latched onto it, willing my mind to grip it, and suddenly, all the noise disappeared. A pulse rippled through my body. I felt...stronger, sharper.

"Hey, Jonathan, let's give this one more try," I said, standing up and shaking out my limbs.

"Man, you wanna hurt yourself. This ain't worth fifty, y'all need to hire someone," he grumbled but trudged back over to me anyway.

"Just humor me," I insisted.

We got behind the piano, and this time, when we pushed, I could feel it—my muscles working harder, faster, like they'd been upgraded. I really was stronger. It wasn't a super human strength, but it was augmented far beyond my normal limits. Inch by inch, the piano inched up the ramp, the wood creaking under the strain, but before long, we were on a flat surface just a few feet from the freight elevator. Jonathan and I looked at each other, his eyes wide with disbelief, and we both let out a whoop of triumph and exhaustion.

Getting the piano up to Celeste's place was a breeze after that. I walked Jonathan out into the hallway, and he stopped me.

"Bruh, I know you said you run a cafe but you smell like straight coffee. Got coffee coming out the pores, man," he said walking towards the elevator. Little did he know it was all because I just expended quite a bit of magic. We dapped each other up, and he headed off, probably happy to never see another piano again.

I turned around to see Celeste leaning against her doorframe, holding the flowers I'd brought her. She was smirking, clearly impressed. "I gotta say, I didn't think you had it in you."

"Yeah, well, I'm full of surprises," I replied, my breath still ragged from the effort but my heart lighter.

She took a step closer, her eyes narrowing playfully. "You mean besides letting me mug you for fifty bucks?"

"Hey, I think of it as a strategic investment," I shot back, feeling a smile tug at my lips.

Celeste laughed, a sound that sent a pleasant shiver down my spine. She reached up and touched my arm, her fingers cool against my skin. "Well, consider it money well spent," she said softly, and for a moment, everything else faded away.

"So this is your place, eh?" I said as she ushered me inside, and for a moment, I just stood there, taking it all in. While moving the piano, I hadn't really had a chance to appreciate her apartment. Now, as I crossed the threshold, I realized just how much it reflected her—elegant, eclectic, and a little mysterious.

The entryway was narrow but inviting, framed by built-in bookshelves on either side that stretched up toward the ceiling. They were crammed with books—hardcovers, paperbacks, some with frayed edges and yellowing pages. It was a bibliophile's dream, and I could see that the spines ranged from modern fiction to what looked like old leather-bound tomes that probably had a century's worth of dust on them.

The entryway opened up into a spacious living room with ceiling-to-floor windows that bathed the space in soft, natural light. The walls were a deep, warm burgundy that contrasted beautifully with the cream-colored furniture scattered across the room—an oversized couch, a couple of plush armchairs, and a low coffee table cluttered with a few well-loved books and a half-finished cup of tea. There were more bookshelves, even taller than the ones in the foyer, lining the walls like sentinels. These books were older, more ornate. I could see gold-embossed titles in various languages, some I couldn't even recognize. A small ladder leaned against one of the shelves, like something out of a library from a bygone era.

Boxes still sat stacked in a corner near a vintage floor lamp, half-packed or half-unpacked, depending on how you looked at it. Celeste had moved in four months ago, yet it seemed like she was still in the process of settling in—or maybe she just liked to keep herself in a constant state of transition. I noticed a few framed photographs on one of the bookshelves: family, friends, maybe a few ex-lovers. She was the type who would have stories for each one, if you asked.

In the center of the living room, like the crown jewel of the whole setup, was the grand piano. Its dark mahogany wood gleamed under the afternoon sun, and the ivory keys were well-polished but not overly so—they had the slight wear of an instrument that had seen some real use. The bench was cushioned with a simple velvet pad, and on top of the piano were sheet music scattered like leaves after a windstorm, along with a metronome and a small framed photo of a much younger Celeste sitting on her dad's knee, her tiny hands on a piano just like this one. Seems like she couldn't wait to get that thing set up because it was only moments ago we were struggling not to rip the cover as we moved it. The box next to the piano had a stack of even more photos and books about music.

I took a slow turn around the room, letting it all sink in, and then turned to Celeste. "How can you afford this place? You can afford this but couldn't spring for a proper mover?" I asked, wandering over to the kitchen island, which was connected to the living room in a seamless, open-concept design. I took a seat on one of the high stools, the coolness of the granite countertop seeping into my forearms.

Celeste rolled her eyes, but there was a smile tugging at her lips. "I saved. I saved and saved and had a little help from my dad," she said, busying herself with rearranging some of the books on a nearby shelf.

"Next time, tell Pops to spring for Two Guys and a Truck," I quipped, raising an eyebrow. "It occurs to me I never even knew you could play the piano," I added, gesturing toward the grand piano that now sat victorious after our Herculean effort.

Celeste paused for a moment, her eyes lingering on the instrument. "Music has always been a huge part of my life. My parents made me learn when I was young. I was pretty good! I didn't stick with it, though. So when I asked my dad if he could help me out with this place, he said only if I took up the piano again. So, he gave me his. Said it was just collecting dust and I'd get more use out of it," she explained, her voice softening as she spoke about her dad.

"I love that. Seems like we both have a huge appreciation for music," I said, leaning back on the stool, feeling a warmth settle in my chest. "Since I was your grand hero today, why don't you play that grand piano for me?" I added with a smirk.

Celeste didn't reply. Instead, she walked over to the piano, moving with a fluid grace that was almost hypnotic. She settled onto the bench, did a couple of stretches—stretches that, admittedly, I watched with more interest than I should have—and then her fingers hovered over the keys. There was a moment of silence, a breath held between us, and then she began to play.

Her fingers danced across the keys with an effortless elegance, like she was rediscovering an old friend. The melody was soft and haunting, with notes that hung in the air like secrets. It was heavily influenced by jazz, a slow, bluesy tune that made me feel like I'd just walked into a smoky club in Harlem in the 1950s. There was a depth to it, a kind of raw emotion that pulled at something deep within me. I didn't recognize the song, but it had a way of making you feel like you'd known it your whole life, like it had always been a part of you, waiting to be heard.

I leaned back, closing my eyes, letting the music wash over me. I could feel the tension in my shoulders begin to melt away, replaced by a sense of calm I hadn't felt in a while. It was like every note was a little thread, weaving together a tapestry of peace and longing and something I couldn't quite put my finger on. My heart pounded in rhythm with the music, each beat syncing with the rise and fall of the melody. I was lost, completely enraptured, and I didn't think there was anything that could make me fall harder for her—but here it was. I opened my eyes and looked at her. She was the most beautiful woman I'd ever seen.

I must have been staring too hard because she glanced over, catching my eye, and flashed a broad smile, the kind that sent a ripple of warmth all the way down to my toes. She didn't miss a beat, though. Without warning, she shifted into an upbeat, almost swing-style song, her fingers flying over the keys with a newfound energy. The music took on a life of its own, filled with playful flourishes and quick tempo changes that made me want to get up and dance right there in her living room.

I chuckled, shaking my head, caught off guard by the sudden change in mood. But that was Celeste—always full of surprises. And maybe that's what I liked about her the most. I watched her, completely captivated, feeling like the luckiest guy in the world just to be here, in this moment, listening to her play. Just then, my phone buzzed in my pocket, shattering the perfect moment like a glass hitting the floor. I hesitated. I didn't want to ruin the vibe, but something in my gut told me to check. I pulled it out and glanced at the screen. It was a text from Tempris, and all it said was, "911. Cellar. Now."

My body went rigid, and a cold wave of anxiety crept up my spine. Tempris didn't just throw out "911" like it was candy on Halloween. My mind raced, trying to piece together what might be happening at the cafe. Was there a break-in? A fire? Did someone spill an entire vat of soup again? My thoughts were spiraling, and the music that had just a moment ago seemed so magical now felt a million miles away.

The piano stopped abruptly, breaking me out of my thoughts. I looked up to see Celeste staring at me, her eyes narrowed, her lips twisted into a mock pout.

"Nolan! If my music is boring you, then maybe I'll play some exit music," she said, her tone laced with mock annoyance. The corner of her mouth quirked up in a smile, but I could see a flicker of something else—concern? Disappointment?

"Yes. No, I mean no. I—you sound great. Really great," I stumbled over my words, feeling a flush creep up my neck. "I just got a message from Toby at the cafe. He said one of the new hires just made a huge mess." It wasn't a complete lie; Toby was there, and a mess was certainly within the realm of possibility. "I'm sorry, I really have to go. You're beautiful—your music—your music is beautiful. You are too. I'm sorry I have to rush off," I rambled, my words coming out in a jumbled mess.

I watched Celeste's face shift from mock annoyance to something softer, more amused. "Did you need me to come help you?" she asked, her eyes sparkling as she wagged a finger in my direction. "I told you I should have done the hiring for you."

I chuckled, despite the knot of worry tightening in my stomach. "No! No, it's fine. I'm sure it's probably not as bad as the text implies," I said, shrugging on my over-shirt in a hurry. My eyes flicked to the counter, where I noticed she'd already put the bouquet of flowers I'd brought her in a vase. The sight of those fresh flowers, carefully arranged in water, put a smile on my face—a quick burst of warmth amidst the rising tension.

For a moment, I felt torn, like I was being pulled in two different directions. I wanted to stay in this cozy little bubble of music and light and Celeste. But that text from Tempris—it nagged at me like a splinter under the skin.

I took a few steps toward the door, then stopped. Something inside me couldn't leave things like this, not after a moment like that. I spun around on my heel, crossed the room in two quick strides, and wrapped Celeste in a big, impulsive hug. She let out a surprised laugh, and I could feel the warmth of her body against mine, her heartbeat matching my own.

When I pulled back, I was grinning like an idiot, and she was too. There was this moment—just a heartbeat—where everything felt still. Her eyes were bright, and for a second, I forgot about the message, the cafe, the impending crisis. All I could see was her.

"You better come back in one piece," she said, her voice soft, almost a whisper. "And with a good story."

My heart fluttered. "Promise," I said, holding her gaze for another second before I reluctantly pulled away.

And then I was out the door, my feet pounding down the steps, my mind already racing ahead to the cafe and whatever emergency awaited. I couldn't shake the feeling of her smile lingering in my mind, or the scent of her perfume clinging to my clothes. I felt both exhilarated and anxious, like I was running from one life to another, each filled with its own kind of chaos.

As I jogged toward the cafe, a hundred thoughts buzzed in my mind like angry bees. Was Tempris okay? What kind of trouble had brewed up in the cellar? Was it something magical, or just a run-of-the-mill disaster? And then, threading through all of it, like a persistent undercurrent, was the image of Celeste's face as I'd left— half-smiling, half-concerned. The way her eyes had softened when she'd offered to help. The way she'd said, "You better come back in one piece."

I wasn't sure which part of me was more worried—the part racing to Tempris, or the part that was already missing Celeste.

# Chapter 14

*Vulnerable.*

I burst through the door of the cafe, eliciting several stares from customers and staff alike. Toby stopped mid-pour over, a bemused expression crossing his face. "You okay, boss? Thought you weren't coming in today."

I forced a smile, trying to shake off the lingering thoughts of Celeste and the music still playing in my head. "Yeah, no, I just forgot something. I won't be long. It looks busy in here! I like it! Keep up the good work," I said, breezing past him. I was moving fast, trying to maintain an air of calm when all I really felt was a growing sense of unease.

I made my way to the cellar door and unlocked it. Weeks ago, when Tempris started teaching me magic, we decided it was necessary to keep the cellar locked at all times. He'd even placed a special ward on it to make the door less interesting to anyone who might notice it. I rushed down the stairs, my mind running through every possible scenario of what could have gone wrong. But to my surprise, everything looked fine. No fires, no broken walls, nothing that screamed "911."

Then I spotted him. Tempris was slumped against the wall in the corner, unmoving. Panic seized me as I rushed to his side.

"Tempris! Tempris, wake up!" I yelled, shaking him.

Yeah, good job, Nolan. Shake the unconscious man who might have internal injuries. Brilliant.

Just then, his eyes fluttered open. He smiled at me and clapped me on the shoulder. "You got my text!" he said, a little too chipper for someone who had just been unconscious.

Tempris nearly jumped to his feet and started toward the warded barrier in the center of the room, his movements a little too energetic. My confusion mixed with annoyance. He seemed perfectly fine—better, in fact! I got pulled away from my perfect moment with Celeste for this?

He was looking around almost frantically, his eyes darting about like a ferret searching for a misplaced nut. A couple of boxes had fallen over, so I decided to pick them up. Beneath one was Tempris' open journal. For as many weeks as I'd spent with him, I had never seen the inside of this beat-up old journal he carried around. He told me not to touch it, but he didn't say I couldn't look inside.

I kneeled and looked at the open page. It was a sketch of a beautiful woman. Her face was framed by long dark hair, and her eyes were incredibly detailed. It was almost like she was peering into my soul. There was something haunting, yet familiar about her. I decided not to be too nosy and called to Tempris.

"Tem, is this what you're looking for?" I asked, rising while still holding a box.

Tempris darted over and scooped up his journal as if it were a child who had tripped and fallen. "Yes! Yes, Nolan. Thank you," he replied quickly, clutching it to his chest.

I took the moment to prod a little further. "So, who's the woman?" I asked, trying to sound casual but genuinely curious.

Tempris seemed to stiffen, his back toward me. He took a moment to turn around before speaking. "She's someone very dear to me, and before you ask, no, she's not dead, no, I can't just go see her, and yes, my research has a little to do with her. Satisfied?"

I could tell this was a sensitive subject for Tempris, but I was tired of being kept in the dark. "Tempris, I've asked very little about what you're researching, and I've let you give me tidbits and put things off, but I need to know what you're doing," I said firmly.

Tempris' face tightened, but after a moment, he seemed to deflate. He sat on a crate, crossing his legs, and leaned toward me. "Nolan, I'm not a powerful mage. In magical society, I'm considered a crackpot, a charlatan, a researcher whose universal magic is his only tool. The woman you saw in my notebook is a researcher of sorts as well. Her name is Alessia. She is someone I look up to because she too was cast aside, ridiculed, and mocked. However, the ones who push through all of that are the ones who make the breakthroughs. Like I said, I'm not powerful, but you are. Once I find the metaphorical jar of knowledge I have been looking for, I'll need you to open it," he said, getting to his feet.

He walked over to me and put a hand on my shoulder. His face looked drawn and old, his eyes haunted by experiences I couldn't possibly comprehend. I could smell sage and cinnamon—remnants of whatever magic had knocked him out before I got here. His eyes seemed to shimmer. I don't know if it was a trick of the light or if he was using his magic to try to regain the strength he'd lost. He cleared his throat before speaking again. "I'm almost there. Almost. You have made tremendous progress. You can expend tremendous amounts of magic before you burn yourself out. I envy you. Will you trust me? Continue to let me teach you, even though I'm more of a novice at teaching than you are at using magic?"

I took a deep breath, considering his words. Tempris wasn't one to open up often—he kept things close, hidden behind his quirky demeanor—but tonight, there was something different. There was a vulnerability in his voice, a kind of urgency that made me realize the stakes were higher than I had allowed myself to think.

"We're both learning," I said, stepping into the circle. I figured since my day with Celeste was officially over, I might as well learn something new. "Alright, what've you got for me today? Maybe a new spell? Something less likely to blow up in my face?"

Tempris stroked his chin theatrically. "It occurs to me that, after what happened a few weeks ago, you should probably learn a bit about combat magic. Self-defense, sure, but you need to know how to fight."

I raised an eyebrow. "Fight? Like, magical street fights? What am I, the next Harry Potter MMA champion?"

He chuckled, shaking his head. "Nolan, you've got potential, but it's not all fun and games. You're learning more about magic, right? That means more people from the magical world will start to notice you, too. And not all of them are friendly. The more you use magic, the more exposed you are."

"Great," I muttered. "That's comforting."

Tempris stepped closer, his tone softening. "I don't mean to worry you. I just want you to be prepared. You've already been attacked by some regular thugs—what if next time, it's someone with magical abilities?"

I shrugged, trying to brush off the anxiety starting to creep in. "Look, those guys were just regular dudes. I don't plan on joining a magical fight club or anything. Besides, if someone threw a fireball at me, I'd probably just...duck?"

"Very funny," Tempris replied, not laughing. "But here's the thing —you're not invincible. Sure, your own magic can't hurt you, and you heal quickly when you use it, but if someone else hits you with magic? That's a different story. It'll take you longer to recover because of the way magical atoms collide. It's...complicated. But trust me, if a magical attack lands, you're going to feel it."

I nodded, trying to process it all. He was serious. But at the same time, the idea of me getting into a magical battle still felt ridiculous. "Alright, I get it," I said, raising my hands in surrender. "You're trying to prepare me for the worst-case scenario."

Tempris sighed, stepping back. "Exactly. I'm just trying to keep you safe, Nolan. Magic isn't all sparks and cool tricks. It's dangerous. The more you know, the better off you'll be."

I crossed my arms, trying to look casual, but inside, my mind was buzzing. I didn't sign up for this level of danger when I asked Tempris to teach me magic. It was supposed to be fun, like learning a new hobby—not life-threatening.

"You ever think I might be better off not learning magic at all?" I asked, surprising even myself with the question.

Tempris looked at me with a kind of sadness in his eyes, like he'd been waiting for me to ask. "There's no going back now, Nolan. You've already opened that door. But how far you walk through it—that's up to you."

I swallowed hard. There was a knot in my stomach that hadn't been there before. Maybe he was right. Maybe I was in too deep to back out. But did I really want to keep going? And what would it mean if I did?

"I don't know, man," I admitted. "It feels like I'm on the edge of something big, and I'm not sure I like it."

Tempris clapped me on the back, trying to lighten the mood. "That's the thing about edges, Nolan. You never know what's on the other side until you jump."

I snorted. "That's some terrible advice."

He grinned, heading for the stairs. "Well, you're not getting any better from me. Come on. Let's get out of here. I think we need something stronger than coffee."

I followed him up, feeling the weight of the conversation settle over me like a heavy coat. When we stepped out into the crisp Detroit night, the air felt different—charged with possibility and tension. Detroit had always been a city of rebirth and mystery, from its rich history of jazz and industry to its modern revitalization. Now, with magic in the mix, it seemed like the city had even more secrets to reveal.

We walked down the street in silence for a bit, past old brick buildings and modern storefronts. The layers of history here always fascinated me—how a place could be both old and new, broken and rebuilt. Tempris must've sensed my thoughts because he nudged me with his elbow.

"Did you know Detroit used to be a hotbed for magic? Back in the 1920s, during Prohibition. Bootleggers weren't the only ones smuggling things in and out of the city."

I raised an eyebrow. "Are you saying Al Capone was a mage?"

Tempris laughed. "Not exactly. But there were plenty of magical speakeasies, places hidden from the mundane world. The magic users were smart—they kept themselves under the radar. If you weren't part of their world, you'd never even know they existed."

"Kind of like now," I mused. "Except I'm in on the secret."

He nodded. "And that's why I'm teaching you. Because one day, someone from that hidden world might come knocking. And I want you to be ready."

I stuffed my hands in my pockets, feeling a weird mix of excitement and dread. "You think there are still magical speakeasies around here?"

"Who knows? Detroit's full of hidden places, Nolan. Maybe one day you'll find one. Or maybe," he added with a sly smile, "one will find you."

We walked in companionable silence again, the neon lights of the city casting strange shadows on the pavement. Despite my doubts, I felt a strange sense of camaraderie with Tempris. We were both out of our depth in different ways—him, the underdog researcher; me, the reluctant student. But together, maybe we could figure this out.

As we passed a bar with flickering lights and jazz music spilling into the street, I glanced at Tempris. "So...what's your breakthrough?" I asked.

He smiled, but there was a guardedness in his eyes. "I'll tell you soon. But not tonight. Tonight, we celebrate the fact that you didn't burn down the cellar."

I laughed, pushing away my worries for now. "First round is on me," I said and we walked into the bar with a fresh sense of where our road would take us.

# Chapter 15

*Autumn in Detroit.*

F all had wrapped the city in its golden embrace, and Detroit Bold was transformed into a Halloween wonderland. Cobwebs stretched across the corners of the café, dangling plastic spiders that seemed to dance with every gust of wind from the door. Ghostly figures floated near the ceiling, their paper forms swaying eerily above the rows of dark roast. Tiny pumpkins lined the counter, and in the middle of it all was a life-sized skeleton sitting at a table with a coffee cup in hand. The cafe wasn't just decorated—it was alive with the spirit of the season, playful yet spooky, with a few ghoulish surprises scattered throughout. A haunted house soundtrack hummed softly in the background, barely audible over the hiss of the espresso machine.

Despite all the eerie décor, something was missing: Celeste. She used to love spending time here, but lately, her visits had been few and far between. I wasn't mad about it; I just missed her, and the café felt a little emptier without her constant energy. The few times she did come in, it was always about how much she loved her new job at the library. I made a mental note to visit her there one day.

Tempris, too, had been a rare sight. His trips out of town for research left me to fend for myself with magic, and though I tried pushing my limits like he'd instructed, it was never the same without his guidance. Still, I had other things to focus on—like Halloween, which had come faster than I expected.

Tonight, I was Dick Tracy, yellow trench coat, fedora, and two-way wrist radio, the whole nine yards. I felt sharp, but none of the college kids filling the café recognized the look. A few stifled giggles suggested they probably thought I was dressed as some random detective from an old cartoon. Didn't matter—Halloween was for having fun, and I was in my element.

I'd just handed over a pumpkin spice latte to the fifth Harley Quinn of the day when the bell on the door jingled. That's when I saw her—Celeste, dressed to the nines as Zatanna. Her top hat tilted low over her face, her waistcoat hugging her form just right, and the fishnets completing the look in a way that made me forget for a second that we were just friends. She made her way to the counter, her movements calculated and teasing. She tapped the brim of my hat with a toy magic wand, leaning in close.

"Trick or treat," she whispered.

I couldn't help but play along. Raising my wrist, I fiddled with the dial of my radio and spoke into it. "Come in, I'm gonna need backup at Detroit Bold. We've got an arsonist on the loose."

Celeste arched an eyebrow. "An arsonist?"

"Yeah, you're so hot you're gonna burn this place down."

She burst into laughter, her voice filling the café. "With that yellow trench coat and those lines, you could totally pass as an ear of corn," she teased, making her way around the counter.

"I admit, not my best work, but you look amazing," I said, trying to recover from her joke.

She reached for a coffee mug from the shelf, inspecting it with mock seriousness before tapping it with her wand. "I'm not just amazing, I'm magic," she said, winking. With a dramatic flourish, she tapped the mug three times, and suddenly, it began to fill with steaming coffee. She calmly applied dark red lipstick while the mug continued to fill, then took a sip, letting out an exaggerated sigh of satisfaction before handing me the rest.

I smelled the coffee—hot and fresh. "How did you do that?" I asked, genuinely curious.

Celeste removed her top hat and gave me a theatrical bow. "A magician never reveals their secrets."

With a flourish, she waved her hand and a plume of thick smoke surrounded us. When it cleared, she was gone. I blinked, half-impressed, half-wishing I could pull off something that slick. When I turned around, she was leaning casually against the door, a sly smile on her face.

"Bravo," I applauded. "That was actually pretty cool, and you didn't even trigger the sprinklers."

"I always know what I'm doing, Tracy. Now, let's blow this popsicle stand." She beckoned me on.

Before leaving, I glanced over at Toby, who was standing by the register in full "Java the Hutt" attire. He was literally an oversized coffee cup, complete with a droopy, foam tail and a garbled impression of Huttese.

"Go ahead, boss. I'll handle the rest," he muttered in a garbled, hilarious version of Jabba's speech. I laughed, unable to resist the ridiculousness of it.

"You're the best, Java," I replied, waving as I followed Celeste out into the crisp autumn night.

Outside, the air was cool and refreshing. "Where are we going?" I asked, watching her scroll through her phone.

"You're the detective—figure it out," she replied, hailing an oncoming ride share. The Kia Sportage rolled up, and I opened the door for her, sneakily grabbing her phone as she slid in.

I held the phone out of her reach with a smirk. "Cliff Bell's, huh? What's a dame like you doing at a joint like that?" I asked, putting on my best detective noir voice.

"You cheat!" she laughed, trying to grab her phone back. I dodged her attempt, enjoying the playful back-and-forth.

"If you ain't cheatin', you ain't tryin'," I said, grinning wide.

She shook her head, giving up as the car pulled away, the excitement of the night building as we headed for the jazz club.

Cliff Bell's was like stepping into another era. The moment I pushed open the door, the sounds and sights of the place hit me all at once. It was more than just a jazz club—it was a living, breathing piece of Detroit's history. The deep, polished mahogany of the bar, the intricate art deco light fixtures, the dim glow that seemed to wrap everything in a warm haze—it was like the past had never left. I could almost feel the ghosts of jazz legends lingering in the air, their notes echoing faintly between the clinks of glasses and the low hum of conversation.

I'd been here before, sure, but tonight felt different. Maybe it was the Halloween vibe, or maybe it was just the fact that Celeste was beside me, still in her Zatanna getup, flashing me that knowing smile like she could read my thoughts.

"Not bad for a detective," she teased, leaning into me as we made our way to a small table near the stage.

I smirked. "Guess I can follow clues after all."

The place was packed, but not in an overwhelming way—more like it was alive, buzzing with energy. The stage was bathed in soft, amber light, where a jazz quartet was warming up, and the whole room seemed to hum with anticipation. We barely had time to sit down before a waitress appeared, almost like magic, and we ordered drinks—an old-fashioned for me, a dirty martini for Celeste.

As we settled in, I couldn't help but glance around. The history here was palpable. This place had been open since 1935, surviving through Detroit's highs and lows. The fact that it was still standing, still vibrant, was a testament to the city's grit. It had seen Prohibition, the Great Depression, and the rise and fall of the auto industry. It had weathered Detroit's near collapse in the '80s and somehow come out on the other side, shining like a hidden gem.

The band started playing "Autumn Leaves," the saxophone's haunting melody drifting through the room like smoke. I leaned back in my chair, letting the music wash over me. There was something about jazz—it wasn't just music. It was emotion, a conversation between the notes, a story being told without words. And tonight, it felt like the music was telling my story.

"This place is incredible," I said, mostly to myself.

Celeste took a sip of her martini, her eyes softening as she listened to the music. "There's something about jazz, isn't there? It's like... every note tells a story."

I nodded, feeling that too. The music, the history, the flickering candlelight—it all seemed to blend together into something timeless. Like the magic Celeste had been playing with earlier, only this was real. Real and alive, right here in this moment.

We clapped as the band wrapped up their final number, and I turned to Celeste. Something about her seemed off—she was fidgeting with her glass, her smile a little less certain. Was she nervous? Did I do something? My mind raced through the night, trying to figure it out. Was this a date? Should I have made a move?

My hands tightened around my glass like it held the answers, and I couldn't tell if my palms were sweating from nerves or if it was just the condensation from the drink. I opened my mouth, ready to blurt out something—anything—to break the tension, but before I could speak, Celeste stood up abruptly.

"Uh, hey—" I started, but she was already moving towards the stage.

For a split second, I was lost. What was going on? Then it hit me when I saw her take a seat at the piano. She was performing. Of course she was performing! How did I not know that? Playfully, she twirled in her Zatanna costume, the top hat tipping just a little as she waved to the audience. I could feel the eyes around the room following her with curiosity and intrigue.

"This one goes out to a special piano mover who helped me get my music back," Celeste said into the mic, her voice smooth and teasing. She shot me a wink and flashed that smile—the one that sent my pulse into overdrive.

The spotlight dimmed as she adjusted the microphone to her height. She settled herself at the grand piano like she was preparing for a duel, fingers gently brushed the keys, her body completely still for just a second. She paused as if drawing in the energy of the room, and in that moment, the whole club seemed to hold its breath with her. The lights reflected softly off the sleek black surface of the piano, casting gentle shadows over her face.

I took a deep breath, I could still smell her scent lingering on my sleeve. It warmed me from the inside out, and before I knew it, I was grinning like a total idiot.

Then, her fingers moved. The music that flowed from the piano was like nothing I'd ever heard before. Soft but powerful, delicate but filled with emotion. The melody seemed to wrap around the room, capturing everyone in its embrace. The audience, once buzzing with conversation, had gone completely silent. Heads tilted, eyes closed, bodies leaning in as if they couldn't help but be pulled closer to the sound.

Her playing wasn't just good—it was hypnotic. Every note seemed to hit me in a different way, filling me with a warmth I hadn't expected. The way her fingers danced over the ivory keys, fluid and confident, was like watching magic unfold in real time. And the way she swayed as she played, completely immersed in her music, sent a shiver down my spine.

I could feel the tension in the room shift. There was something about her song—it wasn't just beautiful, it was intimate. Like a secret she was sharing with all of us, but mostly with me. I could see a few people out of the corner of my eye, whispering to each other, but their words didn't matter. It was like the entire club had been transported somewhere else, somewhere ethereal.

The song started soft, almost fragile, and then it built, rising like a slow wave. Her hands moved faster, the music gaining intensity, yet it never lost its beauty. It swirled around the room, gathering everyone in its tide. I could feel the notes settle in my chest, each one like a spark of warmth that slowly spread through me.

I leaned forward in my chair, completely entranced by the way she played. Every time her fingers struck a chord, I felt like she was telling a story—our story. And when her eyes flicked up to meet mine in between verses, I swear my heart stopped.

Celeste wasn't just playing a piano—she was casting a spell. And I was completely under her enchantment.

When the final note rang out, it hung in the air like a lingering echo of something too beautiful to let go of. The audience erupted into applause, but all I could do was sit there, completely dumbfounded. She looked up from the piano, her eyes finding mine again, and that smile—that damn smile—spread across her face, as if she knew exactly what she'd done to me.

She stood up, gave a graceful bow, and sauntered back toward me, the applause still roaring in the background. As she slid back into her seat, I stared at her, unable to form any words that could possibly capture what I was feeling.

"That was... you were..." I stammered like a lovestruck teenager.

"Magic?" she asked with a wink, picking up her drink and taking a casual sip like she hadn't just knocked the wind out of me.

I chuckled, finally finding my voice. "Yeah, magic."

She tilted her head, her eyes twinkling with a mix of humor and something deeper. "I told you, didn't I?"

I shook my head, smiling like an idiot again. "I didn't realize just how serious you were."

"Stick around," she teased, leaning in closer. "I haven't shown you all my tricks yet."

The warmth of her breath against my ear sent a thrill through me, and in that moment, it was pretty clear—I was hopelessly, completely, and undeniably smitten.

The next performer took the stage—a jazz singer with a voice like velvet, accompanied by a pianist who, frankly, could've been asleep for all the energy he was putting into his playing. I tried to appreciate the music, but after hearing Celeste play, it was like going from a five-star meal to reheated leftovers. My mind was still replaying her performance, every note she touched still dancing in the back of my mind.

"I'll be right back," Celeste said, leaning into me with a soft, warm presence that sent my thoughts into overdrive.

"Where you goin'?" I asked, more curious than concerned.

"Nature calls," she replied with a playful grin. "And let me tell you, using the bathroom in this thing is gonna be worse than a romper."

I couldn't help but chuckle. "Ah, the Zatanna costume strikes again. You should've brought a magician's assistant to help."

She winked, but just as she started to rise, she wobbled, her hand shooting to her temple. Instantly, I was on my feet, steadying her in my arms.

"Whoa, hey," I said, concern tightening my voice. "What's wrong?"

"My head," she murmured, wincing as her fingers pressed against her temples. "These stupid headaches."

Her eyes welled up from the pain, and a jolt of panic shot through me. I quickly snatched her top hat from the table and slipped it under my arm as I pulled her closer.

"Alright, we're done for tonight," I said, already thumbing my phone for a ride share. "Let's call it an early night. I *really* wish you'd get these headaches checked out."

She groaned, leaning into me for support, her weight light but her pain palpable. "You worry too much," she said with a forced smile. "It's probably just from working too hard. Too much time squinting at old manuscripts in the library archives. Occupational hazard."

I wasn't buying it. "You've been getting these headaches for months, long before you started the new job." My voice was firmer than I intended, the concern spilling out.

As we reached the door, she sighed and tilted her head up to look at me. Her expression softened, and for a moment, some of the pain seemed to fade from her eyes. She raised her wand, tapping her forehead lightly with a wink.

"You know what might help a little?" she teased, her eyes glinting with that familiar mischievousness.

I couldn't help but smile, despite the anxiety twisting in my gut. I pulled her close, kissed her softly on the forehead, and for a brief, perfect moment, everything else fell away. She relaxed into me, her breath slowing, and I held her there, feeling the warmth of her body against mine.

Time seemed to blur. We stood like that, just the two of us in our own little bubble, the world outside dimming. My heart pounded in my chest, racing faster with each second that passed. I didn't know how long we stayed there—minutes, hours, a lifetime?—but I didn't care. All that mattered was her.

My phone buzzed in my pocket, snapping me back to reality. I pulled it out to see a text from the driver: **"Arrived. Silver sedan. Parked out front."**

"Ride's here," I said softly, not wanting to break the moment but knowing I had to.

Celeste sighed but smiled, her eyes still a little dazed from the headache. "Thanks, Nolan. You're always looking out for me."

"Someone's gotta keep you out of trouble," I said with a grin, though the worry still gnawed at the back of my mind. Whatever these headaches were, they weren't going away, and no amount of magical wit was going to fix that.

As I guided her outside, the crisp night air hit us, and for a moment, I hoped it might clear her mind. But deep down, I knew something was off. I just didn't know how to help her yet.

# Chapter 16

*Motor City Magic.*

Halloween came and went, leaving behind a haze of pumpkin spice, costumed chaos, and the lingering memory of almost —but not quite—something more with Celeste. There were moments where we seemed on the verge of crossing that invisible line from friendship to something deeper, but we never quite made the leap. Could I even make that leap when I was hiding such a massive part of my life from her? It gnawed at me constantly. Every time I thought about telling her, my mind spiraled into a labyrinth of what-ifs.

I was thrust out of my thoughts quite literally when something smacked me in the head—a bag of coffee beans. The bag exploded as it hit the ground, beans scattering across the floor like tiny brown marbles. I looked up to see Tempris standing there, shaking his head in disbelief, clearly unimpressed with my lack of focus.

"Earth to Nolan!" he snapped, waving his hand toward the mess. "If you can't shield yourself from a bag of dark roast, I shudder to think how you'd fare against dark magic."

He flicked his wrist, and a broom slid across the floor toward me with a *swish*. I caught it mid-slide and stared at the wreckage of my good coffee beans, strewn across the floor like a metaphor for my brain right now.

"Sorry! Sorry!" I stammered, rubbing the back of my head. "My mind was elsewhere." I gestured helplessly at the beans with one hand. "But seriously, you didn't have to waste a whole bag of my best coffee, man."

Tempris folded his arms and gave me a long, disapproving look. "Wouldn't have been a waste if you weren't wasting time. What's on your mind?" He summoned a dustpan with a flick of his fingers and held it out for me to sweep up the mess.

I sighed and started sweeping, the sound of beans clinking against the floor oddly soothing. "Celeste is on my mind," I admitted, more to myself than to Tempris. "I thought we had a breakthrough at Halloween, you know? But it's been another two weeks since I've seen her."

Tempris didn't say anything for a moment, just watched me sweep up the debris of my distracted thoughts. "She's busy," he finally said, his tone softer, though still edged with that no-nonsense vibe. "And you're supposed to be busy too. Busy learning all you can, so you don't get distracted. Not by her. Not by anything."

"I know, I know," I muttered, dumping the beans into the dustpan with a resigned sigh. "It's just...hard. She's all I think about lately."

Tempris snorted, shaking his head. "That's because you're human, Nolan. It happens. But if your mind's wandering, you're not fully present. And if you're not fully present, your magic's going to reflect that. You have to stay focused."

I nodded, but my focus was already slipping, my thoughts drifting back to Celeste—the way she smiled, the way her fingers danced over the piano keys, the way her perfume still lingered on my sleeve long after she left. My chest tightened at the memory of her on stage that night, the music wrapping around me like a spell I couldn't shake.

I barely even registered that Tempris had thrown another object at me until it hit my shoulder—this time a much larger bag of beans.

"Ow!" I yelped, dropping the broom. The bag burst open, and once again, beans cascaded across the floor, scattering in every direction like some kind of caffeinated confetti.

Tempris raised an eyebrow, unimpressed. "And *again*."

The beans continued to roll across the floor, a few of them making soft clinking sounds as they brushed against the dustpan. The sharp sound echoed through the room, matching the splitting feeling in my head every time I thought of Celeste. I looked down at the beans, then back up at Tempris, feeling the weight of his gaze pressing down on me.

"Okay, fine. I'm distracted. You happy?" I threw my hands in the air. "I've been trying to get better at the whole shield thing, but it's hard to focus when my brain is constantly stuck on her."

Tempris sighed deeply, his frustration palpable, but there was a glimmer of understanding in his eyes. "Look, Nolan," he said, stepping closer, "I get it. Believe me, I've been there. But if you can't learn to compartmentalize, you'll never progress. Magic requires discipline. Your mind has to be sharp, or you're going to end up getting yourself—or worse, her—hurt."

I frowned, sweeping the new mess half-heartedly. "Yeah, but it's not like I can just turn off my thoughts, you know?"

Tempris smirked, his eyes twinkling with a hint of humor. "No, but you can stop letting your emotions run the show. Think of it like...brewing coffee. You wouldn't let the beans soak in water forever, would you? They'd get over-extracted, bitter. You have to time it perfectly, balance it just right."

I glanced at the scattered beans on the floor. "So...what, I'm supposed to put a timer on my feelings for Celeste?"

Tempris chuckled, the sound surprisingly light. "Not exactly. But you can learn to separate them from your magic. Trust me, you don't want to be in the middle of casting a complex spell and suddenly have your brain short-circuit because you're thinking about how good she looked in that Zatanna costume."

I flushed, rubbing the back of my neck. "Okay, point taken."

He gave me a small, almost fatherly pat on the shoulder. "You'll figure it out. Just...try not to let it consume you. Otherwise, the only thing you'll be good at is making coffee—and trust me, magic's a lot more exciting than that."

With one last amused glance at the coffee bean carnage, Tempris gestured for me to try again.

This time, I managed to put up a decent shield, but the sound of those beans splitting open still echoed in the back of my mind.

Training was short today—Tempris had other things to attend to, and the shop was quiet with only one staff member on duty. The college crowd had thinned out after midterms, leaving us with a lull I wasn't complaining about. I strolled over to Toby, who was lost in the process of steaming milk, completely oblivious to me thanks to the massive headphones covering his ears.

As I walked by, I noticed his laptop propped open on the counter, and a podcast titled "Motor City Magic" filled the screen. There was a subheading, but I couldn't quite make it out. I waved to catch his attention, startling him just enough that he almost dropped the milk pitcher. He laughed and pressed the side of his headphones, pulling them down to his neck.

"Hey! Sorry about that, man. It's so slow in here I thought I'd catch up on some podcasts," he said, pouring the frothy milk into a cup of espresso.

"No worries," I replied, leaning over to look at his laptop. "Motor City Magic? Sounds more like a coffee blend than a podcast."

Toby grinned as he slid the finished drink onto a tray and grabbed a napkin. "It's a podcast Celeste recommended to me. She knows I'm into all that lore, Renaissance Festival, geeky stuff, so she thought I might like it. The host talks about magic—like, real magic—and he's super into it."

That's when it hit me. *Mr. Motor City Magic*—was this the guy Celeste had gone on that date with? Sure, the date didn't go anywhere, but the guy had guts. I mean, here I was, still debating if I should even ask her out, while this guy was out here talking about mystical forces over a microphone. I knew magic *actually* existed, but the real magic in my life wasn't spells or shields—it was Celeste.

This was it. The final straw. No more playing around with "will they, won't they?" I was done waiting. If some podcaster could shoot his shot, I sure as hell could.

"Toby, I'm heading out for a bit," I said, grabbing my jacket from the coat rack.

"Cool," he replied, barely looking up from his laptop. "Need me to do anything while you're gone?"

"Yeah. Wish me luck," I said, throwing on my jacket and stepping out into the chilly autumn air.

Ten minutes later, I was standing outside the Detroit Public Library Main Branch. I always loved this building—a grand, Beaux-Arts structure that felt like stepping into another century. The place radiated history, from the stone-carved details outside to the towering shelves of ancient books inside. But I didn't come here nearly enough, which was a problem, because I had no idea where to find Celeste.

I headed inside and approached the front desk, where an older gentleman sat, flipping through a worn paperback. His glasses were so thick they practically magnified his eyes to twice their size, and his beard was...impressive, to say the least. He glanced up at me over the rims of his glasses.

"Hi, I'm looking for Celeste. She's the head archivist," I said, trying to sound casual, though my nerves were already buzzing.

He gave me a knowing smile. "Ah, but is Celeste looking for *you*?" He chuckled at his own joke. "Just kidding. I recognize you from the coffee shop. She's setting up documents for a lecture in the main hall."

He gave me directions that should have been easy to follow, but—being me—I got turned around three times before finally arriving at the main lecture hall. The room was grand, with high, arched ceilings, rows of stadium-style seating, and large, stained-glass windows that made the place feel more like a cathedral than a classroom.

At the front of the room, there was a raised platform with a lectern and a cart full of old documents. And there she was—Celeste—wearing white gloves, handling a centuries-old manuscript with the kind of grace that made everything else disappear.

She looked up as I approached, her face lighting up in a smile that made my heart race.

"I didn't know you were into 17th-century literature," she teased, pulling off her gloves.

"Oh yeah, big fan," I replied, trying to keep it light. "Got any Dr. Seuss in that pile?"

She laughed, and it was the kind of laugh that echoed in my chest. It felt so good to see her like this, in her element, comfortable and confident. But I wasn't here to make jokes.

"I'm actually here to ask you out," I said, suddenly feeling like every word was a leap of faith. Her eyes widened slightly, and her smile grew even bigger.

"It only took you half a year," she teased, stepping a little closer.

"I like to wait for the right moment," I stammered.

"And what makes this moment so right?"

My heart was pounding, but I reached for her hand anyway. "If you can't tell someone how you feel about them during the holidays, then when can you? The Christmas tree lighting is in a week and a half. Come with me. Let's go together—as a date."

She didn't say anything right away, just looked at me for a long moment, like she was letting the words sink in. And then her smile softened, and she stepped even closer.

"It's a date," she said softly, and kissed me on the cheek.

"Now either take a seat up front so you can learn everything you can, or get outta here!" she teased, eyes twinkling with mischief.

Beaming like an absolute idiot, I started backing away, my feet moving on their own, nearly tripping over a group of stuffy, collegiate-looking guys who had just walked in. One of them gave me the side-eye, probably wondering what kind of fool would get that flustered in a lecture hall. But I didn't care. Hell, I could've knocked over a whole bookshelf, and it wouldn't have wiped the grin off my face.

I caught one last glimpse of Celeste as I reached the door. She was still smiling, her head tilted slightly, looking at me like I had just made her day. That smile—it was everything. The kind that made my stomach flip like I'd just stepped off a rollercoaster.

As I stepped into the hallway, the cool air from the library's ancient ventilation system hit me, and I took a deep breath. I actually did it. I asked her out, and she said yes. I could practically hear

Tempris' voice in my head, mockingly slow-clapping, but hey, even *he* couldn't ruin this moment.

The lecture hall's grand double doors closed behind me with a heavy thud, and suddenly the echo of quiet library halls surrounded me. The musty smell of old books lingered in the air as I strolled down the long corridor, each step feeling lighter than the last. Everything around me seemed more vivid now—the marble floors gleaming under the soft light, the intricate wood paneling along the walls, the faint rustle of turning pages from distant rooms.

I almost wanted to laugh out loud. Here I was, feeling like I'd just conquered the world by asking a girl to the tree lighting. A girl who literally works with rare documents older than the city itself, while I struggled to remember where I parked my car.

As I passed by a row of portraits of former library directors, an old man sitting at a bench near the window looked up from his newspaper and gave me a curious glance. His thick, bushy eyebrows lifted in amusement.

"Young love?" he asked, with a knowing grin.

"Something like that," I said, still grinning like a fool.

He chuckled and shook his head. "Enjoy it while you can. You'll never be as brave as you are now."

I laughed and gave him a mock salute before pushing open the main doors of the library. Outside, the crisp autumn air greeted me, sharp and invigorating. The trees lining Woodward Avenue were dressed in gold and crimson, the late afternoon sun casting long shadows over the historic buildings around me. Detroit's heartbeat felt steady and strong, like it always did in these cooler months.

I checked my phone, noticing a few messages from the shop and a reminder to call Tempris back. But none of it seemed important right now.

The real magic wasn't in my training with Tempris, or the occasional enchanted mishap at the shop. It was in this. In moments like this, when the world was just a little brighter, when the noise in my head quieted enough for me to take a leap of faith. Celeste wasn't just a part of my life; she was the spark that made it all worth it.

I slipped my hands into my pockets and took off down the street, a little quicker than usual, because, for once, the world felt like it was on my side.

And besides, I had a date to plan.

# Chapter 17

*In a sentimental mood.*

D owntown Detroit really comes alive during the holiday
season. Woodward Avenue runs the length of Detroit,
stretching from the riverfront facing Canada all the way to
Pontiac, a city north of Detroit. Spanning almost thirty miles, it
serves as a dividing line between the east and west sides of the city.
Along its downtown stretch, the street is lined with shops,
restaurants, and businesses. At Christmastime, these storefronts are
decked out in such elaborate lights and decorations that even Kris
Kringle himself would probably take notes.

In the center of it all lies Campus Martius Park, the beating heart
of Detroit during the holidays. It's home to an enormous Christmas
tree, the kind you'd expect to see in movies. Every year, thousands of
people gather around for the tree lighting ceremony, and this year,
Celeste and I were making an evening out of it. We'd planned to meet
after I closed up shop and she ended her shift at the library.

Business at the café was slow, so I closed early and caught an
Uber downtown. Normally, I would've walked—it wasn't far—but
tonight, the cold winter air felt like knives against my face. Michigan
winters are never something you fully get used to, even after a
lifetime of living here. The wind off the Detroit River could chill your
bones if you weren't prepared.

As the Uber approached Campus Martius, I was greeted by the sight of families, couples, and groups of friends all bundled up in scarves and hats, strolling under the twinkling holiday lights. The entire park was buzzing with life and excitement, a mix of laughter, music, and the occasional jingle of bells from street performers. Snow flurries drifted through the air, adding an extra touch of magic to the scene.

The massive Christmas tree towered in the center of the park, easily over 60 feet tall, transported from Kingsley, Michigan, hundreds of miles north. Beneath it, an ice rink had been set up, with skaters twirling and gliding under the tree's twinkling lights. The rink at Campus Martius is even larger than the one at Rockefeller Plaza in New York—though I only share that fact when I'm trying to impress someone.

I stepped out of the Uber, adjusting my scarf as the cold hit me. The entire scene looked like something out of a winter postcard, the kind you'd send to family bragging about how picturesque the holidays were in the city. I wandered through the crowd, weaving between people, wondering just how many of them knew the things I knew now. How much of this holiday magic was *real* magic?

"Nolan!"

I turned and saw Celeste walking up the street towards me. She wore a huge smile, and a cranberry red peacoat with the lipstick to match. Her hands were covered with fluffy white mittens strung with balls that dangled when she waved to me. It was in that moment I realized I always knew magic was real. Without a moments notice, snow began to fall. Flurries covered her enormous twist-out and she took a twirl reveling in it. I found myself smiling uncontrollably as I made my way over to her. She twirled into me with a hug and our faces came close enough that I could make out the snowflakes on her eyelashes and smell the shea butter on her skin.

"Merry Christmas! I brought you something," she said without breaking contact.

Her arms were wrapped around me and I could feel her shaking one of them as she pulled back and handed me a small paper bag I had not noticed before. My smile widened when I read "Avalon

Bakery" on the wrinkled paper. Avalon's baked goods were legendary, and since their hours mirrored mine, I rarely had the chance to visit. I reached into the bag and pulled out a puff pastry that had a clear bite taken out of it. Remnants of red lipstick rimed the torn edges. My eyes met hers with a good natured glare.

"How'd you know? I always wanted fresh baked leftovers for Christmas!"

"I'm sweet like that," she replied and for the first time I noticed flakes of pastry down the front of her scarf and a few stuck to her lips. I started to tell her, started to reach towards her face to wipe the crumbs—then I just went for it. I pulled her in to me, her body warm even in the cold night air. She craned her neck to look up at me and didn't say a word. It wasn't planned—nothing about that moment was—but it felt perfect. I kissed her. Neurons fired in my brain as our lips met and every ounce of pent up desire was finally let loose. I felt her body respond, her lips and tongue probing mine, searching, feeling, and embracing this long awaited moment. I couldn't tell you how long we stood there on Woodward Avenue in that embrace. When we finally pulled back, our foreheads resting together, Celeste's giggle broke the silence. I suddenly felt self-conscious.

"What? What's funny?" I asked.

She pulled out her phone, snapped a picture of me, and held it up to show my reflection. My lips and chin were smeared with her bright red lipstick.

"I didn't know you shopped at the Lip Bar too," she teased, barely able to contain her laughter.

"Hey, I make this color work," I replied, grabbing a napkin from the Avalon bag to wipe it off.

"You know, I have another shade I think would look *perfect* on you," she said with a mischievous glint in her eye.

"I'll try the whole collection if it means—"

Before I could finish, she leaned in and kissed me again. This one was softer, shorter, but just as sweet. When we pulled away, we stood there for a long time, holding each other, the world bustling around us.

"You cold?" I asked, noticing her shivering.

"Freezing!" she said, her teeth chattering slightly.

"That's it. We're getting you the biggest, hottest hot chocolate in Detroit," I declared, grabbing her hand and leading her toward Campus Martius.

"I thought I already had the biggest, hottest hot chocolate," she said with a sly grin, nestling closer into my arm.

I laughed, pulling her in tighter as we made our way toward the ice rink. Campus Martius was a sea of twinkling lights, music, and excited chatter. The Christmas tree towered over the crowd, standing tall at over 60 feet, its branches covered in thousands of shimmering lights. People were packed together, some skating on the rink, others gathered around waiting for the tree lighting ceremony to begin. Performers dressed as elves and reindeer were twirling on the ice, earning cheers from the crowd.

"Did you know," I said, pulling Celeste closer as we walked, "the rink here is bigger than the one in Rockefeller Plaza?"

She gave me an exaggerated eye roll. "Only you would drop random Detroit trivia during a romantic moment."

"Says the librarian," I teased.

"Head archivist, buddy. And don't you forget it," she corrected, poking me in the ribs.

"I don't think I could forget anything about you, even if I tried," I said, giving her a playful nudge.

We were about to kiss again when the countdown for the tree lighting began. The crowd around us erupted in excitement, and we both turned our eyes to the massive tree. The final seconds ticked down, and then, with a flick of a switch, the tree came to life, bathed in vibrant, colorful lights. The crowd cheered, and I instinctively pulled out my phone, trying to capture the perfect photo of the two of us in front of the tree.

An older gentleman, one of the regulars from Detroit Bold, appeared out of nowhere and offered to snap a few shots for us. "I better get a discount next time I'm in," he joked as he handed my phone back.

"Drinks are on me," I replied, looking at the photos. They were perfect—Celeste's smile as bright as the tree behind her.

We walked around Campus Martius for a while, hand in hand, basking in the holiday atmosphere. There were kids on their parents' shoulders, couples dancing under the lights, and vendors selling roasted chestnuts and hot cider. It felt like we were in the middle of a Hallmark movie.

As the night wore on, Celeste tugged on my arm, pulling me toward the street.

"Come on, you're coming home with me," she said with a smile.

I raised an eyebrow. "Whoa, buy me dinner first."

She laughed, swatting me playfully. "It's freezing, and my heat's on the fritz. You're gonna help me fix it."

"Oh, so you're just using me for my technical skills?" I asked, grinning.

"And your lips," she replied, leaning in to kiss me again.

"Fair trade," I said, as we headed toward her apartment, the city lights twinkling around us like stars.

# Chapter 18

*Love spell.*

Celeste's apartment was freezing, which came as a great surprise to both of us as we crossed the threshold. Her place was a newer build, so I assumed it had something to do with the smart thermostat.

"Fix it, fix it, fix it! I am putting on tea to go with these sweets!" she shouted through trembling lips.

I kicked off my boots and hastened to the thermostat, sliding to a stop on the polished wood floors as I approached. I fiddled with the settings for a few moments and realized it was a very simple fix. The "smart" thermostats we've come to know and love aren't always that smart. They learn routines that make absolutely no sense. I reset the internal schedule, cranked up the temperature, and could immediately hear the hum of the furnace initiate and felt a satisfying whoosh of air that began blowing through the vents.

"Fixed it!" I shouted over my shoulder as I headed back towards the living room. I turned to see the room aglow with candlelight. Celeste had taken it upon herself to light an army of candles around the room.

"I know what not to buy you for Christmas. I think you already have every candle in Metro Detroit."

"Shut up and come here."

She was on the couch, her figure lit by the soft glow of the candles. Shadows danced on her face, and I could see she was already cutting through the strings of the bakery container. The box was already open by the time I sat beside her, the sweet smell of baked goods washing over me. I leaned back to get comfortable and was taken by surprise when she swept her legs up over mine and scooted closer. She had a blanket drawn over her lap that was dotted with powdered sugar and flakes of what had to be chocolate croissant or baklava.

"You're getting awful comfy for someone who's gonna have to get up to move the kettle any minute," I said as I caressed her leg under the blanket.

"Please, you should know by now that I'm the master of multi-tasking," she replied.

I brushed crumbs from the blanket.

"Looks to me like you're the master of making a quick mess."

She kicked me with the back of her heel and took a huge bite out of a pastry I still couldn't make out in the dim candlelight.

"Nolan, is this... are we..."

Celeste returned from the kitchen, no tea in hand. She climbed atop me, straddling my legs, her hips grinding into mine. She moved with the grace and intensity of a jungle cat. My hands gripped her thighs and made their way up her body until I had her face cupped in my hands. I wasted no time as I brought her lips to mine. They were soft and tasted of honey, with the faintest hint of pistachio. The baklava, then. We kissed for what seemed like an eternity, lips and tongues getting lost in each other.

Her legs swung wildly across the coffee table, scattering chess pieces across the floor.

I kept one breast in my hand as I brought it to my mouth. She gasped as I sucked and nibbled, her nails clawing into my shoulder. Without warning, she pulled away and looked into my eyes. There was something in the way our eyes met that spoke volumes. More was expressed in that one look than in the past year of knowing her, learning her, loving her.

Celeste rose and took my hand, leading me to the bedroom. We collapsed onto the bed, a tangle of arms and legs, hands groping for each other hungrily. We vanished into a world of our own making.

# Chapter 19

*Magic in the morning.*

It was the next morning. I woke before Celeste and watched her sleep. We lay naked on her platform bed, sheets and blankets all but forgotten. Blades of light cut through the curtains turning I would describe our time together, but my words wouldn't do it justice. The way my hand felt caressing the small of her back. Knowing how I've trained tirelessly for months and in this one moment I finally understood what magic was. It was also in that moment I knew I had to tell her everything I'd been doing the last few months. The magic, the training, Tempris, all of it. If Celeste was going to be part of my life, there was no way I could keep this from her. I felt bad enough hiding everything from her till this point and now that we were whatever we were, it was only right. Come to think of it, what were we? One thing at a time I thought and began gathering my thoughts. Celeste stirred, her body gently moving closer to me, her hand finding my chest. Her eyes fluttered open and she smiled at me. I smiled back and decided now was the time.

"Celeste, there's something I—" my words were cut off by Celeste bolting upright at the sight of the bedside clock.

"Oh, shit! I have a meeting!" She said, pecking me on the lips and rolling out of bed. I watched her still naked form dart towards the bathroom. The sound of the shower turning on came drifting from the bathroom.

"This isn't one of those let me get out of an awkward or uncomfortable situation by pretending I have a meeting the morning after things is it?" I asked jokingly.

Celeste hurried back into the bedroom pinning her hair up into a shower cap as she walked. She kissed me, long and deep.

"What do you think?" She asked as she stood and tip-toed back to the bathroom. I heard her enter the shower and watched steam cascade from the the now half closed door. There was no doubt in my mind her shower was the approximate temperature of Mount Vesuvius.

"I'm gonna go change and open the cafe. There's still something I want to talk to you about. Talk later?" I asked raising my voice over the shower.

"I'll come by after my meeting. We can have lunch. You're not going to tell me you love me or something are you?" she replied with mock disgust in her voice.

"Geez! Of course not! I love you!" I shouted as I walked out the door.

# Chapter 20

*Truth hurts.*

Cleaning usually puts me at ease. So I cleaned and I cleaned and I cleaned. Although the cafe was still tidy from the evening before, I put a little extra elbow grease into getting things spotless. I wiped under the counters, stopping to scrape gum off every minute or two. I hefted the espresso machine and wiped underneath that. Doorknobs got polished, fixtures dusted and glasses rearranged. This is what happens when I'm faced with a tough conversation, I start doing things. I knew at any moment Tempris would be walking in the door and I was going to let him know Celeste would need to be brought into my world. Although really she is the one that brought me into hers. I'd been in love before, at least I think I had. However after the events of the past few weeks, especially last night, I wasn't so sure anymore. Love had a new meaning. I had a whole new lease on love! A customer cleared their throat and I looked over realized I'd been staring into space with a handful of stirs in my hand and a stupid grin on my face. We were so slow I forgot we were even open. One black coffee to go later I was back at it, cleaning the toaster oven. I imagined how the conversation would go. Would Tempris be understanding and excited for this new chapter of my life or would he get so mad he'd immolate my store before hopping off into another dimension? I guess I could hope for something in the middle, right?

I heard the chime of the bell at the front of the cafe and in walked Tempris, a wide grin on his face. He was waving his journal frantically as he approached.

"I've done it! It's done! Years of research have finally paid off! The coordinates, are complete and I know how to reach where we need to go! Best of all we can do it from right here! Well from your training ground below. I couldn't have done this without you! Thank you my friend," he said slamming his journal down on the counter with almost schoolboy glee.

"Woah woah woah, that's great news! I really wasn't much help, all I did was provide you a place to work," I replied.

"You have done so much more than that, you will never know! What's on your agenda for today? We can go right now! Close up shop!"

I squared my shoulders as I approached Tempris, my magic teacher, feeling a knot of anxiety twisting in my stomach. We had sworn to keep our training sessions hidden from the world, but I couldn't bear to keep Celeste in the dark any longer.

"Tempris, there's something I need to discuss with you," I started, my voice steady despite the turmoil raging inside me.

He looked up from his journal, his expression guarded. "What is it, Nolan? You seem troubled."

I took a deep breath, shaking off the nerves. "It's about Celeste, Tempris. You know, beautiful, funny, makes a great cuppa Celeste? Things have been going really well between us lately, like REALLY well. I've fallen for her. Hard. But I can't keep our training a secret from her any longer. There's this huge part of my life I've been hiding from her for months and she has to know."

Tempris's eyes narrowed, a flicker of anger sparking in their depths. "You made a promise, Nolan. A promise to keep what we're doing hidden from outsiders. Do you not understand the gravity of your actions?"

"I understand, Tempris. But she deserves to know the truth. You know Celeste, and you know she's a cute above the rest. She might get a little freaked out but part of me thinks she will understand, and she will keep our secret as well," I insisted, my heart pounding in my chest.

His body twisted away from me, his hands trembling with suppressed fury. "You are risking everything, Nolan. Everything we've worked for. Do you not care about the consequences?"

"I care about her, Tempris. I love her," I replied, my voice cracking with emotion.

He shook his head, his dark hair falling over his face creating an ominous shadow. "Love is not enough to protect her from the dangers of our world, Nolan. You are being selfish, blinded by your emotions."

The weight of guilt pressed down on me as I watched him turn further away, his form rigid with anger. "I'm sorry, Tempris. But I can't keep hiding who I am from the woman I love."

He turned back to me sharply and raised a finger, jabbing it in my chest. "I forbid you to tell her. That's final."

"First of all, you can't forbid me to do anything. We're doing each other a favor remember? Now I know I'm being a total jerk by going back on my word but circumstances have changed. I thought you of all people would understand," I gestured around us and gestured at my hands, spreading my fingers as if holding something. "This is too big, too important to hide from someone I am trying to build a future with."

Tempris closed the distance between us and loomed over me, using his considerable height difference to emphasize his point. The smell of sage was strong, and I could feel magic radiating off of him. "What do you understand about building a future? About this world and this magic you were so eager to exploit me for? You haven't even begun to grasp the enormity of what you have bulldozed your way into. Tell Celeste and you will regret it more than if you kept her in the dark."

With that, he stormed out of the cafe, blowing past Celeste as she walked in. She must have noticed the guilt and regret on my face. "What was that about? Did you have a bro fight? Need a White Claw and an MMA pay-per-view to cheer you up?" she said mockingly.

I looked past her at the door, her verbal jab barely registering. "Be right back."

Tempris was only a few steps beyond the threshold, I could see he'd turned back, maybe for round two. Although I'm sure this wasn't a conversation he wanted to have in front of Celeste. "Coming back to threaten me some more? To yell at me some more? To reinforce what a huge mistake I'm making? Well It's my mistake to make. You've been a great friend to me and by all means I'm breaking your trust and I'll totally understand if you don't want to train me anymore. I'm sorry. I'm really, really sorry, but this is the way it has to be. I'll make sure Celeste keeps your secret, don't worry."

He put his fingers to his temples and rubbed as if he was nursing a headache. "I'm not worried, Nolan, and thank you for that. I just turned back to get my journal."

"Oh, yea it's on the counter," I replied feeling the guilt creep back in at the memory of how excited he was just moments ago.

A wave of nausea washed over me and I felt a rush of magical energy, the smell of sage and anise flowing around me. At first I thought Tempris had finally snapped and was taking his well earned frustration out on me, but I looked up and saw Tempris' shocked expression, all the color drained from his face. Focusing, I could tell the magic was coming from the cafe. "Celeste!"

We both rushed through the door and Celeste was nowhere to be found. I rounded the counter and there she was laying on the floor unconscious, Tempris' journal splayed open next to her. I knelt beside her and checked for a pulse. Her heart was racing but her skin was like ice. "Tempris! Do something! Do something now!"

I turned and saw Tempris had his phone to his ear. I could hear the faint sound of a dispatcher, tinny and thin coming from his device. "911, what's your emergency?"

# Chapter 21

*Grace.*

There was no constant beep of an EKG machine, nor were there doctors rushing around frantically trying to perform miracles. In the hospital room there was just me, and Celeste. Doctors couldn't explain the random changes in her heart rate, temperature, or brain functions that seemed to be fluctuating at random with no signs that she was either braindead or waking up any time soon. As far as they knew she was just unconscious. They'd asked me an endless stream of questions. "Did she ingest something poisonous? Is she allergic to anything? To the best of my knowledge was she on any kind of drugs prescription or otherwise? What were we doing at the time of the incident?" I couldn't rightly tell them "She touched a magic tome and fell into a deep slumber from which she may never awaken." Could I?

I sat by Celeste's bedside in the sterile hospital room, my heart heavy with guilt and worry. The fluorescent lights overhead cast a harsh glare, illuminating the pale lines of her face as she lay unconscious, her chest rising and falling in steady rhythm. How could I have let this happen?

It had started with a simple argument with Tempris. Words had been exchanged, tempers had flared, and in the heat of the moment, Celeste had unwittingly picked up Tempris's book. A book filled with ancient wards and protective spells, designed to keep prying eyes at bay. Tempris was nowhere to be found. He stayed behind after calling the ambulance and reassuring me he'd try and find a solution to the problem. His words echoed in my mind "I can't reverse the effects of the wards, but magic did this, magic can undo this."

But Celeste, innocent and unaware of the dangers lurking within its pages, had fallen victim to its magic. Now, she lay in a deep slumber, her mind trapped in a realm of dreams and shadows, while I struggled with the weight of my secret.

I couldn't tell the doctors about the book. I couldn't explain how its magic had ensnared Celeste without revealing the truth about my own abilities. The consequences would be too great, not just for me, but for everyone involved.

So, I sat in silence, watching over her as the minutes stretched into hours, feeling utterly helpless in the face of her unconsciousness. Each passing moment only served to deepen the ache in my chest, a constant reminder of the consequences of my actions.

But as I gazed upon her peaceful face, a flicker of determination sparked within me. I couldn't undo what had been done, but I could do everything in my power to set things right. Even if it meant delving into the dangerous world of magic once more.

With a heavy heart and a resolve born of desperation, I reached out and clasped Celeste's hand in mine, silently promising her that I would find a way to wake her from this unnatural slumber. No matter the cost.

And as the steady beeping of the heart monitor filled the room, I whispered a prayer to whatever gods might be listening, hoping against hope that they would grant me the strength and courage to face the trials that lay ahead.

Lost in my thoughts, I glanced up and froze as I caught sight of Tempris standing in the hallway outside the door. His presence sent a shiver down my spine, a mixture of fear and hope swirling within me. Could he truly help Celeste?

Without hesitation, I rose from my seat and approached him, the urgency in his gaze mirroring the turmoil in my own heart. "Tempris, what do you know? Can you help her?"

He nodded solemnly, his eyes glinting with determination. "I believe I have found a way to break the curse that binds her, but time is of the essence. We must act quickly if we are to save her."

Relief flooded through me, mingled with a renewed sense of dread. Could I trust Tempris to save Celeste, or was I only leading her into greater danger?

Despite my reservations, I nodded, my voice barely above a whisper. "I'll go with you, Tempris. Just promise me you can fix this."

He placed a reassuring hand on my shoulder, his touch surprisingly gentle. "I will do everything in my power, Nolan. But we must hurry."

Before I followed him out of the room, I turned back to Celeste's unconscious form, my heart heavy with guilt and determination. "I promise you, Celeste. I will fix this. I will bring you back."

With those words lingering in the air, I followed Tempris into the unknown, praying that his magic held the key to saving the woman I loved.

# Chapter 22

*Been here before.*

A s we entered the cafe, my agitation bubbled to the surface like a pot boiling over. Celeste lay unconscious in the hospital, a consequence of our heated argument and the secrets we had kept. And now, Tempris wanted to lead me on some wild goose chase through my own cafe? It was infuriating.

"Why are we here, Tempris?" I demanded, my voice sharp with frustration. "We should be at Celeste's side, figuring out how to help her, not back at my cafe having tea and crumpets."

Tempris sighed, his irritation evident in the furrow of his brow. "I'm not British! Nolan, you must trust me. The answer we seek lies within these walls, I assure you."

I scoffed, my patience wearing thin. "The answer is back here at the scene of the crime, eh?"

He fixed me with a steady gaze, his eyes piercing through my doubt. "The research I've been conducting has led me to a discovery, one that could hold the key to saving Celeste. But we must act swiftly."

His cryptic words only fueled my frustration, but I followed him down into the basement nonetheless. As we descended the stairs, I couldn't shake the feeling of unease that settled in the pit of my stomach. Something about this whole situation felt wrong.

As we reached the bottom of the stairs, I noticed that the runes scribed on the floor looked different than before. Tempris had changed them, I realized, his intentions becoming clearer with each passing moment.

"What have you done, Tempris?" I asked, my voice barely above a whisper.

He turned to me, a determined glint in his eyes. "I have etched out a portal, Nolan. One that will lead us to knowledge and power beyond our wildest dreams. And with that knowledge, we can bring Celeste back from the curse she's under."

I hesitated, uncertainty gnawing at the edges of my resolve. I didn't want power beyond my wildest dreams. I just wanted enough power to save Celeste. But when Tempris laid a hand on the circle of runes and instructed me to do the same, I knew there was no turning back.

As Tempris and I placed our hands on the magic runes etched into the floor of my cafe, a sense of foreboding washed over me. The air crackled with energy, and I could feel the power emanating from the rip in space and time that snapped open before us. It was unlike any portal I had ever seen, its edges jagged and uneven, as if torn open by some immense force.

I turned to Tempris, my voice filled with uncertainty. "What... What is on the other side, Tempris? This doesn't feel right."

He met my gaze, his expression unreadable. "It is difficult to explain, Nolan. But trust me when I say that we must go through immediately. Time is of the essence."

His words did little to assuage my fears, but the urgency in his voice left me with little choice. With a deep breath, I steeled myself for whatever lay ahead and stepped through the portal.

As I emerged on the other side, a wave of disorientation washed over me. The world around me seemed to blur and shift, the colors swirling together in a dizzying kaleidoscope. I stumbled forward, struggling to maintain my balance as I tried to make sense of my surroundings.

The air here felt heavy and oppressive, thick with the scent of ozone and something darker, something ancient. I glanced back at the portal, but it had already begun to close behind us, sealing us off from the familiar surroundings of my cellar.

"Tempris, what have you done?" I demanded, my voice echoing in the strange, unfamiliar landscape.

He turned to me, his expression grim. "We have entered a realm no one has been for over a millennia, Nolan. A place of ancient power and forbidden knowledge. But relax, we've got each other's backs, right?"

His words offered little comfort as I looked out into the unknown, an ominous presence looming on the horizon. Whatever lay ahead, I knew that our journey was far from over, and that the true dangers had only just begun.

As the disorientation from our journey through the portal began to fade, I took in my surroundings with a mix of confusion and awe. We stood in a cavern, its walls lined with jagged stalactites and stalagmites, illuminated by the faint glow of bioluminescent fungi. It was a common enough sight for caves, yet something about it felt off, out of place in the bustling city of Detroit.

"Tempris, where are we?" I asked, my voice echoing off the cavern walls.

He turned to me, a gleam of excitement in his eyes. "Nolan, my boy, we are below the Eastern Market in Detroit."

My eyes widened in surprise. The Eastern Market was only a few short blocks from my cafe, yet I had never suspected that such a cavern lay beneath it. It seemed impossible, yet here we were, standing in its depths.

Tempris grinned, his eyes sparkling with excitement. "Ah, Nolan, my boy, trust me. We're exactly where we need to be. This cavern lies beneath the bustling streets of Detroit, right below your very own cafe."

I arched an eyebrow, unconvinced. "Sure, it's under Detroit, but how do we know it's not some other random cave?"

Tempris chuckled, clapping a hand on my shoulder. "Because, Nolan, magic has a way of leading us to the most unexpected places. Now, come on, let's explore! Who knows what wonders we might find down here?"

I rolled my eyes, but couldn't help but feel a twinge of excitement at the prospect of adventure. "Fine, fine, lead the way, oh wise and knowledgeable magic mentor. But let's make it quick. We need to find a cure for Celeste, remember?"

Tempris's eyes gleamed with determination as he clapped me on the back. "Of course, Nolan! But think of the discoveries we could make down here. Ancient artifacts, lost treasures... Who knows what wonders await us?"

I looked around suddenly wishing I packed some chainmail and a broadsword. "Let's just hope one of those wonders happens to be the cure we're looking for."

With a playful grin, Tempris led the way deeper into the cavern, his excitement infectious despite my lingering apprehension. As we delved deeper into the unknown, I couldn't help but wonder what other surprises lay in store for us beneath the Eastern Market.

# Chapter 23

*Into the depths.*

The cavern smelled old and the air was thick with humidity. Tempris lead us to a narrow tunnel that looked out of place in a cavern like this—as if I'd been in many caverns myself. As we walked, I could make out a dull light at the end of the tunnel. We reached the end and the light blinded me. Light and heat seemed to cover everything and nothing all at once. For a moment I felt as if I was going to throw up but it passed quickly and I blinked the light from my eyes. Before us was a short path that lead to a large stone door, but that wasn't the part that blew my mind. Although we were underneath the Eastern Market, above us was an overcast sky filled with pockets of blue and purple between the clouds. Tempris looked back at me with a grin.

"This is one of the pocket dimensions I told you about. Not quite in mundane space and not quite in magical space. Come on, keep up," Tempris said as he strode forward.

I knew I was in for surprises but I had no idea a place like this could exist so close to the material plane I was used to. The last thing I wanted was to get lost so I picked up my pace and followed after closely after Tempris.

To my surprise, there was loose debris and stones that looked misplaced. "Are you sure no one has been here in a long time?"

Tempris chuckled and turned to me unconcerned. "The amount of training we have been doing so close to the entrance to this plane, and the natural tectonic shifts have no doubt, loosened the entrance. That should work in our favor."

Tempris studied the markings on the door. He'd shown me many books but I didn't recognize a single line or character etched on its surface. He pulled out his journal it looked like he was comparing things he'd scrawled on the weathered pages. Smiling, he clapped the book shut and pointed to one of three depressed spots on the surface of the door. "Fire, here."

I looked at him confused and stepped a little closer. "You want me to use fire magic on the door?"

Tempris jabbed a finger at the spot "Yes! Come, come! Just a little fire here. Air here, and universal magic in the middle," he finished, pointing at three different areas.

I nodded, understanding dawning on me as I focused my energy on the task at hand. With a wave of my hand, flames flickered to life on the first depression, dancing with a fierce intensity. Then, I summoned a gust of wind to swirl around the second depression, its invisible force stirring the air around us. Finally, I poured my energy into the third depression, a surge of power flowing from within me and into the stone door.

As if in response to my magic, the door lit up with characters I had never seen before, glowing with an otherworldly brilliance. With a low rumble, the door began to open, revealing a cavern beyond.

Before we could step through, Tempris cornered me, his eyes flashing with urgency. "Nolan, listen carefully. Once we enter, I need to maintain a particular spell at all times. It will keep us both safe, but it leaves you in charge of dealing with any threats we encounter."

I nodded, a sense of responsibility settling over me. "What kind of threats are we talking about?"

Tempris's expression grew grave. "Creatures, constructs, who knows what else. But remember, don't hold back. Your magic could be the difference between life and death. As long as I maintain the spell, we should be fine."

With a deep breath, I steeled myself for the challenges ahead. Together, we stepped through the door and into the unknown, ready to face whatever dangers lay in wait within the cavern.

# Chapter 24

*Dungeons no dragons.*

The cave was warm, but not uncomfortably so. Illumination was provided by strange blue crystals on the cavern walls and occasional holes in the ceiling which created an otherworldly ambiance. Yet, despite the beauty of our surroundings, a nagging question lingered in the back of my mind—what sky were we under? What sky we're beneath? I mean, we were supposed to be underground, but it felt like we were in a whole other world.

Turning to Tempris, I voiced the other question plaguing me. "Tempris, you've vaguely spoken about what you're doing in Detroit and your research, but what the hell are you looking for?"

He chuckled softly, his eyes twinkling with amusement. "Ah, Nolan, always with the philosophical questions. As for what I'm looking for, it's quite simple, really. My research deals with the very nature of magic itself."

I raised an eyebrow, intrigued by his response. "And what exactly does that entail?"

Tempris shrugged nonchalantly. "Understanding, pure and simple. I don't have any grandiose plans to bring anyone back from the dead or conquer the world. Just a humble quest for knowledge."

I couldn't help but laugh at his casual dismissal of world domination. "Well, maybe if you had a bit more understanding, my training wouldn't have been so rough these past few months."

Our shared laughter was cut short by a shuffling noise echoing from the darkness ahead. My heart skipped a beat as I instinctively reached for my magic, ready to defend against whatever lurked in the shadows. Something was coming, and I had a feeling it wouldn't be friendly.

As the creature emerged from the darkness, my heart leapt into my throat. Its grotesque features were illuminated by the faint shafts of light filtering through the cavern. Grey, pockmarked skin stretched over a flat, bulldog-like face, its red eyes devoid of focus as it shuffled closer to us. Its tattered clothes hung loosely from its frame, but what caught my attention were the bullet holes peppering its shirt.

"Handle it, Nolan," Tempris's voice cut through the tension, snapping me out of my paralysis.

I stood frozen, suddenly unable to summon the courage to draw upon my magic. How could I attack or defend against such a creature? It looked like something straight out of nightmares, and I was utterly unprepared.

Just as the creature loomed upon me, ready to strike, Tempris sprang into action. With a powerful shoulder charge, he sent the creature careening into the cavern wall. As it staggered, dazed and disoriented, Tempris delivered a crushing boot to its face, smashing it against the wall with a sickening thud.

I stumbled back, my heart racing with fear and disbelief as Tempris took a knee beside me, concern etched into his features. "Are you alright, Nolan?"

Terrified but still clinging to my sense of humor, I managed a weak smile. "Oh, just peachy, Tempris. Just another day in the life of a magic apprentice."

I couldn't help but ask, "What was that thing, anyway?"

Tempris sighed, brushing off the question with a lazy wave of his hand. "Just a cave troll, Nolan. Nothing to worry about. Let's focus on the task at hand and push forward."

Despite his nonchalant demeanor, I couldn't shake the feeling of unease that lingered in the air. What had caused the usually docile creature to attack us with such ferocity? But as Tempris urged us to continue, another troll leaped from the ceiling above, tackling me to the ground. I kicked it off, surprised by how light it was. This one looked even smaller and more malnourished than the last one. It glared at me and opened its mouth to show row upon row of sharp, jagged teeth. It sprung forward and I punched, a plume of fire spraying from my fist on impact. The troll flew back several feet and crunched on the cavern wall unmoving. My nose wrinkled at the smell of burnt hair and flesh. I could see the creature was still breathing but was clearly unconscious. The sound of applause drew my attention. Tempris was clapping.

"Bravo! Well done! You took it down in one blow and managed to control your fire magic enough to only wound the creature. Dare I say I'm the best magic teacher in Detroit!" Tempris said.

I shook my fist which was tight from the attack. "You're the only magic teacher in Detroit."

Tempris clapped me on the shoulder and winked. "You got that right! Now, if we run into any more of those, I want you to switch up your magic types. Just roulette through all the magic you know as we make our way through. A little practice in control and switching on the go!"

I gave Tempris a withering look, and was about to ask if he really expected us to run into more of them but just as the words were beginning to leave my lips, two more shuffled into our path. I swept them both with air magic then blew them into the far wall making sure I poured enough juice into it to knock them out. "Like that?" I said to Tempris.

"Just like that, Nolan. Keep it up!" Tempris replied.

I could tell his mind was still occupied. He was holding some kind of spell he said would keep us safe but clearly it wasn't working. However it did look like he knew where we were going. I glanced at my watch, wondering if time worked the same here and hoping Celeste was getting better while we searched for a cure.

As Tempris and I pressed deeper into the cavern, I could sense his unwavering focus, his attention consumed by whatever spell he was holding. Perhaps it was leading us towards whatever he sought, guiding us through the labyrinthine depths of the cave.

We halted before the mouth of a larger cavern, its walls adorned with even more of the luminescent crystals that illuminated our path. I couldn't resist picking up a fallen crystal, jesting to Tempris that perhaps if my endeavors in magic and running the cafe failed, I could try my hand at becoming a jeweler.

Tempris chuckled, but his response was sobering. "Keep your day job, Nolan. That shard is worthless."

I turned the crystal over in my hands, admiring its beauty despite its lack of value. Before I could say anything else, a rumbling from the corner drew our attention.

A towering troll, three times the size of any I had faced before, rose to its feet amidst a cascade of crumbling crystals. It gnawed on one of the glowing shards as if it were a meal. The towering troll stood before us like a mountain of raw, brute strength. Its massive frame loomed over me, casting a shadow that seemed to swallow the light from the luminescent crystals around us. Its gray, pockmarked skin stretched taut over bulging muscles, veins pulsating beneath the surface like thick ropes. With each gnash of its jagged teeth against the crystal, a low rumble echoed through the cavern, sending shivers down my spine. Its red eyes, unfocused and vacant, seemed to pierce through the darkness, fixating on its makeshift meal with a primal hunger. As it chewed, drool dripped from its twisted, snarling lips, sizzling as it made contact with the ground below. The sight of the troll, its grotesque features contorted in ravenous delight, filled me with a sense of dread unlike anything I had ever known.

I couldn't help but joke, "Well, at least someone appreciates the crystals."

Tempris chided me lightly, his expression serious. "This is no laughing matter, Nolan. This troll is formidable, and hand-to-hand tactics won't work. You're on your own for this one."

The reminder of our purpose here, to save Celeste, fueled my resolve. With a deep breath, I charged the massive troll, summoning flames to engulf it. But the creature barely flinched, retaliating with surprising speed as it swiped at me, knocking me off balance.

I scrambled to my feet, dodging the troll's thunderous stomps. A puddle at my back caught my attention, water dripping from a stalactite above. In a split-second decision, I used air magic to trip the troll, causing it to collapse.

As I summoned the power of lightning, a surge of electricity crackled and danced along my fingertips, casting an eerie blue glow in the cavern. With a determined focus, I directed the energy toward the water pooling at my feet, watching as tendrils of electricity danced across its surface, illuminating the chamber with an otherworldly light.

The lightning surged forward with a deafening crack, illuminating the cavern in a blinding flash. The bolt struck the water with a resounding crash, sending ripples cascading outwards like a shockwave. Instantly, the troll convulsed in agony, its massive form writhing and contorting as tendrils of electricity coursed through its body.

The air was filled with the acrid scent of burnt flesh as the troll let out a deafening roar, the sound reverberating off the cavern walls like thunder. Its muscles tensed and spasmed uncontrollably, its limbs thrashing wildly as it struggled to withstand the onslaught of energy.

Finally, with one last convulsive shudder, the troll fell to the ground, its body smoking and charred from the electrical assault. The cavern fell silent once more, the only sound the crackle of fading energy and the echo of my own ragged breaths.

As the adrenaline began to ebb, I couldn't help but feel a sense of awe at the destructive power of the magic I had wielded.

"I guess the troll really knew how to conduct itself," I joked. This elicited a shake of the head from Tempris. But his smile told me everything I needed to know—we had arrived at our destination, one step closer to saving Celeste. With a weary but determined grin, I turned to Tempris, ready to face whatever challenges lay ahead.

# Chapter 25

*For my next trick.*

The cavern mouth opened up into a large almost circular space. There were far fewer crystals in this room but that didn't make it any darker. A soft glow seemed to shimmer from the very center of the room. In the center was a chest which seemed to be made out of the same stone and crystal the cavern was comprised of. As we stepped into the vast circular chamber, I couldn't help but be awestruck by the ethereal glow emanating from the center. My heart quickened with excitement as Tempris hastened his pace, indicating the chest nestled amidst the stone and crystal.

"This is it," Tempris declared, his voice filled with urgency.

My pulse quickened with anticipation, hope blossoming within me like a budding flower. Could this be the key to saving Celeste? I took a step forward, eager to uncover its secrets, but Tempris's hand shot out, halting me in my tracks.

"Stay back, Nolan," he instructed, his tone grave and serious. "If anything happens, I want it to happen to me first."

His words struck a chord deep within me, a testament to the bond we had forged in the short time we had known each other. Despite our differences, Tempris had become more than just a mentor—he was a friend, a confidant, and now, a protector willing to sacrifice himself for my safety.

Touched by his selflessness, I nodded in silent agreement, staying rooted to the spot as Tempris approached the chest with careful reverence.

When I first met Tempris, I'll admit I didn't think much of him. In fact, I thought he was a bit of a mysterious jerk. Celeste seemed to have a crush on him, which only added to my initial annoyance. He was aloof, enigmatic, and seemed to have this air of superiority that rubbed me the wrong way. At the time, I couldn't understand what Celeste saw in him, and I certainly didn't think he would become such an integral part of my life.

But oh, how wrong I was.

As I reflect back on those initial impressions, I realize now that Tempris was so much more than just a mysterious figure who had caught Celeste's eye. He was my link to a brand new world—a world of magic and discovery that I had never imagined existed. And as much as I resisted it at first, Tempris became my mentor, my guide, and eventually, something akin to a brother.

Our bond was forged in the fires of adversity, tempered by the challenges we faced together. From the moment he begrudgingly agreed to teach me magic, to the countless hours we spent training in my cafe, our relationship evolved from one of reluctant teacher and student to something deeper, more profound.

Tempris pushed me to my limits, challenging me to unlock the potential that lay dormant within me. He saw something in me that I hadn't even seen in myself—a spark of magic, a thirst for knowledge, a hunger for something more. And with his guidance, I began to blossom, to grow into the person I was always meant to be.

But our bond went beyond just mentorship. There was a camaraderie between us, a shared understanding that transcended words. We laughed together, we argued together, we faced danger together. And through it all, there was a mutual respect and admiration that bound us together like brothers in arms.

As I stood here in that cavern, facing an uncertain future, I couldn't help but feel a swell of gratitude for the man who had become not just my mentor, but my friend. Tempris may still be enigmatic and mysterious in many ways, but I now see him for who he truly is—a kindred spirit, a fellow seeker of truth, and a steadfast ally in the journey ahead.

While Tempris focused on the task at hand, I couldn't help but glance around the chamber in wonder, my mind racing with questions about its origins and purpose.

But amidst my curiosity, something else caught my eye—a glint of light amidst the dust and debris near the chamber entrance. With a furrowed brow, I bent down to investigate, my fingers brushing against something unexpected—a lip gloss.

Before I could dwell on the strange discovery, a bone-rattling hum filled the air, drawing my attention back to Tempris and the chest. I watched as he opened the chest, unleashing an ominous light and a swirling mist that cascaded towards me.

Panic surged within me as I called out for Tempris, but he remained focused on the chest, seemingly oblivious to the danger approaching. With no other choice, I summoned my magic, unleashing a gust of air to push back the encroaching mist.

But to my horror, the mist hungrily consumed the air magic, only accelerating its advance towards me. With a sinking feeling in my chest, I realized it wasn't just any mist—it was something far more sinister, something that seemed to defy the very laws of magic itself.

"Screw this," I yelled, my voice echoing off the cavern walls as I unleashed a barrage of fire, lightning, and kinetic magic at the encroaching mist. But to my horror, each spell only seemed to accelerate its advance, closing in around me like a suffocating shroud.

With a sense of desperation gnawing at my gut, I turned and ran, my heart pounding in my chest as I sprinted through the chamber. But as I glanced back over my shoulder, I realized with a sinking feeling that the mist had shifted, surrounding me on all sides.

"Tempris, HELP!" I cried out, my voice laced with panic and confusion. But when I looked to him for aid, all I saw was a sidelong glance before he returned his focus to the chest, seemingly unfazed by my plight.

Confused and desperate, I made myself as small as possible, trying to ward off the encroaching mist as it swirled around me. I could feel its insidious pull, not physical but something different—it was tugging at my magic, draining me from within.

With a frantic kick, I pushed back against the mist, but it clung to me like a malevolent shadow, wrapping around my limbs and engulfing me in its icy embrace. I fell to my hands and knees, the harsh stone floor biting into my palms as I struggled to resist its pull.

It was like giving blood, but a thousand times worse. Every ounce of magic within me was being siphoned away, leaving me weak and drained. And as the cold seeped into my bones, I couldn't help but feel a sense of despair wash over me.

But through the haze of exhaustion, I managed to lift my head and gaze up at Tempris, who stood before the chest with a look of fierce determination. His hands were raised above it, emanating a shimmering silver field that seemed to repel the darkness of the mist. I managed to get out some words.

"Tempris...what's happening? I feel weak,"

"That is the feeling of the booby trap inside the chest devouring you. The entity inside this chest devours magic and magic users. It's drawn to power, and it has been down here so long I'm sure it's very, very hungry,"

As Tempris's words sank in, a sense of fear and betrayal washed over me like a tidal wave. How could he have known about the danger lurking within the chest and not warned me? How could he have knowingly put me in harm's way?

"You, you're more powerful than I am," I managed to croak, my voice barely above a whisper, the weight of his betrayal pressing down on me like a heavy stone.

Tempris's response was chilling in its candor. "That's true, but right now you are practically radioactive with magical power. I, on the other hand, have barely used a drop. Why do you think I've had you do everything? I'm not holding some kind of spell. I was just making sure you were the proverbial pie on the windowsill for whatever was inside."

His words struck me like a physical blow, leaving me reeling with disbelief and anger. How could he have manipulated me like this, used me as bait to lure out whatever dark entity lay within the chest? And why had I been so blind to see it until now?

"Why are you doing this?" I demanded, my voice trembling with a mixture of fear and fury. The betrayal cut deep, slicing through the bonds of trust we had forged over months of training and camaraderie. But even as I awaited his answer, I couldn't help but feel a sinking sense of dread at what his response might reveal.

As Tempris spared me a glance, a twisted smile curled upon his lips, sending a shiver down my spine. His gaze bore into me with an unsettling intensity, as if peering into the very depths of my soul.

"This isn't the first time I've taught you magic," he began, his voice dripping with a malevolent edge that made my blood run cold. "Did you ever wonder why you could use so many different types of magic? You've been a bit of an experiment for me. We've met over and over, and I've taught you over and over. Somehow, your magical ability was able to harness and control a magnitude of magic types. It's quite remarkable."

His words hung in the air like a sinister specter, casting a shadow of doubt upon everything I thought I knew. I felt a surge of anger and betrayal rise within me, a sickening realization dawning upon me like a thunderclap. Tempris had been manipulating me from the very beginning, using me as a pawn in his twisted game of power and control.

"The only drawback," Tempris continued, his voice oozing with malice, "is that every time I needed to start a new kind of lesson, I'd have to start from scratch as far as your memory is concerned. I needed someone uniquely powerful in order to not be subject to the entity in this chest."

His revelation struck me like a physical blow, leaving me reeling with disbelief and rage. How could he have played me for a fool, exploiting my abilities for his own gain? The realization sent a wave of revulsion coursing through me, a sickening knot forming in the pit of my stomach.

But even as I seethed with anger and betrayal, I couldn't help but feel a twisted sense of awe at the extent of Tempris's deception. He had woven a web of lies and manipulation so intricate, so diabolical, that I had been blind to his true intentions until now. The light of Tempris' magic grew as he concentrated. The mist pulled back and I felt some of my strength return.

"Wait, what?" I asked. At the same time, I noticed some of the energy return to my body. With great effort I was able to return to my feet and face Tempris. He was standing over the chest now, concentrating, but he took another moment to glance over his shoulder at me smirking. That smirk. It was evil. Awful. It had malice and something else in it. His eyes shot down for half a second. I followed his gaze. The trail of smokey mist billowed along the ground thick and unnatural. It was making a beeline straight towards me again. Bits of it reached my feet and swirled around me. The sensation my my magic being pulled out of me returned instantly and I stumbled backwards away from the growing mist. The stuff seemed to be alive! Aware! I nearly yelped and pushed out with my magic sending a telekinetic burst along the floor. The mist dissipated ever so slightly, but the disturbing part was that it seemed to absorb most of the force held in my blast!

I looked along the floor and noticed the mist was beginning to rise higher and higher in a stunted column that rose a dozen feet above my head. My blood ran cold when I saw what was happening. The myst began to take shape. It was forming—something—something huge and dark, and unnatural. It was vaguely humanoid, with craggy skin, that seemed to shimmer in and out of mist form. It had a misshapen lump which I could only gather was its head that sat atop horned shoulders and a barrel chest that glowed from within. My mouth was agape, and my legs were frozen in place. It was the kind of instinctive fear that lies within all people. The type of fear that relays mortal danger and imminent death. Thoughts began to stream through my head. How did I end up here? I'm a coffee shop owner who just wanted to learn a little magic. Now I'm in a trans-dimensional cave, standing before a twenty foot mist monster that eats magic. I was going to die here and no one would ever know what came of the flippant, charming, small business owner with the heart of gold. Sure, I probably wasn't going to be remembered that way but I was scared too shitless to process how I would be remembered

—and by who. Who? Celeste. I wondered if she was okay. I wondered if when she woke up would she go looking for me, and if she did would she somehow end up here. With this thing. With Tempris?!

That thought snapped me back to the problem before me. Snapped me back just in time too! I backpedaled and barely avoided an enormous arm that came down inches from where I was standing. Shards of sharp stone sliced into my skin, as I rolled and narrowly avoided the creature's backswing. I concentrated, and used a burst of fire from both of my palms, to launch myself away from the rampaging beast.

Looking up, I noticed large stalactites jetting from the ceiling. I focused my will, and attempted to create the thinnest, sharpest burst of air I could manage. My first attempt was too narrow and slammed into the cavern ceiling. Showering me with rock. I re-focused and my second try hit home. Two large stalactites were cleaved, cleanly and crashed down hard into the creature. The floor beneath me rumbled and the monster disappeared into a pile of rubble. Through the haze of dust, I can no longer see it but I could hear the creature growling. Although it wasn't an angry growl, it was...delighted? I risked a glance at Tempris and I could just make out his fingers finally making their way through the energy field surrounding the chest. I sprang to my feet and darted towards him pumping magic into my movements in hopes of augmenting my speed. All it did was make the beast even more attracted to me and I could see it in my peripheral vision emerging from the rubble in misty streams and gaining ground.

I reached out my hand readying a blast of fire that would have taken Tempris straight in the back, but I was lifted from my feet by a whip of mist that caught me around the waist. The mist flung me backwards through the air and I crashed into the cavern wall with tremendous force. Crumbling rocks rained down all around me. I coughed and spat blood on impact and crumpled to the debris strewn floor, rocks stabbing into me painfully. I laid there surprised I didn't lose consciousness from that assault, but also fairly certain I was going to pass out at any moment. Somehow, I gathered the strength to sit up. I sat with my back to the cavern wall. The beast was making its way towards me, but it had thrown me quite some distance. I could see it opening its huge, gaping maw and I could feel it drawing the magic out of me slowly. The closer it got, the stronger the drain. As far as ways to go, this wouldn't be so bad I thought. Not really a blaze of glory, but I went down fighting—fighting for myself and fighting to see Celeste just one more time. It was comforting in those last moments, thoughts of her flooded my memory. I could see her lopsided smile, and the crease that appeared between her eyebrows when she was upset or confused. What's more I could hear her voice calling my name in that melodic lilt. But the best part was her smell. Coconut and shea, the memory as strong as if she were standing right in front of me. My eyes fluttered open and I was still on the cavern floor, but something was different. I saw smooth dark wrist adorned with a hospital band. My heart began to race and my eyes shot open as I looked up. Celeste's face filled my vision, and there was that eyebrow crease. This time it was filled with concern. I couldn't imagine what I looked like at this moment, but none of that mattered. Celeste was here, and she was awake. I sat bolt upright ignoring my protesting joints and muscles.

"Celeste! You're awake!" I cried, pulling her into a tight embrace, my heart pounding with a mix of relief and fear. "I can't believe you're here! And in a cavern, no less. Did they start offering magical cave tours in the hospital now?"

Her familiar scent of coconut and shea filled my senses, grounding me in the moment despite the chaos around us. But my joy was short-lived. I glanced up and saw the mist that had nearly drained me reforming on the ceiling, swirling and coalescing into the shape of the creature once more.

"Celeste, I don't want to ruin the moment," I whispered urgently, my voice trembling with a mix of panic and affection, "but we might be in a bit of trouble. That thing up there is about to come down on us like a ton of magical bricks. And the cinnamon and sage guy from the cafe, well, he's a total asshole who set this whole thing up. Apparently, I'm some sort of magical snack for that mist monster."

She pulled back slightly, her eyes wide with surprise and a hint of amusement. "Coffee shop guy did this? What did you do? Get his order wrong? I always knew there was something off about him. But don't worry, I have a plan."

I couldn't help but laugh despite the dire situation. "Of course you do. You always have a plan. Just promise it doesn't involve more mist monsters or any more of Tempris's crazy schemes."

Celeste smiled, that familiar lopsided grin that made my heart skip a beat. "Trust me, this one's all me. But you need to trust me and follow my lead. We can get out of this, Nolan. Together."

I nodded, feeling a renewed sense of hope and determination. "Alright, lead the way. Let's show that mist monster what happens when it messes with us."

With that, Celeste took my hand, and we both stood up, ready to face whatever came next. Her confidence was infectious, and for the first time since this whole ordeal began, I felt like we might actually have a chance.

"So, what's the plan?" I asked, half-expecting her to pull a rabbit out of a hat or some other cliché magician's trick.

Celeste's eyes twinkled with a mischievous glint. "I need you to let the mist capture you."

I blinked, processing her words. "Wait, you want me to what? Celeste, I think you might need to go back to the hospital. Maybe lie down for a bit. Have they checked your head since you woke up?"

She chuckled softly. "No, seriously, Nolan. You're not the only one who has been keeping secrets. And you're not the only one who knows magic."

I stared at her, slack-jawed. "You know magic? But... but the mist monster is attracted to magic! How is this supposed to help? I mean, isn't that exactly what we're trying to avoid?"

She gave me a reassuring smile, the kind that made everything seem possible. "Don't worry. My magic is more passive. I'll be fine. You'll be drawing all the attention."

"Great," I muttered, rolling my eyes. "So I'm the magical bait in this brilliant plan of yours. Awesome. What about Tempris?" I glanced over to see him still engrossed in his spell, seemingly oblivious to our conversation. "He's still there, doing his creepy spell thing."

Celeste's expression hardened for a moment. "One thing at a time, Nolan. First, we deal with the mist monster. Then we handle Tempris. Trust me on this. We can do it."

I took a deep breath, my mind racing with a mix of fear and determination. "Okay. Let's do this."

We moved closer to the center of the cavern, the mist swirling more aggressively as it sensed our approach. Celeste positioned herself behind me, her hand resting gently on my back. "Ready?" she whispered.

"Ready as I'll ever be," I replied, trying to muster some confidence. "Just don't forget to pull me out of the fire when it gets too hot."

As the mist began to envelop me, I couldn't help but think about how surreal this whole situation was. Celeste, my supposed non-magical girlfriend, revealing her own hidden powers and asking me to trust her with my life. I guess love really does make you do crazy things.

The mist tightened around me, and I felt that familiar draining sensation, like my very essence was being siphoned away. Through the haze, I could see Celeste's determined face, her hands moving in intricate patterns as she cast her own spell. Despite the fear, I felt a spark of hope. We were in this together, and maybe, just maybe, we had a chance.

I stepped forward, my heart pounding in my chest. With a shaky hand, I threw a weak and ill-aimed bolt of electricity at the mist, now nearly reformed into its monstrous shape. The creature's eyes, red and glowing, locked onto me. The scent of coconut and shea filled the air, growing stronger with each passing second. I glanced back at Celeste, who stood a few steps behind me, her face etched with determination.

All this time, I thought that scent was her natural fragrance or some hair product she used, but now I realized—it was the smell of her magic. I couldn't help but smile to myself at the realization. The mist monster, however, snapped me back to reality with its guttural growl.

Focusing again, I aimed four fiery punches at what could only be the leg of the mist monster. The flames licked harmlessly at the vaporous form, doing no visible damage but definitely grabbing its attention. The creature swiped at me with a massive, smoky limb, missing me by inches.

"Guess you missed the mark, huh?" I quipped, trying to keep my voice steady. But my bravado was short-lived. The mist monster's second swipe didn't miss. I was snatched up in the clutches of its gigantic hand, the cold, ethereal touch sending a shiver down my spine.

"Nolan!" Celeste shouted, her voice breaking through my panic. I struggled against the creature's grip, but it was like trying to break free from a steel vice. The more I fought, the tighter its hold became, draining my energy with each passing second.

"Celeste, now would be a good time for that plan of yours!" I called out, hoping she had something up her sleeve that could turn the tide in our favor.

She didn't respond immediately, her focus entirely on her spellwork. The scent of coconut and shea grew almost overpowering, wrapping around me like a comforting blanket. I felt a strange mix of fear and calm wash over me. This was it—the moment of truth.

The mist monster roared, a deafening sound that echoed through the cavern, and I felt my strength waning. Celeste stepped forward, her hands glowing with a soft, warm light. She chanted something under her breath, the words unintelligible but powerful. The mist monster hesitated, its grip loosening slightly.

"Don't give up, Nolan!" Celeste yelled, her voice filled with determination and something else—love. It was enough to give me a second wind. I channeled every bit of remaining magic I had into a final, desperate push.

"Let's see if you can handle a bit of a shock," I muttered through gritted teeth, summoning the last of my lightning magic. The bolt surged through the creature's misty form, causing it to shudder and convulse.

I heard as much as felt several ribs break as its hand tightened out of reflex. With all of my might, I pounded at it's barely corporeal fingers to no avail. I hoped Celeste knew what she was doing, but it was far too late at this point to change my mind. I began to feel weak as if from oxygen and blood loss, but I knew it was because the monster was consuming me on some level. Was it eating my magic? No. My soul? I shuddered at the thought—not that I knew much if anything about that kind of thing. Below me, I could see Celeste concentrating, pale fuchsia light emanating from her outstretched palm. It was not long before the light swirled around the creature and I. The beast's grip loosened and I watched its hollow eye sockets turn towards Celeste. I had to maintain the creature's attention, but I was running on fumes. Pain shot through me as I took as deep a breath as I could and shot a weak burst of fire right into its face. Fingers squeezed into me and my vision blurred.

"Celes—" I couldn't get the rest out and I began to dangle limply.

The light that was funneling from Celeste's hand intensified and I could see ribbons of it curling around the monster and through me. I fell from its grip and crumpled to the cavern floor. Above me the creature began to shrink and its ominous glow began to lessen. It only lessened because it was flowing into me. Celeste's ribbons of magic seemed to chain this thing to me and I felt a odd sensation all over. It wasn't like using my magic or magic being used on me. For an instant I could sense the entire cavern, the grotto outside and the coffee shop above. My senses were heightened. I could smell the leaves of the trees far beyond the cavern walls, taste bits of metal from the stone, and feel all of the moisture in the air though the cavern was bone dry. I could hear a faint voice in the distance. No. Was that voice coming from inside my head? The voice, the sensations, the magical ribbons and strands of power all cut off abruptly and I was simply laying there on the floor of the cavern.

I began to take stock of things. The pain in my body was gone and as far as I could tell, my injuries had healed. My clothes were little more than a ragged ruin as I tried to get to my feet. I stumbled and fell forward, landing flat on my face. Celeste rushed forward to help me. She took my hand in hers, and when she did, she yanked it away with a large gasp. When I looked up at her, she looked afraid, and her skin was ashen.

"Celeste! What's wrong?!"

"You...you're...wrong," she replied.

What did she mean I was wrong? The creature was gone, but had she somehow bound it to me? Panicked, I asked her what she did. Celeste wasn't paying attention, though, because behind me, Tempris was finishing whatever magical work he was doing. Celeste prompted me to turn around just as we saw magic flow from the chest into Tempris' notebook. Magic swirled and sparked around his hands and arms where he held the notebook. The light faded, and Tempris looked over at the two of us, smirking.

Celeste strode forward, furious. "You! You did this to me. I've been down here before. I remember everything!" Tempris, unfazed and glib, responded to her. "Yes, but unlike Nolan there, you were a failure. Your magic is just too weak and your mind too strong. It was all I could do to shut away your memories while I went to work on lover boy over there."

I cursed and asked Tempris what he did to me. Tempris said, "Five times, I have erased your memory five times. Well, more of a reboot than a wipe, but we won't get into the logistics. Didn't you wonder why you could use so many different types of magic? You thought you were special? No, you're just an especially good lab rat."

I couldn't believe what I was hearing. "So for the past few months you've done what? Given me false memories?"

Tempris chuckled. "Not false, Nolan. More like...recycled memories. Like that movie you love so much where they keep replaying the same day. Except, in this case, I was playing God with your brain."

I glared at him. "You could've at least made me remember the lottery numbers."

Celeste turned to me with concern and dread in her eyes. "Months? Nolan, it's been almost a year since he walked into the cafe," she told me. My mind raced, and the world seemed to spin as I dropped to my knees and vomited. Tempris' laugh echoed through the cavern, drawing our attention. He gave us a small salute and vanished into thin air.

Celeste came to my side, being careful not to touch me, and tried to cheer me up with humor. "Why do all the men in my life like to keep secrets?"

I looked up at her, my vision blurry with tears and the remnants of nausea. Out loud I asked "Celeste, what the hell are we going to do now?" But in the back of my mind I was asking "What the hell did you just do to me?"

She sighed, her eyes full of determination. "First, we get out of this cave. Then, we find someone who can help us. We're not alone in this, Nolan. We have each other, and we'll figure this out together."

I nodded, trying to muster some semblance of hope. With her help, I got to my feet, I noticed she made sure not to touch my skin. We began walking back through the cavern. The echo of our footsteps felt like the slow ticking of a clock, counting down to when we'd have to face everything that happened to us. Each step felt like a journey through the fractured shards of my own memories. How much had I truly lost? How many times had Tempris rewired my mind, erasing pieces of myself? Worst of all, had I forgotten anything that mattered between Celeste and me? The questions swirled relentlessly, each one feeding the dull ache in my head that I desperately hoped was just a headache.

# Chapter 26

*This guy?*

It felt good to be back in my cafe even if we did have to walk through the basement which was full of delightfully painful memories now. Of course they were memories I mostly couldn't remember. Celeste and I had walked back mostly in silence but there were a million and one questions I needed to ask her. Like how long had she been doing magic? What kind of magic could she use? The most important question of all, what did this mean for us? The familiar smell of coffee greeted us when we finally arrived in the basement cellar.

We both looked at each other, exhausted. She started laughing at me.

"What? Do I have something on my face?" I made a show of displaying the dried blood I knew had to be caked to almost every inch of me.

I assured Celeste that I felt great. I looked in the mirror and saw the horror that was my favorite pair of jeans and a Detroit Tigers T-shirt that was practically falling off in tatters. I began rummaging through some of the gear I kept there when Tempris started training me. Celeste put her hand on her hip.

"Well, get changed. I'll go make us something to drink. We've got a lot to talk about."

She went upstairs and left me alone with my thoughts. I cleaned up in the utility sink the best I could and threw on a Wayne State University t-shirt and cargos. As I inspected myself in the mirror, I was shocked that I didn't have a scratch on me. When I was beaten up by those guys outside of the cafe, it took me nearly all weekend to get better. It hasn't even been an hour, and I feel brand new. What was that power Celeste sealed inside of me? Only one way to find out. I grabbed a jacket and headed upstairs.

When I opened the basement door, I saw Celeste staring out the front window.

"You know, I don't smell coffee! What do I even pay you for?" I joked.

Celeste didn't move. Her focus was transfixed on whatever she saw outside.

"Celeste! Celeste! What is it?" I went to her side and followed her gaze. There were four seemingly ordinary-looking people outside. They might have been dressed a little light for the weather, but I wouldn't have paid them any mind. That was until I noticed what one of them was doing. A short woman was tracing runes in the air with her fingertip. They glowed, and the air seemed to shimmer in an almost translucent fashion.

"Celeste, who are those guys?"

Celeste turned to me, panic and worry in her eyes. "Nolan, I need you to go out the back and...and," she trailed off and seemed like she was struggling to figure something out. She took a pen and napkin from the counter and began writing something down. She thrust the napkin into my hands, recoiling sharply when our hands touched, and started rushing me towards the delivery entrance. "Go to that address, tell him I sent you, and tell him I'll be there soon," Celeste said in a hurry.

"Wait, who are those guys? Whose address is this?"

"It's Arthur's address."

"Arthur? The guy you went on a date with Arthur?"

"Yes! I'll explain everything, but you have to go now. Go!"

The look on her face told me she was deadly serious. I looked at her a moment longer, then nodded and rushed out the back door.

As I ran, I couldn't help but shout back, "Make sure the coffee is ready when I get back! And maybe bake some cookies!"

Celeste's frantic voice carried after me, "Just go, you idiot!"

I couldn't help but smile a little despite the chaos. This was going to be one hell of a story to tell—if we survived it.

# Chapter 27

*Man of myth and legend.*

This was going to be humiliating. Not only did Celeste save my tail but now I'm seeking help from the guy she went on a date with. I took solace in the fact that she wasn't interested in him—or at least she said she wasn't. A light snow had begun to fall and I turned the collar of my jacket up in a feeble attempt to stay warm. The address took me to an apartment building near the Fox Theatre. It was an older building but I could tell it had been updated fairly recently. The front door had a silver keypad and buzzer. The button for 3E had no name, but this was what Celeste wrote down. I signed and reached out to press the button, and as I did, a group of tenants came out the front door laughing and paying very little attention to their surroundings. I took advantage of the moment and slid in behind them.

The lobby still smelled of new paint and fresh ambition. I could tell Celeste's friend either had money or came from it. For years, Detroit has been going through a new wave of gentrification, which has come with a mixture of reactions. The historic charm of the city was being polished up and given a glossy finish, but it still had that undercurrent of grit that kept things interesting. I was currently on the positive reaction train because the heat was working in the building, and it was knocking the chill off my bones. I made my way up the stairs to the third floor and was surprised to see this level consisted of only a handful of apartments that were clearly oversized. The kind of place where rent probably cost more than my cafe's monthly income.

On Celeste's friend's door was a mixture of stickers and magnets with quotes from nerd culture. Things like "Answer me these questions three," "You shall not pass," and "When someone asks if you're a God you say yes!"

Reluctantly, I knocked on the door three times in rapid succession. Before long, the door opened and a portly white guy in a Square-Enix t-shirt stood in front of me, wiping what looked like Cheeto dust onto his jeans.

"Gosh, that was quick!" he said, then looked at me quizzically and continued, "Where's the pizza?"

I stared back just as quizzically and said, "I'm not the pizza guy, I'm a friend of Celeste. Can I come in?"

His eyes went wide and his smile even wider as he motioned me in with a, "Nolan! Yeah, come on in, man! Any friend of Celeste is a friend of mine!"

I walked across the threshold and took a look around. The apartment was neat, modern, and filled to the brim with memorabilia and replicas. On one wall was a full suit of armor, and beside it was original Stormtrooper armor. A whole corner contained classic arcade machines of all different sizes, eras, and types. The floor looked like refinished wood, but certain areas had real-looking claw marks bored in. Hanging on the wall were legit-looking World Title Wrestling belts, one of which was inscribed "A. Pendragon."

I turned to my gracious host and asked "A.P.? Pendragon? As in Arthur Pendragon?" I knew magic was real, but I wasn't expecting to meet a man from myth and lore.

He scratched his head and looked at me sheepishly before answering. "No! Not Arthur. Although I do go by that sometimes. Old name. Um... Aragorn Pendragon. You see, I changed my name and I couldn't settle on a favorite story, so I took one of each," he said, extending one orange-tinged hand in my direction.

I looked down at the hand and paused before shaking it. "I'm not calling you Aragorn Pendragon," I said.

"You can call me Aragorn, or Pendragon. How about AP?"

"Pen. I'll call you Pen," I replied, completely lost as to why Celeste sent me to meet Mr. Nerd-merica.

"Pen, I like that, Nole!" replied Pen.

"Don't do that."

Pen laughed, a loud, hearty sound that echoed through the apartment. "Alright, alright. Come on in, Nole. Make yourself at home."

"Nolan, just Nolan."

I couldn't help but marvel at the place. It was like stepping into a geek's paradise. Action figures lined the shelves, and posters of every superhero you could think of covered the walls. It was clear Pen had poured his heart, soul, and probably a small fortune into decorating his lair. I wondered if he had an actual Bat-cave somewhere in the building.

Pen flopped down onto a couch that looked like it belonged in a spaceship and gestured for me to sit. "So, what brings you to my humble abode? Celeste didn't give you much detail, but she told me to let you know I know about magic—its existence anyway. Can't do any myself unfortunately."

I sat down cautiously, half-expecting the couch to start levitating or something. "She just told me to come here and that you could help. You're only the third person I have met who knows about...well you know. We just got beat up by a giant corporeal mist which Celeste sealed inside of me somehow, and when we finally made it back to my cafe there were some sketchy guys outside. Celeste told me to come here."

Pen's eyes widened. "Oh boy, sounds like you've had quite the adventure. But don't worry, you're in good hands now. We'll figure this out. Want something to drink?"

I couldn't help but feel a bit more at ease. Pen's enthusiasm was contagious, and despite the oddness of the situation, I felt like maybe, just maybe, things were going to be okay. Plus, I couldn't wait to see what kind of drinks a guy like Pen would whip up for us.

Probably something out of a sci-fi novel with a name like "Elderberry Elixir" or "Space Juice."

"So, Nolan, let me fill you in. I run this podcast called Motor City Magic where I discuss and expose all the mysteries of the unseen. Ghosts, cryptids, urban legends—you name it. I always knew magic was real, but I didn't have any solid proof until Celeste agreed to go on a date with me."

I raised an eyebrow, curiosity getting the better of me. "Wait, how did that date even come to be? No offense, Pen, but you don't seem like Celeste's type."

Pen laughed, not taking any offense. "None taken. The truth is, I kind of blackmailed her into it. I told her that either she'd go out with me or I'd try and uncover her ability. I had a few hunches and some minor evidence, but nothing concrete. Of course, I would never have really done it. But, magic has been my life's work, and my podcast audience deserves to find out more."

I couldn't help but chuckle at the absurdity of it. "So, you blackmailed Celeste into a date for the sake of your podcast? How big is your audience, anyway?"

Pen puffed up with pride. "I've got 312 followers as of yesterday."

I laughed to myself but thought better of making fun of the guy who was helping me. "Well, you've got 313 now."

Pen blushed and looked genuinely touched. "Thanks, Nolan. I appreciate it."

Taking the chance to get some answers, I asked, "So, Pen, what exactly is Celeste's power?"

Pen was about to respond when his phone buzzed. He pulled it out, glanced at the screen, and his eyes went wide. "It's a text from Celeste: 'Get out of the apartment now!'"

I jumped up, my heart pounding. "What? Why? What's going on?"

Pen looked around frantically, his jovial demeanor replaced by sheer panic. "I have no idea, but if Celeste says to get out, we get out!"

We bolted for the door, but Pen couldn't resist grabbing a few essentials—a laptop, a couple of books, and, oddly enough, a replica lightsaber. "Just in case," he muttered.

As we hurried out the door, I couldn't help but throw one more question at him. "Seriously, Pen? A lightsaber?"

He shot me a look that was half serious, half amused. "Hey, you never know. Besides, it looks cool."

We burst out the front door just as we saw someone or something rising into the air outside of Pens window. We stopped for the briefest of moments and witnessed the whole front of Pen's apartment explode outward, glass and bricks hovering mid air. That's all it took to kick us into high gear.

# Chapter 28

*The Demon, the Dragon, and the brick wall.*

**W**e ran. We ran for everything we had. Darting through alleyways and snowy side streets breathless and on edge we made it to Woodward Avenue. Traffic had died down since the snow picked up, but that didn't mean we could just dart out into traffic.

I could see Pen was winded and at the brink of exhaustion. I wouldn't be surprised if this was the first real exercise he'd gotten in his lifetime. As if on cue, Pen stopped and leaned heavily on a lamppost.

"I can't—I can't run anymore," Pen said through gasping breaths.

I looked back towards his building and I could just make out two figures in standing in his living room. The side of the building was sprawled open, and one of them pointed in our direction.

"Look, if we don't keep moving, whoever those are will catch up to us and do whatever whoever they are do!" I replied pulling on his arm.

He didn't move and I couldn't move him. I took a closer look at him and what I originally thought was sweat turned out to be tears streaming down his cheeks. Pen was terrified. Could I blame him? Up until now, his conviction about magic was all theory and circumstance. This was his moment to take it all in and in the middle of it we were being chased by forces unknown who undoubtedly meant us harm. I put my hands on his damp shoulders and met his eyes.

"Pen, we're going to get out of this. I won't let anything happen to you, but we have to get moving," I pleaded. He nodded and lumbered forward. An idea struck me and I motioned him to follow.

Moments later, both exhausted, we entered Greektown and caught our breath beside an old church. Greektown is a very old, very historic part of the city. It's well known for it's dining, entertainment and what I was looking for most, crowds. There was a winter festival yesterday which meant the whole weekend would be pretty busy. Even with the snow picking up, there were a good number of people in the narrow streets, coming and going from one bar to another. We might not be able to outrun them, but I had a good bet we could lose them in the throng of people. My heart sank and I realized I bet wrong. A block away I could see one of them scouring the crowd moving sluggishly through the crowd in our direction.

"We're not out of the woods yet," I muttered to Pen.

Pen was no longer standing next to me. In a panic, I looked around frantically. About 20 feet away, I saw him waving me over. I hurried over and huddled in a corridor next to him.

"The people mover! Let's get on the people mover, ride it a couple of stops and lose them that way!" he said decisively.

"I don't have any better ideas!" I replied.

We dashed through the doors to the Detroit People Mover which was essentially an automated above ground subway system which covered three miles of downtown Detroit in a circle.

Nearly spent, we reached the top of the stairs just as the People Mover slid into the station, its quiet hum signaling a brief moment of respite. The doors whooshed open, and a few scattered passengers disembarked, moving with the sluggish pace of downtown commuters. Pen and I stepped inside, heading toward the back of the nearly empty cabin. The People Mover is rarely crowded—it makes slow loops around the heart of downtown, more of a novelty than actual transportation. Tonight, it seemed deserted, save for us.

The overhead speaker chimed, announcing the next stop, and the soft hiss of the doors closing filled the cabin. Just as they were about to slide shut, a figure slipped between them with a dancer's grace, smooth and fluid, as if the narrow gap were made just for her.

She stood in the center aisle, her pixie-cut blonde hair glinting beneath the dim cabin lights. Her skin was pale, almost translucent, as though she rarely saw the sun, and her slight frame was draped in a dark tunic that looked both modern and timeless. The fabric clung in places—practical, fitted—but moved with her like a second skin as she rocked gently from side to side, perfectly balanced on the moving train. There was something disarming in the simplicity of her appearance, yet everything about her radiated the quiet tension of someone accustomed to confrontation.

She looked young—too young, maybe early twenties, a few years younger than me. But the moment her gaze locked on mine, I saw experience etched into those pale blue eyes. She'd seen things, done things, and there was a calm confidence about her that set off alarm bells in my mind. This wasn't someone you could reason with. She exuded the kind of stillness that comes from being in control of every situation, the type of stillness that felt more dangerous than any outburst.

Her hands rested loosely by her sides, but something about the way her fingers twitched made my stomach knot. She didn't need to make a move to be threatening; just standing there was enough. The way she swayed ever so slightly as the train began its slow crawl forward was hypnotic—like a cobra waiting to strike. There was no doubt about it—she was there for us, or more specifically, me.

"Uh, what's she doing with her hands?" Pen asked, his voice quivering with panic.

"Nothing good," I replied, trying to sound braver than I felt.

Circles of vibrant color danced and rippled in my vision as her fingers weaved patterns that seemed impossible, as if she were knitting the air itself. The feeling was surreal, like being on the edge of sleep, that strange liminal state where nothing makes sense but everything feels real. My stomach lurched as my feet left the floor—she'd manipulated the gravity around us.

Coffee cups, discarded receipts, crumpled wrappers, and plastic stirrers slowly floated around us like cosmic debris in a miniature orbit. Even the faint sound of the People Mover's wheels on the track was muted, replaced by the eerie stillness of weightlessness.

Pen let out a gleeful, panicked laugh. "If I wasn't terrified, this would be the coolest thing I've ever seen!" His arms flailed wildly, as if swimming would somehow get him back to the ground. A stray coffee cup drifted past him, and he batted it away like an awkward cat.

"Focus, Pen! This isn't the time to channel your inner astronaut!" I hissed, trying to stay calm, though my heart pounded in my chest. Every nerve ending in my body screamed *danger*.

The woman's fingers continued their delicate movements, her expression serene. She was enjoying this. Each motion was fluid, controlled, as if she'd spent her whole life mastering the art of manipulating gravity.

She took a slow, deliberate step toward us, her eyes locked on mine with unnerving calm. There was no malice in her face—just intensity, as though she were conducting a familiar dance and knew exactly where each step would lead. I was just a pawn in a game I didn't know the rules to.

"Gravity it is, then," I muttered, my mind racing for an idea.

Pen spun slowly in midair beside me, his arms still flapping uselessly. "Should I try to swim or should I just... I don't know, *float better?*" he asked, half laughing, half panicking.

"Just stop doing *that!*" I shot back, motioning vaguely to his awkward paddling.

I twisted and flailed, trying to reach for anything solid to push off from, but there was nothing close enough. My feet swung wildly, kicking at thin air. The woman's calm footsteps echoed in the hollow cabin as she closed the distance between us, floating debris swirling lazily around her.

Panic surged. I was running out of options.

I channeled a small burst of kinetic magic to my palms, just enough to give me a push. A sharp blast shot out, propelling me backward. The force sent me spinning through the air like a human pinball.

Pen yelped as I slammed into him. "Hey! Watch it!"

We collided in a tangle of limbs, and the two of us glided backward into the cold metal wall of the cabin with a heavy thud. The impact knocked the air from my lungs, and Pen groaned as a plastic lid smacked him in the face.

"Okay, new plan—less *crashing into things,*" Pen wheezed.

"Yeah, I'll pencil that in for next time, genius," I muttered, twisting in the air. I had to move fast.

I shoved Pen aside, his body spinning gracelessly off again, and kicked off the wall as hard as I could. The force propelled me toward the small woman, but the moment she noticed my approach, her fingers stopped their weird movement.

She raised one hand, palm flat, and the entire People Mover jolted.

The cabin groaned ominously as if the train itself was under some immense pressure. The gravity slammed back into place—and then some. I hit the floor like I'd just been body slammed.

I let out a strangled grunt as the air was knocked from my lungs. The impact was brutal—every bone in my body screamed in protest, and the floor vibrated under the weight of both my body and the sudden gravity surge. Bits of junk crashed to the ground all around me: crumpled wrappers, half-empty soda cans, someone's abandoned scarf.

I could feel the crushing weight pinning me down, like an elephant had decided to make my ribcage its favorite chair. My limbs felt leaden, pinned to the floor by the sheer force of her power.

The woman tilted her head, studying me with an expression that was almost... curious. Not smug, not angry—just curious, like a cat watching a bug it had trapped under its paw.

"Well, this sucks," Pen muttered from somewhere behind me. His voice was strained, but somehow he was still finding the humor in our impending doom. "It was great meeting you, Nolan, but next time knock on someone else's door,"

"You are not helping, Pen!" I managed to say, straining against the incredible pressure.

The woman didn't say a word. She didn't need to. Her silence was more unnerving than any threat could have been. Every movement she made was deliberate, precise. There was no wasted effort, no unnecessary gestures—just pure, terrifying control.

I tried to push myself up, but it felt like gravity had multiplied tenfold. My muscles screamed in protest, and my limbs trembled with the effort. I could barely lift my head off the ground, let alone fight back. Panic clawed at the edges of my mind.

"Okay, okay, think, Nolan. Think." I gritted my teeth and tried to focus. There had to be a way out of this.

The woman took another slow, deliberate step forward, her expression unreadable. The air around her seemed heavier, charged with an unseen force. I was starting to think I knew very little about how to really control magic.

"Pen, if you've got any brilliant ideas, now's the time!" I hissed, sweat trickling down my temple.

Pen groaned from his spot on the floor. "I got nothin', man. This lady's got us beat. Gravity lady wins. Game over."

"Thanks for the pep talk," I muttered, straining against the crushing force.

A grinding noise sounded from beneath us, halting her advance. It seemed like her little gravity trick affected more than just Pen and me. The grinding noise beneath us grew louder, like metal on metal, as if the very guts of the People Mover were being torn apart by her gravity magic. The cabin trembled violently, lights flickering, sending shadows dancing wildly across the walls. It was clear that her powers were wreaking havoc on more than just us—she couldn't fully control the gravitational fields without also disrupting the fragile mechanics of the train. All of a sudden, the crushing feeling disappeared. I breathed hungrily and rose to one knee. Concern was painted all over the small woman's face. I guess she wasn't as confident as I thought. Her delicate, precise control of gravity had limits, and those limits were now painfully obvious inside a moving steel death trap.

Without hesitation, I pushed off the floor and lunged toward her, my heart pounding in my chest. But before I could close the distance, the small, shimmering spheres orbiting her began to zip through the air like angry hornets. One shot toward my leg, and the weight slammed down on me again, pinning it to the floor as if an invisible anchor had locked it in place.

The weight was intense—crushing, painful—but this time it was localized, isolating my leg with unbelievable  precision. I gritted my teeth and extended my hand, summoning a plume of fire that erupted toward her with a sharp, scorching hiss. The air shimmered with heat, and the cabin was filled with the brief, blinding glow of flames.

But one of her spheres darted into the fire's path, absorbing it like a sponge. The flames dissipated, leaving only thin trails of smoke curling in the air. Another sphere latched onto my arm next, locking it into place. I stood there looking like a worried marionette.

"Okay, no fire," I muttered, the pressure on my arm and leg dragging me closer to the floor. I tried to stay calm, but panic buzzed in the back of my mind—a relentless, nagging feeling that I was quickly running out of options.

I raised my free hand and sent a burst of kinetic energy that rocketed toward her, but she twisted, dodging it like she had choreographed the whole fight.

The kinetic burst smashed into the metal frame of the cabin, leaving a deep dent.

"Not blocking anymore..." I whispered, sending three more bursts in rapid succession. Each shot missed, obliterating a pair of seats and shattering a fluorescent light overhead. Sparks rained down, and the train groaned under the strain of our battle.

"Hey! Can we get a time-out? I think I left my dignity at the last station!" Pen shouted, trying to lighten the mood despite the precarious situation.

I grinned despite myself. "Focus, Pen!"

This was it. I only had one more shot before the gravity pinned me completely. I summoned a larger ball of kinetic energy, about the size of a beach ball, and launched it straight toward her with every bit of force I could muster.

The woman's eyes widened slightly, and her fingers flicked, moving the gravity wells away from my attack. But she was unsuccessful.

The kinetic energy and gravity well nicked each other, creating a swirling vortex of light and magic. It was breathtaking—a brilliant rainbow of swirling colors, spinning wildly in the air between us. The vortex expanded outward, its edges shimmering like the surface of a bubble, unstable and growing by the second.

For a moment, time seemed to stretch, and everything slowed.

Then the edge of the vortex brushed against the metal wall of the People Mover, and the cabin exploded outward with a deafening roar.

The steel siding peeled away like paper, and a gust of freezing winter air blasted into the train. Snowflakes whipped into the cabin, swirling violently in the chaos, as the exposed cityscape spun dizzyingly by outside. I caught a glimpse of the Renaissance Center, its mirrored towers glinting ominously in the afternoon sunlight, looming over us like silent sentinels.

The force of the blast knocked the woman off-balance, her tunic whipping wildly in the wind. She staggered, trying to regain control, her concentration faltering. The gravitational pressure lifted, and I could move again.

This was my chance. No more hesitation.

I planted my foot firmly on the floor and unleashed a final burst of kinetic energy, aiming directly at her chest. The magic hit with a dull thud, and she was sent flying backward—straight through the gaping hole in the side of the train.

She tumbled through the air, her small frame spinning helplessly as the wind carried her away from the People Mover.

"I hope she's got a good insurance policy for that landing!" Pen quipped, though his voice trembled with residual fear.

A sickening wave of guilt crashed over me. My heart pounded in my ears as I stared at the hole where she had disappeared into the Detroit Sky.

What if she couldn't land safely? What if her abilities weren't enough to save her? What if I just killed someone? It was really only a story or two, right? She could be okay.

The thought sent a shiver down my spine, sober and cold, cutting through the adrenaline of the fight. This wasn't just some game or training exercise. This was real, and I had to live with the consequences.

I tried to shake the thought, but it stuck, gnawing at the edges of my mind.

The People Mover shuddered again, struggling to stay on track after the blast. The wind howled through the open side of the cabin, carrying with it the distant hum of the city below.

"We should...we should probably get off this thing before it derails," I muttered, swallowing the lump in my throat.

Pen gave me a shaky thumbs-up. "Yeah, good call. Also, let's never do that again."

I nodded, forcing a weak grin, though my mind was still racing. The fight was over, but the weight of what had just happened lingered, pressing down on me with the same crushing force as her magic.

The people mover rocked raggedly into the next stop and came to a shuddering halt. The doors slid open and Pen and I stepped through. There was no moment of relief because the second person we saw at Pen's loft stood in the corridor before us flanked by two other people all in the same uniform. The man was huge. He was an older black gentleman, probably well into his 60s, with a build that suggested he could bench-press the people mover itself. His salt-and-pepper beard sat below a dangerous scowl, and his eyes looked like they had seen more than their fair share of conflict.

"Okay, this guy clearly skipped leg day," I muttered under my breath.

Pen, still reeling from our gravity-defying escapade, added, "Why do the big scary ones always have to be so... big and scary?"

I squared my shoulders and took a step forward, trying to project confidence. "Look, man! I respect my elders, and I don't really want to kick your ass, but if you don't move out of my way right now, I'm going to move you myself."

The old man raised an eyebrow, clearly unimpressed. "Elders, huh? Boy, I was throwing people around before you were even a twinkle in your daddy's eye."

Pen piped up, his voice still shaky. "Uh, we don't want any trouble, sir. We're just trying to—"

The old man cut him off with a deep, rumbling laugh. "Trouble? Son, you two are the very definition of trouble. And I'm here to put an end to it."

He gestured to the smoking, ruined people mover car we just exited.

"It was like that when we got here," I said trying to suppress a smile.

I glanced at Pen, who was now visibly sweating. "Pen, you wanna handle this one?"

Pen shrugged helplessly. "You're the one with the magic fists, dude. I just press buttons and talk about conspiracies."

I sighed and took a step closer to the old man, who crossed his massive arms over a barrel chest.

"Last chance, big guy. Move, or I'll make you move."

He smirked, clearly relishing the challenge. "I'd like to see you try, kid."

I drew in my magic and focused it on my right hand. I balled up my fist and hurled a kinetically charged haymaker directly into the man's sternum.

Two things happened all at once. First, every ounce of magic I'd drawn into my fist exited all at once. Second, he grabbed the front of my shirt and struck me in the face three times in rapid succession, each blow bringing stars to my eyes. Out of one immediately swollen eye, I saw Pen recoil, his jaw slack. It was quiet, even his subordinates seemed to be still after the swift and severe violence.

A familiar voice broke the silence.

"Daddy!" That voice! It was Celeste!

The big guy released his grip on me, and I fell forward, leaning against his chest.

"Nice to meet you, sir," I garbled out through the bloody ruin that used to be my face.

He rolled his eyes at me, then sidestepped. I fell forward, landing hard on my face.

Celeste yelled again as she made her way forward and knelt by my side.

"Don't worry, my face broke my fall," I said, rolling onto my back. I could already feel my split lip and swollen eye mending. I was healing much faster than before. Maybe this thing inside me wasn't so bad.

"Celestia! What are you doing here?" said the big man in his deep, rumbling voice.

I coughed violently and spit blood onto the gritty floor of the People Mover station. Celeste touched my arm but recoiled sharply, hissing under her breath.

The man I knew only as "Daddy" was on me like lightning, wrapping a huge, meaty hand around my entire face. I tried to peel his fingers free, to loosen his hold even a little bit, but his grip was like iron. I would have had better luck trying to scream underwater.

I could feel myself passing out. Was this it? Would I die here, never knowing the answers to all of my questions? Never being able to hold Celeste again?

Celeste.

I could barely make her out through the cracks of his fingers. She pulled at his arm, striking him uselessly as he pressed the life out of me.

Her face was the last image I saw before my world turned to darkness.

# Chapter 29

*You again.*

I awoke to a familiar blue and purple sky. Gasping, I sat up slowly and took a few deep breaths. Surprisingly, all of my aches and pains were gone. I felt, I felt brand new. I also felt a presence behind me. When I turned around, I recognized my surroundings. I was in the cavern, Tempris, and I had visited. My eyes searched my surroundings, but I saw no one. Again, I felt a presence, stronger now. I fixed my gaze at one point and knew something was there.

"Who's there?" I got nothing but silence in return. "It's you, isn't it? The thing from the box."The air shimmered and I heard a low rumble. Wind whipped around me and for the first time I realized I was wearing a Mystic Ground T-shirt and jeans.

"Am I dead? Is that what this is? Are you here to make some kind of deal? You can save your breath, it's not happening," I said as I brought myself to my full height. Still, silence.

"You know, if you're really inside of me, I'm sure you could have helped me out back there. I got beaten and choked out, and now I'm —here," I said, gesturing around me.

The silence stretched out, and I began to feel uncertain about whether I felt a presence or not. Shadows shifted around the room, and I heard a weird noise that almost sounded like speech but was definitely entirely foreign to the reality I knew.

"Are you there? Say something! Help me out here. I've got to get back. I've got to get back to Celeste!" I said, my emotions flaring. The room shook, and power flowed into me from every direction.

"Whoa, okay! That's... that's a lot of power!" I shouted, feeling like I was being supercharged like a magic battery. "Didn't mean to wake up the neighbors!"

The power surged through me, filling every fiber of my being. The cavern around me seemed to pulse in response, almost as if it were alive.

"Alright, alright! Enough already! I get it, you're powerful!" I yelled into the void. The shadows danced more aggressively, almost mocking me.

Suddenly, my eyes snapped open, and I found myself back in the people mover station, still suspended by the big man. I placed my hand on his chest and a burst of energy came forth. At the moment of impact, a blinding light bloomed into existence. I had to squeeze my eyes completely shut to keep from being blinded. Slowly I opened them, and began blinking away spots. Celeste's father had vanished without a trace. What have I done? Not only could the woman I love not touch me, but now she would probably hate me if I killed her father. I turned towards Celeste. Her eyes were as wide as saucers. To my surprise, she wasn't looking at me. To my right stood Pen. He wasn't looking at me either. I followed their gaze down the terminal. Twenty feet away was an enormous crater in the concrete wall with Celeste's father lodged in it. More of the dust began to settle, and I could see him stirring chunks of concrete and debris spilled off of him as he rows to his feet. And I squinted my eyes to get a better look, and I'd be damned if he wasn't smiling.

"Shit, dude," Pen said looking at me with astonishment.

I turned towards Celeste and she was staring at me with a troubling expression.

"You fucked up," she said shaking her head.

Her father began making long strides towards me, covering the distance fast. I focused my breathing and assumed a fighting stance, readying for impending confrontation. Without hesitation, Celeste stepped between us, halting his advance.

"Daddy, no! This is Nolan. He's my friend. You're not fighting him anymore," she exclaimed.

His expression softened and he looked down at her with what I could tell was pure, deep, genuine love. He placed his hands on her shoulders and kissed the top of her head before preceding to lift her up ever so gently and placing her out of his way. He strode forward and got in my face.

"Do that again," he demanded.

"Do what, um, sir?" I said more sheepishly than I care to admit.

"Do whatever you did to knock my ass in a wall. Do it! That was not magic," he replied, his tone becoming even more demanding.

I don't know if it would be a good idea to tell him he just got punched by a mist being in a box. I looked to Celeste who stood a couple of feet away with her arms crossed.

"I'd do what he says," she said flatly.

"Sorry in advance, sir," I said as I pulled back my fist and began to focus.

The blow landed just as pillow soft as the original punch I threw at him. What's more, there was no bright flash.

"I don't understand," I said puzzled.

"I told you. That was not magic. Take him!" the big man said before two people in similar black uniforms blinked into existence next to me. Without preamble, they secured my arms behind my back with some kind of binders. I couldn't draw any magic and maintaining my balance became a chore.

"Take him? Me? Take me where? Let me go!" I shouted as I struggled uselessly against my bonds.

"Daddy, you don't have to do this," Celeste pleaded.

Her father simply shot her a look before a split in the veil opened up, similar to the tear I saw Tempris escape through. They ushered me through. I was able to take a glance back at Celeste and Pen who stood beside her dictating into his phone. She stepped forward and began to shout something after me.

"Don't worry! I'll find y—" her words were cut off as the portal closed.

# Chapter 30

*Warm Welcome.*

S pots danced in my eyes and I had the sudden urge to vomit. Luckily I held the feeling at bay and became acutely aware that I couldn't remember the last time I actually had something to eat. As my vision adjusted, I took in my surroundings. I was in...I was in a police station. No, it wasn't a police station but it looked a lot like one. The same familiar benches, open office cubicles, and style that was in dire need of updating. It was familiar alright, but everything was much more...bespoke. The desks were rich, natural wood, the fixtures were incredibly elaborate works of art and I could have been concussed but I swear they were made of real gold. My veneration was cut short when I was pushed forward by a pair of large hands on my back. I looked back and had to crane my neck to see Celeste's dad urging me forward. Somewhere between the time I was thrust into that portal and now, my legs where magically manacled and my arms were bound behind my back by something that felt far larger than handcuffs. So I was basically frog marched through the foyer of the building. Glances came my way every so often and I could hear murmurs over the random chatter of the offices. I'm not a particularly prideful man but enough was enough. I stopped in place.

"Hey, could you tell me what's going on? Where am I and what am I doing here?"

Celeste's dad gave me a flat stare before turning on his heel and walking back the way he came, leaving me standing in the middle of a corridor. A cheerful man in glasses approached me. He had the bushiest mustache I can ever remember seeing outside of civil war reenactments

"Name please," he said with a wide smile.

Reluctantly, I spoke my name. "Nolan West," I felt a pop and a jolt of electricity and I was no longer standing in the corridor.

I sat in a room that wasn't the similar from the interrogation rooms I'd seen on TV. The major difference, this one had windows. I don't know when it happened, but my wrists and forearms were now bound in front of me. Runes, some of which I recognized, swirled across glowing metal bracers. I couldn't bring my arms apart or conjure any magic. My legs were free, but I could still feel an odd pressure where they had been bound just moments before.

Thankfully, I wasn't restrained to the table so I decided to stand up. I crossed the room to the window and peered out. What I saw took my breath away. I could see a beautiful horizon and a lush cityscape. It was like looking at Detroit's Grand Circus Park only there was so much greenery. Trees, manicured bushes, beautiful vines and flowers all came together perfectly with the stone and concrete structures. If I wasn't a prisoner I'd be in love.

I was several stories up so leaping out of the window was not an option unless I wanted to break both legs and drag myself along the cobblestone street till they mended. Taking a closer look at the window I noticed something. There was something in the windows, in the glass. If I got close at let my eyes go out of focus, I could see runes scrolling across the pane. Even if I could use my magic I was certain it wasn't going to make a dent in these things. I was imprisoned, alone, confused, and powerless. My thoughts drifted to Celeste, or should I say "Celestia?" Isn't that what her father called her? My head thudded against the window pane and I audibly sighed. The woman I was madly in love with was somehow part of all of this. I closed my eyes and imagined her face. She saved my life and all I was left with was the memory of tears in her eyes as I got hauled off by magic Johnny Law. In that moment, I made a promise to myself. I would find my way out of here and see her again. That much was certain. Just then, the door opened and a pale man with fiery red hair strode in carrying a large tumbler of what I assumed was coffee. He was tall with intense eyes and a five o'clock shadow that was s red and manicured as the hair on his head. He wore a similar outfit to the one the crew that came to abduct me wore. I could have been imagining things but it looked like he was staring daggers at me. Pulling a seat out for himself, he motioned for me to take a seat. I straightened up and returned to the seat I arrived in, struggling to get comfortable due to my bindings. He watched me struggle for several moments. My knee struck the table spilling some of his drink before he was able to right the cup. I was right, it was coffee and to my surprise even the spill was steaming. The man slammed his hands down on top of my binding and they vanished in a stream of particles.

"Thanks," I said as I rubbed my tingling wrists. "Can I uh  can I get one of those?" I pointed at the still steaming coffee with a sheepish grin.

"Listen, shit snack, you're going to answer every question we have, and if we like the answers, maybe you want to spend the rest of your life in a deep, dark hole," he nearly shouted at me in reply.

Well if this guy wasn't going to be pleasant, I could at least show him how it's done.

"Wait, did you just call me shit snack? What the hell is a shit snack?" I shot back.

"You are a shit snack, a little tiny shit small enough to eat that's fits in a—"

"So are you trying to call me a piece of shit? Or a sack of shit?"

"Dogs eat shit and they like snacks and you're a shit snack shit snack!" he retorted with rising exacerbation.

"Wait, wait, now are you trying to call me a piece of shit or are you trying to call me dog shit? I tell you, buddy, you're gonna have to work on your insults."

The coffee boiled over in his tumbler and created a huge mess on the table, steam rising from each small puddle.

Behind him, the door opened and in walked the woman I threw from the people mover. Well, to be honest it was gravity and unstable magic that did most of the work. She looked a little worse for wear with a bandage on her cheek and one arm in a sling. She made her way over with a slight limp and placed a hand on the man's shoulder.

"Take it easy there, hot head! Now you see why they let me handle the field work," she said and plopped a manilla folder down next to him. I noticed her wince with the movement.

"I'm sorry. I'm really sorry. This is all very new to me," I said earnestly.

Both of them just stared at me. The woman's expression seemed to soften, but the man looked like his rage was beginning to bubble over again.

"I feel like you mean that. Thanks, slugger," she said with a smile that was as brilliant and genuine as a sunrise. Behind all that power and demeanor, she really was very pretty.

"Slugger! I get a nickname too? Now I feel like part of the gang. Isn't that right, Hot Head?" I said directing the last part at my fiery friend. His hands clenched into fists and he began to rise.

"My name is Nash!" he said, his eyes beginning to glow. The acrid scent of burnt popcorn flooded the room.

The young woman must have sensed something I didn't, because she decided to intervene. With the barest touch of her hand, she forced him back down in his seat. The scent of wildflowers filled my nose. She just used magic to keep this guy three times her size in his seat. I think she noticed my look of astonishment because she smirked and looked at me again.

"I'm Gravitas, and my affinity is gravity magic. It doesn't play so well with kinetic magic. That's why you opened up that hole in the People Mover," she said with a slight bite in her voice.

"Your name is a little on the nose, isn't it? We. We tore up the People Mover," I replied.

"Maybe I should change your nickname to Dumb-Dumb. It's magic 101! Everyone knows magic types and what they shouldn't be combined with," she said slightly puzzled.

I said nothing, but simply slid my gaze away from the both of them. Not only was I a fish out of water but apparently I didn't even know what land was. Had Tempris really used me this much? Should I even attempt to use my magic again knowing I know so little?

"Nash, if you've got any more questions to ask him you better finish up quick, she's on her way in to talk to him," Gravitas said tousling his hair before sweeping out of the room taking with her the sweet smell of flowers and leaving the over roasted popcorn scent. I brought my attention back to Nash, his face was beat red and his focus seemed to be entirely elsewhere. Suddenly it all became so clear.

Oh! Oh! I get it! You like her! You're pissed at me because I roughed up your girlfriend!" I said in an exasperated whisper.

"She's not my girlfriend!" he said fervently.

"Does she know? If you call her back in here I can tell her how you feel. It's no big deal. We're bros, right?" I replied with an elbow nudge in my voice.

His cheeks flushed, and for the first time his scowl was replaced by a look of surprise.

"I'll kill you!" he replied. But this time he was far less angry and far more timid.

"You'll do what?"

The voice came from the entryway, but it was a voice I knew all too well. A voice I wasn't sure I'd ever hear again. Celeste moved into the room like a vision, graceful and composed, with a presence that made everything else feel small and dim. Her eyes locked onto mine, and I felt an intense swirl of emotions—relief, desire, guilt, even a touch of fear. The gaze she held was complex, a fusion of mirth and sadness that seemed impossible to unravel. She had never looked more striking or more untouchable.

Every detail hit me at once. Her black tunic, the same as Nash's, was sleek and structured with gold piping that shimmered as she moved. Runes, intricate and almost alive with faint energy, laced through the fabric, their patterns catching the light just right. Her half-cape, draped over one shoulder, flowed with her, adding to the air of authority and mystery that now enveloped her. This was a side of Celeste I'd only glimpsed before, like seeing someone you thought you knew in a dream that was both familiar and entirely alien.

I couldn't take my eyes off her as she crossed the room toward us, every step deliberate. I felt my pulse quicken. A hundred things I wanted to say flooded my mind, but none of them made it past my lips.

"I don't think your supervisor would relish the idea of his enforcers threatening homicide, do you, Nash?" she said, her voice cool, almost amused, and laced with a subtle authority.

"N-no, ma'am," Nash replied, practically tripping over himself as he got to his feet and began gathering his things.

"Geez, don't call me ma'am! We went to the same school!"

"Sorry, Celeste," Nash mumbled, then hurried out, clearly rattled.

As the door clicked shut, Celeste turned her full attention on me, her expression softening just a fraction. Our eyes met, and I couldn't help but get lost in her gaze. The urge to reach across the table, take her face in my hands, and apologize, explain, even just hold her— anything to bridge the distance that had grown between us—was almost unbearable. We stayed like that for what felt like an eternity until I finally broke the silence.

"Let me guess. Your dad is the supervisor."

"Ding-ding-ding! He's correct! What does he win? An all-expenses-paid trip to telling me why the hell you've been lying to me all this time," she replied, her voice carrying an edge that pierced me.

Her smirk faded, replaced by a mixture of anger and raw hurt that twisted my insides. She wasn't going to let me off easy—not this time. And who could blame her? This was my mess. Hurting Celeste was the last thing I could ever imagine doing, but my actions had led us to this moment.

"Celeste, I'm sorry. It's a long, long story," I said, the weight of my regret thick in my voice.

"Well, you're not going anywhere, and I've got time," she replied, sliding a coffee across to me.

I paused to take a sip, and my eyes nearly rolled back in my head. It was definitely coffee, that much I could tell, but I'd never tasted anything like it. In all my travels I'd had hundreds of roasts, blends, and beans, but this was next level. Whatever I'd done to deserve this cup was a mystery, but I wasn't complaining.

"This is amazing. You've been holding out. Do you know what people would do to get their hands on a cup of coffee like this?" I said, taking another long draw from the dark, heady brew.

Celeste crossed her arms and just stared at me. Clearly, this wasn't the time for jokes. I reluctantly set the cup down.

"A few months ago, the guy you clearly had some kind of crush on came in one day while you weren't there. I saw him heat up a cup of coffee with his hands! So I convinced him to teach me, and I learned magic was real. I also learned I had some kind of innate affinity for it. In exchange for his instruction, he said I had to help him track down an artifact he was looking for. Then you go into a coma after touching his notebook, and when you show up, I find out I wasn't Tempris' first choice. You know what happened after that," I said, condensing the story as best I could.

Straightening up, Celeste ran her fingers through her hair and bit her bottom lip, her expression softening as she considered my words.

"Why didn't you tell me?"

"What was I supposed to say to the woman I'm falling for as this burgeoning romance is happening? 'Oh hey, do you like close-up magic? Then throw a lightning bolt or something?'" I replied.

"You can throw lightning?"

"I'm better with fire, but I can manage," I admitted, giving a small shrug.

"Wait, just how many magic types are you able to use?" she asked, her eyes widening with curiosity.

"So far I can use fire, lightning, and I think air. My kinetic magic is pretty good as well, but I'm not so good with the fine control," I explained.

"That's not normal."

"That's what I've heard."

Celeste fell silent, her face shifting into an expression of deep contemplation, as if trying to piece together a puzzle. But I couldn't shake the feeling there was more she hadn't told me either.

"What about you?" I asked, my tone softening. "What kind of magic can you use? Whatever you did to me was pretty... unusual."

"I'm a sealer," she replied, almost reluctantly, not offering much else.

I stared at her, my brow raised, silently urging her to elaborate. She sighed heavily, drumming her fingers lightly on the table as she continued.

"I can lock and unlock everything within an object. Information, history, memories, things like that. I can place my hand on a book and tell you how old it is, where it's been, who's held it, and what kind of magic it's been in contact with. But it's different with living things. I can't touch you and reveal your life story, or place my hand on the ground and learn the whole history of the earth. Their own flow of magic disrupts my ability in that way. My magic is mostly for inanimate objects," she said, her palm glowing faintly as she placed it on the table for emphasis.

"That's why you like books so much, why you wanted to work at the library so badly. The sheer amount of information in and out of that place must be staggering. Wait, you said 'mostly' inanimate objects," I said, my tone questioning.

"While I can't unseal living things, I can seal things within them. If I wanted to, I could share memories, thoughts, experiences, and histories, but only temporarily. Again, the flow of magic from a living thing is ever-moving, ever-changing, and would disrupt my ability," she explained, the excitement in her voice clear as she spoke about her power.

"So kind of like how paper gets old and weathered or old media formats can degrade?" I asked, catching on.

"Exactly! Only much quicker," she replied, looking pleased.

Now came the big question, the one I knew she was waiting for me to ask.

"Celeste...how did you seal whatever that was—the thing in the cave—inside of me?"

"I don't know. When I felt its power, I knew it wasn't magic. It was old, powerful, and it didn't seem malevolent. So I trusted in my magic, and you trusted in me," she said, giving me a look that felt like pride and apology all wrapped into one.

"Didn't seem malevolent? I think you and I have two very different definitions of that word," I replied, trying to lighten the tension with a smile.

"Come on. I want you to talk to someone," Celeste said.

She rose, turning sharply, her cape billowing behind her. I watched her walk toward the door, admiring the fluidity in her movements, the confidence in her posture. Everything about her in this moment exuded strength and purpose, and I felt a pang of regret that I had kept so much from her.

"You coming?" she asked, glancing over her shoulder with a look that was both challenging and inviting.

If there was one thing that could distract me, it would always be Celeste. I slid out of my chair, following her toward the door.

"Nice outfit. While we're on the topic of secrets, do you work here or something?" I asked, studying her from head to toe.

"I used to. Not for a long time, though," she replied flatly, leaving it at that.

I waited for her to continue, but she simply walked through the door, leaving me momentarily in the room alone. Maybe she was still upset, or maybe her role here was a sore subject. Either way, I decided to table it while I sought answers to the questions that had led me to this room in the first place. I started after her but darted back to grab my coffee. This little cup of magic seemed to be the one thing that hadn't gotten me in trouble today.

# Chapter 31

*What's up, Doc?*

We walked through the offices to a long hallway with several elevators on each side. Celeste waved her hand over a glowing flat panel on the outside of one of the elevators. The doors slid open revealing three glass walls that faced the outside of the building. She waved her hand again on another panel and we began traveling to the lower levels of the building. The ride was smooth and although it looked like a pretty ordinary elevator, I could sense magic as it sped down through the floors.

"Is this powered by—"

"By magic? Yes," Celeste replied before I could finish.

"How—how does it work? That would be an amazing power source for the mundane world! Is it infinite? Like cold fusion or something? Can it be stored in batteries?"

"I'm a researcher, not a scientist. Can you explain regular electricity, battery storage, conductivity, and molecular science to me right now?" Celeste replied a little more curt than normal.

"I uh, well you charge a battery with electricity and it works...I think," I replied quietly.

"Okay, you know even less than I do! Chemical energy is stored and converted into electrical energy. The same basic principal is applied with magical energy only on a much more involved scale,"

"Thanks for the magical science lesson,"

"Don't thank me yet. Wait till you meet the Doc,"

We turned a corner, and the hallway opened up into a huge laboratory. Inside were a handful of people in lab coats milling about and working on various projects. To my surprise, I recognized one of them. Pen stood next to one of the men, laughing. Celeste and I walked over, and Pen's eyes lit up.

"Nolan! Celeste! You made it!" Pen rushed over to greet us, a broad smile on his face. "I'm so glad you're both okay!"

"Pen," I said, feeling a surprising wave of relief at seeing him. I had only met him a few hours ago, but his presence was reassuring.

"You're stoked to be here, aren't you?" Celeste asked with a grin.

"Absolutely!" Pen replied. "This place is incredible! I never imagined I'd get to see something like this in person."

Celeste turned to me, her smile widening. "Pen is kind of a celebrity, you know."

I raised an eyebrow, glancing between her and Pen. "A celebrity? With a few hundred followers in the mundane world?"

She nodded, hovering a hand over a nearby laptop. The screen shifted, displaying Pen's Motor City Magic YouTube page. To my astonishment, it was lit up with activity, showing millions of views and countless comments.

"Here, in the magical society, Motor City Magic has millions," Celeste explained.

Pen looked at the screen, his eyes widening in surprise and excitement. "Wait, really? I'm a celebrity here?"

"Yeah, you are," Celeste confirmed. "Your videos have been a huge hit. People love how you explain magic in a way that's both entertaining and informative. And they love how you get a lot right and a lot wrong. That's the comedy of your page."

Pen stared at the laptop, his mouth agape. "I... I don't know what to say. This is amazing! I was wondering why that lab tech asked for my signature! "

"You've earned it," I said, patting him on the back. "You've got a way of making things accessible and fun. It's no wonder people love your stuff."

Pen beamed, looking around the lab with renewed enthusiasm. "This is just... wow. I never imagined I'd get to be part of something like this."

Celeste chuckled. "Well, get used to it. You're in the big leagues now."

As Pen continued to marvel at his newfound fame, I couldn't help but feel a sense of camaraderie. Despite everything that had happened, we were in this together. I no longer felt jealous or out of sorts that Celeste went out with him, that was for sure. The man in the lab coat who was standing next to Pen cleared his throat. Celeste took it as a cue for introduction. "Nolan, I'd like you to meet Dr. Vihaan Subramani."

He was a dark skinned man of Indian dissent. He had a shock of salt and pepper hair on top of his head and his long wrinkled white lab coat and 5 o'clock shadow gave me reason to believe he spent way more time in his lab than he did at home.

"Nolan and I have met once before!"

He stared at me and smiled a familiar smile.

"You! You're the doctor from Celeste's hospital room!"

"The one and only! I hope you don't mind but I stole a little DNA and a sample of your magic when we ran into each other the first time,"

"You did what? When? How?"

"It's far easier than you'd think, and the results from your sample are exceedingly interesting—have a look,"

Dr. Subramani waved his hand over a console and a holographic display of a brain with several different metrics beside it came into view, hovering in midair.

"This is a normal, healthy human brain that is accustomed to magic. Starting at the parietal lobe you see colored lines forking through the rest of the brain all the way down to the brainstem,"

Red and green lines spread lightly and evenly throughout the holographic brain. Some forked in random directions but for the most part they followed a pattern. Another brain winked to life next to the brain we were already looking at.

"This, Nolan, is your brain,"

It looked similar to the brain on the left however this one had more colored lines than I could count running down throughout it. They forked, criss-crossed, and some of them even seemed to wind around different sections of the brain. Every color in the rainbow and more seemed to cocoon the cortex. I turned to look at Celeste. She was holding her hand to her mouth and it looked like she was almost drawing back from the display.

"Let me guess, this displays my colorful personality?"

My attempts to lighten the mood fell flat as both of them gave me blank stares. Dr. Subramani expanded the hologram of my brain and stepped forward taking his glasses off to clean them.

"Nolan, the lines and color variations represent your magic type and your affinity with it. You shouldn't have more than one, two at the most. They should also be tightly connected to the parietal lobe and branch from there. This, as you see, is for lack of a better word—a mess. I am not able to completely determine the number or kind of magic types that exist in your brain. Elemental and non-elemental. Fire, air, force, illusion, spatial, the list goes on. I've been studying this for quite a while now and the only conclusion I can come up with was that this was done deliberately and intentionally. However, the most fascinating thing is how you're not dead or in a coma. These types of magic shouldn't be able to exist together in one person—not without serious repercussions. Nolan, you are an anomaly," Dr. Subramani finished.

"The fact that I'm okay is a good sign, right?"

"You're a danger to everyone around you," Celeste interjected.

"What Celestia is trying to say is yes and and no," Subramani crossed to a desk on the sidewall which clearly acted as the coffee area of this particular lab. Celeste and I followed.

Dr. Subramani picked up an old, battered toaster from the table. "Imagine this toaster is your brain. A simple device with a simple function: toasting bread. He placed a slice of bread in the toaster and depressed the button. The bread disappeared into the toaster in one fluid movement. Now, let's say we start adding other functions to it. We put in a microwave function, a blender function, and maybe even an espresso machine. All these appliances crammed into one device."

He pointed to the holographic brain. "Your brain is like this toaster. It wasn't designed to handle so many different types of magic. Each type of magic is like a different function or appliance. They have their own power requirements, their own mechanisms. Trying to run them all at once is like trying to toast bread, blend a smoothie, and make an espresso all at the same time with one device. It's not designed for that."

"But I've managed so far," I said, trying to wrap my head around the analogy.

"Barely," Subramani replied. "The issue is control. You might be able to get one or two functions to work, but not without risking overload. Each time you use a different type of magic, you're pushing your brain to its limits. The fact that you're still functional is remarkable, but it's also unpredictable. Any moment, any use of magic, could be the one that causes everything to short-circuit."

Celeste nodded. "Think about it, Nolan. You've been using different types of magic without understanding the full scope of what's inside you. It's dangerous because there's no way to control all the functions and abilities you now have."

Subramani continued, "Imagine if you were in a high-stress situation, trying to access multiple types of magic simultaneously. The mental strain alone could cause catastrophic failure, not just to your brain but potentially to those around you. You're walking a tightrope without a safety net."

The gravity of their words sank in. I realized the extent of the danger I posed, not just to myself but to everyone around me. It was a sobering thought.

As if to punctuate his point, the toast popped up from the toaster a blackened, charred mess, wisps of smoke rising from the top of the device. My stomach growled involuntarily and I began eyeballing the box of donuts that sat open taunting me. Dr. Subramani must have noticed the donut lust in my eyes. He reached out and slid the box towards me.

"Bless you!" I exclaimed as I tore into the half stale but still delicious donuts.

"You're not taking this serious at all, are you?" Celeste said.

I tore myself away from stuffing my face to see Celeste staring at me with a mixture of anger and concern in her eyes.

"The fact that this magic experiment you've been put through hasn't killed you is a miracle. Now you're eating donuts!" Celeste exclaimed.

I put down the half eaten cruller in my hand and dusted crumbs from my fingers.

"Look, I know this is serious and I know I have a lot to be thankful for. I just learned my brain has been tampered with and I should probably be comatose. But just an hour ago I thought I might never see you again and you being here with me through this just makes me feel...like things are going to be okay," I replied and wiped my mouth with my sleeve.

We stared at each other for a long time and I could see Celeste begin to soften. Pen bit into a loud chip, the crunch breaking the silence and making both Celeste and I jump. "Don't stop on my account," he said, grinning widely. "This is the perfect magical soap opera. I'm definitely adding this to my next Motor City Magic video."

"Pen," Celeste began, her voice warning.

"What? People need to know about the epic love story blossoming amidst magical chaos," he said, winking at me. "Besides, you two are giving me all the best material."

I chuckled, despite myself. "You're a fool, you know that?"

"Part of my charm," Pen replied, popping another chip into his mouth with a dramatic flair.

Celeste rolled her eyes but couldn't hide the small smile tugging at her lips. "Pen, you play too much. Nolan's situation is serious."

"I know, I know," Pen said, holding up his hands in mock surrender. "But a little humor never hurt anyone. Besides, you both needed the laugh."

I shook my head, still smiling. Dr. Subramani cleared his throat, drawing our attention back to him. "As entertaining as this is, we have more pressing matters to discuss. Tempris and his plans are far from over."

Subramani waved a hand, changing the holographic display behind us. Hovering above the projector was a face I'd grown to know all too well. Tempris was shimmering in the middle of the room with his name and statistics beside him. I felt my body move closer to the bastard floating just feet from where I stood. I began reading:

'Alan Tempris, Age: Unknown. Magic Type: Unknown. Place of Origin: Unknown. Last Known Location: North America. Affiliations: The Subversive. Classification: Red.'

There was an area with known associates. Instinctively, I reached out and began swiping through them in the air. This must have been a very intuitive holographic projection because the dossier of known associates rotated to show pictures of different people. I stopped abruptly when I saw someone I knew. Me. It was a picture of Tempris and me at Eastern Market right before Thanksgiving.

"What is this?" I said to no one in particular.

I suddenly became very aware of a fear that started bubbling up inside of me. Tempris had been messing with my mind. Where, when, and for how long? I looked down and noticed Celeste had moved beside me.

"Nolan, I'd like to reintroduce you to Alan Tempris. For lack of a better explanation, he's a magic terrorist. He is wanted for crimes against the human and magical world. As you can see, we have not been able to gather much information on him. However, your encounter with Tempris has given us more than we could have imagined. While we can't necessarily pinpoint his magic type, I can surmise that he definitely used a type of mind magic on you. Celeste as well, but another variation. While he has definitely rewritten and augmented a lot of your parietal lobe, that wouldn't explain why Celeste was unable to piece together the things she'd forgotten. For that reason, I believe he also uses some sort of illusory magic, mind control, and telepathy," Dr. Subramani said.

"Telepathy?" I asked, feeling a chill run down my spine.

"Not in the traditional sense," Subramani continued. "He can't necessarily read your mind, but he can read your emotions, your intentions, and your magical state of being. It's like he has a sixth sense that allows him to understand what you're feeling and thinking based on your magical aura. This makes him incredibly dangerous because he can anticipate your actions, manipulate your perceptions, and alter your memories without you even realizing it."

I looked at the holographic display of Tempris, feeling a mix of anger and fear. "So he's been inside my head, twisting my thoughts and memories to suit his needs?"

"Yes," Subramani confirmed. "And not just yours. He's done the same to Celeste and who knows how many others. His ability to blend different types of magic—mind magic, illusory magic, and telepathy—makes him a formidable adversary. He's been playing a long game, manipulating events from the shadows."

Celeste stood beside me, her presence a comfort even though we couldn't touch. I could see the worry in her eyes and knew she felt the same.

Dr. Subramani adjusted his glasses, his expression becoming more intense. "Celeste's concerns are not to be taken lightly. I'm sure Tempris expected you to either die or be trapped in that cavern. However, you survived, and in doing so, you essentially became both strong and uneducated. He taught you very little about the theory of magic and almost nothing about the necessary safeguards. Imagine a child playing with fire—now magnify that tenfold. You are more like a child playing with a nuclear warhead. The risk to the rest of the world is just as great, if not greater, than the risk to yourself."

Subramani paused, letting the weight of his words sink in. "Your magical abilities are unprecedented, chaotic, and incredibly potent. Without proper knowledge and control, you could cause catastrophic damage. Tempris has turned you into a ticking time bomb."

My heart pounded in my chest as I processed his words. The comparison to a nuclear warhead made my blood run cold. "So what does this all mean? And what am I supposed to do now?"

Subramani took a deep breath, looking around the lab. "It means we need to act quickly and decisively. First, we need to understand the full extent of your abilities. This requires rigorous training and study, under controlled conditions, to ensure you learn how to wield your magic safely."

Celeste nodded, her eyes filled with determination. "We have resources here in the magical community that can help you, Nolan. But it's going to be a long, hard road. You'll need to commit fully to learning and controlling your powers."

Pen, still crunching on chips, chimed in. "Sounds like a magical boot camp. Intense, but necessary. And just think of the content! 'Nolan's Journey: From Magic Novice to Master'—it'll be epic."

I managed a weak smile at Pen's attempt to lighten the mood. "Yeah, epic. But I'm more worried about not blowing anything up."

"Again," Pen interjected, grinning. "Remember the People Mover?"

I winced at the memory. "Yeah, that was an accident."

Pen laughed, shaking his head. "You know, it's not every day you get to say you derailed public transportation with your mind. I think it's kind of impressive."

Celeste couldn't help but chuckle. "Only you, Nolan."

I groaned, but I couldn't help but join in the laughter. "Alright, alright. Point taken. No more blowing things up."

"Again," Pen echoed, giving me a thumbs up. "But seriously, we need to keep you in check. That magic of yours is no joke."

Dr. Subramani, who had been watching our exchange with a bemused expression, cleared his throat. "Indeed. Humor aside, we must be vigilant. The consequences of uncontrolled magic are severe. However, we cannot keep you here against your will."

"Like hell we can't," said a deep rumbling voice.

We all turned to see Celeste's father walking into the lab, flanked by Gravitas and Nash. The moment he stepped into the light of the laboratory, the contrast between him and the sterile surroundings was striking. He was tall and built like a linebacker, his presence commanding the space with an almost physical weight. His salt-and-pepper locs brushed his shoulders, and his eyes were a pale, steely grey that seemed to see straight through everything. His expressionless face met mine with a look that spoke volumes.

"You know, I don't really think we were properly introduced. Donut?" I said, my tone a mix of bemusement and challenge.

I reached past Dr. Subramani, holding up the nearly empty box of donuts with a sheepish grin. The look on his face was a mix of incredulity and mild disgust. He glanced at the box briefly before turning his attention back to Celeste.

"You mean to tell me this is the guy you're dating?" he said, his voice dripping with emphasis on "this guy."

Celeste moved to my side, her stance protective but assertive. "Hate to bring up fresh wounds, but you already know he's more than meets the eye," she replied, her tone smug yet affectionate.

"Can we not bring up how I put your dad through a wall? Trying to make a better impression this time," I whispered to her, my voice tinged with nervousness.

Celeste suppressed a laugh, and as she did, her hand brushed gently against mine. A jolt of electricity seemed to pass between us, making her stiffen slightly and stagger. Her father's eyes snapped to the contact, and in an instant, he was on me. His massive hands gripped my shirt, lifting me off the ground with ease. I struggled, but his grip was as unyielding as iron.

"I definitely think you're a wee bit hangry," I said, trying to maintain a semblance of humor as my feet dangled in the air.

Commander Okoro stepped forward, his eyes narrowing with a mixture of anger and concern. He released my hand, but his grip had left my fingers tingling. "You know, West," he said, his voice low and filled with menace, "it might be better if you stayed here for a bit longer. We're not some secret black-bag organization that'll hold you against your will, but we've got some... unique circumstances to discuss."

I glanced at Celeste, hoping for a hint of what he meant. She gave me a reassuring smile that didn't quite reach her eyes. "He's right, Nolan. It would be safer if you stayed for now. Besides, we have a lot to catch you up on."

As I stood there, the gravity of the situation hit me. I was caught in a world of magic, danger, and intrigue—far removed from the simplicity of running a café. My mind raced through the chaos of the past hours, grappling with the reality that I was no longer a regular coffee shop owner but a player in a world with far-reaching consequences.

In the calm before my response, I found myself reflecting deeply. My café, with its comforting aroma of roasted beans and the hum of everyday conversations, seemed a world away. I had been thrust into a whirlwind of magical mayhem, my life turned upside down by forces I barely understood. The weight of my new reality pressed down on me, making the idea of retreating to the safety of my familiar world even more tempting.

Despite the peril I faced, the thought of leaving Celeste behind tugged at my heart. I had just begun to understand the depth of our connection, and the thought of leaving her in this turmoil made me uneasy. Yet, I also knew I couldn't just walk away from the magnitude of what was happening. Celeste looked at me with a mixture of concern and something else. Nash stood stone faced beside Gravitas who was half smiling. Commander Okoro had his arms crossed, waiting for me to say something.

"Yeah, about that," I said, trying to keep my tone casual despite the turmoil inside. "I kind of need to get back to my café. Got some things to process, and maybe a few less life-threatening situations to handle."

Commander Okoro nodded thoughtfully, his expression softening slightly. "I understand, Nolan. But if you choose to leave, you need to know what you're walking away from. Remember, this is not just about you anymore. Your actions affect everyone around you." He gestured, and a shimmering portal opened up, revealing the familiar sight of my cafe. The smell of coffee and pastries wafted through, making my stomach rumble.

I stood there, my mind a whirlwind of thoughts and emotions. The portal beckoned, promising a return to normalcy but also signaling a retreat from the fight that had suddenly become so personal. I looked at Celeste, who had moved to my side again. "You wanna come with me?" I asked, half hoping she'd say yes.

She shook her head, her eyes sparkling with mischief. "I'm going to stay here a little longer. Make sure my dad doesn't throw any more surprises your way."

I nodded, a little disappointed but understanding. "Alright, I'll see you soon then."

As I stepped through the portal, I turned to give Celeste one last look. Her smile was warm, and for a moment, everything felt right. But then, all hell broke loose.

Alarms started blaring, loud and insistent. Lights flashed red, and the atmosphere changed from calm to chaotic in an instant. Dr. Subramani rushed into the room, his face pale. "We've got a problem! The integrity of the veil has been challenged at several locations all at once. There's no immediate threat, but we need to reinforce it until we can pinpoint what's happening."

Commander Okoro turned to him, his expression tense. "What's causing it?"

Subramani's eyes widened with realization. "It's Tempris. Whatever he took from that cavern must be really powerful because he's tearing the veil in a major way. We won't be able to open any more portals any time soon." They all looked at me standing alone on the other side of the portal which began to fray at the edges.

I turned back to Celeste, my heart pounding. "Celeste, wait!" I shouted, but the portal started to shimmer and destabilize.

"Nolan, you have to come back through!" Celeste urged, her voice full of concern.

Just as I took a step towards the portal, it snapped shut abruptly, cutting off my words and leaving me standing in my cafe. The familiar, comforting smell of freshly brewed coffee filled the air. It was like an anchor to reality amidst the chaos I had just left behind. I walked over to the counter, every step feeling heavier with the weight of what had just happened.

First things first: coffee. It always grounded me, helped me think clearly. I grabbed my favorite mug from the shelf—a simple, sturdy thing with a small chip on the rim. I filled the kettle with water and set it on the stove to boil, listening to the rhythmic ticking as I reached for my grinder.

As I scooped beans from the jar, their rich, earthy aroma enveloped me. These were my favorite beans, a dark roast from a small farm in Guatemala. I poured them into the grinder and began to crank, feeling the satisfying resistance as the beans were crushed into a fine, fragrant powder. Each turn of the handle seemed to pull me further from the bizarre and the inexplicable, and closer to the familiar and the routine.

The kettle began to whistle, and I removed it from the heat, pouring the steaming water in slow, deliberate circles over the grounds in my pour-over dripper. The water darkened as it seeped through the coffee, releasing a plume of aromatic steam that filled the air. I watched as the liquid streamed down, forming a dark pool of rich, inviting coffee in my mug.

As I waited for the last drops to filter through, my mind started to wander back to the events that led me here. The strange, dangerous world I had just left, the unexpected revelation about Celeste's father, the chaos that erupted with the alarms... and Tempris. The name sent a shiver down my spine. Whoever—or whatever—he was, he had something incredibly powerful, something that was tearing apart the very fabric of reality.

The final drops of coffee dripped into my mug. I removed the dripper and took a deep breath, savoring the smell before taking a long, slow sip. The warmth spread through me, calming my nerves just enough to think clearly.

If the portals were closed, then getting back to Celeste and the others wasn't an option, at least for now. Which meant I was on my own. I took another sip, feeling the weight of that realization settle in. Somehow, it seemed like it was up to me to figure out what to do next, to find a way to stop Tempris.

I leaned against the counter, my fingers tracing the rim of my mug as I thought about what I knew. Tempris had something powerful from that cavern, something capable of challenging the veil. And if the portals were closed, he might be planning to use that power on this side, in my world.

I took another sip of coffee, feeling the caffeine start to sharpen my thoughts. Maybe I couldn't go back to Celeste and the others, but I could start looking for answers here. There had to be clues, something that would help me understand what Tempris was after and how to stop him.

Finishing my coffee, I set the mug down with a sense of resolve. This wasn't just about getting back to Celeste—it was about protecting both our worlds from whatever Tempris was planning. What did I know? I knew Tempris was tampering with the fabric of the veil. I remember him telling me that the veil is at its most physical state along the ley lines that cover the earth. I knew one passed beneath Eastern Market and split off under my cafe. Maybe if I look at a map I can kind of follow it along.

I pulled out my phone, which was cracked and close to dying, and opened a map. The screen flickered a bit, but it was functional enough. "Come on, you can do this," I muttered, swiping and pinching to zoom in on the map of Detroit. I paced back and forth, trying to figure out which way the lines would go.

As I passed by the window, something caught my eye—violet light rolling and pulsing in the sky near downtown. It looked like a cosmic disco ball on steroids. "Well, that's not ominous at all," I muttered, squinting at the glowing spectacle.

Which direction was that? I traced a loose line with my finger from my cafe, through the market, and towards the direction of the light. It was directly over Comerica Park. "Great, I hope Tempris isn't a Tigers fan," I thought to myself.

I needed to get over there and fast. "It's not baseball season but let's play ball," I said aloud to no one in particular. I grabbed a winter coat from the coat rack behind the counter. It was an old, oversized coat that smelled faintly of espresso and had seen better days. But it was warm and had deep pockets—perfect for a night of supernatural sleuthing.

As I headed out the door, I gave my cafe one last look. "Keep the place warm for me," I said, patting the doorframe. I stepped outside, pulling the coat tight around me as the chilly night air hit. The streets were eerily quiet, and the violet light in the sky seemed to pulse with a life of its own.

I hurried down the sidewalk, my breath coming out in puffs of steam. As I approached Eastern Market, I couldn't help but think of the history of the place. Once a bustling hub of commerce, it now had an almost mystical air to it—like the ghosts of old traders and farmers still lingered in the shadows, whispering secrets about the veil and the ley lines beneath.

Navigating the market at night was a bit like playing a game of hide-and-seek with ghosts. "Hey, Old Man Jenkins," I joked, waving at a particularly spooky-looking vegetable stand. "Still selling those haunted carrots?"

I reached the edge of the market and paused, pulling out my phone again to check the map. The violet light was still glowing ominously in the distance, and I traced the ley line in my mind, imagining it running beneath my feet and leading straight to Comerica Park.

As I continued my trek, I couldn't help but wonder what Tempris had planned. Was he trying to harness the power of the ley lines for himself? Was he planning to open some kind of portal? Or maybe he just really, really hated baseball. Whatever it was, I had to stop him.

Finally, I reached the outskirts of Comerica Park. The violet light was now directly overhead, casting an eerie glow on the stadium. I took a deep breath and steeled myself. "Alright, Tempris," I said, adjusting my coat and marching forward. "Let's see what kind of game you're playing."

As I stepped into the shadow of the stadium, I couldn't help but mutter, "And here I was hoping for a quiet night with a cup of coffee." But there was no turning back now. It was time to play ball.

# Chapter 32

*Double header*

The ball park was dark. The moonless evening giving the hash shadows even more purchase as dusk turned to night. It wasn't hard snapping a lock with magic and finding my way into the stadium. Security was non existent given the off season and the evening's previous snowstorm left the streets of downtown Detroit pretty empty. I made my way to the field passing covered kiosks and storefronts filled with the jerseys of last years players. I came across an overturned hotdog cart and my stomach rumbled reminding me I hadn't eaten since I the donuts I stole from Dr. Subramani's office. If I made it through this alive, I was going to have a feast—a feast of something that wasn't going to set my mouth ablaze. I felt the tick of magic, and increased my pace.

I took the stairs down to the baseball diamond two at a time and hopped the barrier when I arrived at the field. I stood and took in my surroundings before I carried on. Tempris was nowhere in sight but I could feel his magic getting stronger. The map of magical ley lines said the point Tempris would be looking for was near center field. I starting making my way forward but the snow made traversing the terrain much more difficult. More than once, I slipped and almost face planted in the thick snow.

"Screw this," I said, looking at my breath visible in the air.

I drew my fists back towards my ribs, called on my magic then threw my palms forward. A wave of flames cascaded towards the pitchers mound instantly melting every bit of snow in its path and then some. I began to whoop in triumph until the flames came to a crashing halt ten feet from the mound. The fire spread into an arc before disappearing. At the same time, a familiar shield covered in runes glimmered into view and in its center stood Tempris. His back was to me but I could see that his palms hovered over a pale purple orb of light. Was I too late? He'd already started the ritual. It was now or never. My legs shook as everything I leaned about Tempris came flooding back. He was a murderer, he'd killed countless people in incredibly ruthless ways. He violated my mind for who knows how long, and he did the same to Celeste. It was the latter thought that kicked me into gear. I'd die to protect Celeste and the maniac just feet in front of me put her in the hospital. Fury rose inside of me unlike anything I had ever experienced before. I reached for my magic.

"Someone is angry! I guess I can't blame you. I'd be livid too if I failed as incredibly as you. There is one consolation, Nolan. You haven't failed me,"

"I'm gonna wipe that smug look off your face and stop you from... whatever you're doing,"

"Isn't it so delicious? I taught you so much and yet you're still like a child. You couldn't begin to comprehend what I'm going to accomplish. It's a bit sad really. If only my first choice could have held her mind together. She may have been able to appreciate my machinations,"

All I could see was red as I exploded. Jets of fire sprayed from my outstretched arms increasing in intensity. The flames turned blue as they grew hotter and hotter. Steam rose all around us, the snow evaporating in seconds. Through the blaze I could see a crack begin to form in Tempris' shield. My mind went to something Pen said. "Magic is only limited by the practitioner's imagination." I pulled in my focus drew my hands closer together. The flames began to form into one solid pillar of super hot magical energy. I shouted till my voice cracked and my throat became raw, pouring every once of fire magic into the assault. The shield shattered like glass and I fell to my knees, the magic dissipating and my mind beginning to tingle. This was no time to stop thinking but I knew I couldn't burn out yet. Looking straight ahead, I took a few seconds to clear my mind. Seconds were all I had because when the smoke and steam began to clear, Tempris was gone, but the purple orb of magic remained, more brilliant than ever.

I approached cautiously, feeling its energy thrumming in the air making the hair on my arms stand straight up. There was no heat or pressure radiating off it, but I could tell it was doing *something*— shifting the atmosphere, bending reality in a way I couldn't understand. I reached out to touch it, curious and reckless as ever.

Before my fingers could make contact, Tempris's voice cut through the silence like a blade, low and menacing.

"You've now become more than a minor annoyance. I guess it was my fault. I seem to have created a monster instead of just releasing one. It's time to put you down for good," his hands came up in a flash and all around him dirt flew into the air in big chunks.

Chunks of dirt and rock erupted into the air, raining down like shrapnel. I coughed, trying to clear my vision, wiping at my eyes as dust clung to my lashes. Through the debris, I saw movement— something clawing its way out of the earth.

Rock-like creatures, their craggy bodies glowing with a sickly orange hue, dragged themselves free from the ground. Their broad shoulders and squat frames made them look like something straight out of a myth—or maybe a nightmare. Their eyes burned with the same orange intensity, locking onto me with eerie precision.

Golems.

The nerd in me wanted to whip out my phone, snap a picture, and send it to my old D&D group with a caption like, *"Guess who rolled a natural 20 on summoning!"* But the survivalist in me knew better. This was no game.

I counted five of them, and more were still clawing their way out from beneath the pitcher's mound.

My heart pounded, each beat echoing like a drum in my chest. I tried to keep my breathing steady, but fear gripped me like a vice. I may have seen some strange things recently, but I wasn't sure I'd ever get used to this.

Tempris stood at the center of it all, arms crossed, his expression smug as his rocky bodyguards lumbered around him. He looked like a bored parent watching a kid struggle with a math problem— completely unfazed by the chaos he'd unleashed.

And it was *his* stupid face that finally made me act.

"Let's see how you like this!" I shouted, hurling a fireball at the nearest golem. It was a good one—bright, hot, and crackling with raw energy.

It splashed harmlessly across the golem's rocky chest.

"Fantastic," I muttered. "Fire-resistant golems. Because of course they are."

The creature lumbered toward me, its glowing orange eyes fixed on mine like it had all the time in the world. Which, apparently, it did. At least they weren't fast.

I darted to the side and threw a kinetic blast at the next closest one. It hit square in the chest, and for a moment, I thought I'd done something. But no—nothing. It didn't even stumble.

"Great. They're not just fireproof; they're Detroit tough."

Before I could rethink my strategy, something slammed into me from behind. Pain exploded in my shoulder as I was launched forward, sprawling onto the dirt. Grit scraped my cheek as I skidded to a stop. Groaning, I rolled over just in time to see it—a severed stone arm flying toward me like a heat-seeking missile.

"Oh, come on!" I rolled to the side, narrowly avoiding decapitation by rogue limb.

I scrambled to my feet, heart hammering in my chest. The golems were missing chunks—arms, fists, pieces of their craggy bodies—but it didn't slow them down. If anything, it seemed to make them angrier. I was officially out of ideas.

Tempris's laugh echoed across the field. "Having fun yet, Nolan? I know I am!"

I gritted my teeth. Fear and frustration churned in my gut. Just a few weeks ago my biggest worry was the espresso machine going on the fritz. Now I was fighting for my life against real life monsters.

Nothing I'd tried had worked, and every passing second brought me closer to an untimely demise. But I wasn't about to let Tempris have the satisfaction of watching me give up.

I charged at the nearest golem, ducking under its massive swing. Its fist crashed into the ground, sending a shockwave through the dirt. I vaulted over its back and crouched low. Behind me, I heard a sickening crunch as another golem's fist collided with its companion.

"Yes!" I shouted, throwing my arms up in triumph. "Rock beats rock!"

The remains of the shattered golem showered me in debris, but I didn't care. I was alive, and that was enough for now.

The remaining four golems weren't so easily fooled. They adjusted their approach, closing in on me from all sides. My heart pounded as I glanced around, searching for anything I could use. My eyes landed on the jagged remains of the destroyed golem. Perfect.

"Nice try, Tempris," I called out, darting toward the debris. "But if you think these oversized paperweights are going to stop me, you're dumber than you look."

Tempris scoffed, his voice dripping with condescension. "Nolan, if you're going to die, at least try to be original. Insults like that just hurt my feelings."

The nearest golem swung at me, and I ducked, grabbing a shard of rock from the ground. With a roar, I drove it into the glowing crack in its chest. The light flickered and died, and the golem crumbled into dust.

"Three to go," I muttered, spinning to face the next one.

The second golem was on me in an instant, its stone fingers flying toward me like jagged missiles. I raised my arms to shield myself, the impacts sending jolts of pain through my body. Blood trickled down my temple, warm and sticky.

I staggered back, barely staying on my feet. My vision swam, but I forced myself to focus. I darted toward the golem on my left, ducking under its swinging arm. As I emerged on the other side, I grabbed its wrist and yanked with all my strength, using its momentum against it. It stumbled into the third golem, their heads colliding with a thunderous crack.

"Seriously, Tempris," I called out, panting. "Did you buy these things at a discount golem store? Two-for-one special?"

The last golem hesitated, its orange eyes flickering. Maybe it realized it was outmatched. Or maybe I was just hallucinating from blood loss. Either way, I wasn't going to give it a chance to recover.

I charged, feinting to the right before leaping into the air. With a burst of kinetic energy, I planted both feet on its chest and kicked off, flipping backward. The golem teetered, then crashed onto a jagged piece of debris. Its chest shattered, and it fell still.

I stood there, chest heaving, sweat dripping down my face. For the first time since the fight began, I allowed myself to feel victorious.

I turned to face Tempris, my chest heaving with exertion. The purple orb in the center of the field pulsed ominously, casting an eerie glow on the snow. Tempris stood there, a sinister smile spreading across his face.

"Impressive, Nolan. But it's time for the seventh inning stretch." Tempris looked past me with an almost mirthful look on his face. I looked down and noticed broken pieces of golem were rolling past me. I audibly gulped and turned around. Directly behind me chunks of all sizes rolled, flew, and gathered into what was becoming one massive golem. My bones shook with every click and clack of pieces snapping together. This golem was seven feet tall and as broad as three linebackers. Orange light spilled from even more cracks on it's hodgepodge surface. It collected every piece of the golems I defeated so there was nothing to attack it with. I didn't have much time to think because despite its size, this golem was much faster. It barreled towards me with a tackle. I narrowly missed its arms and didn't miss it's backswing. The back of its enormous hand crunched into my midsection sending my flying several feet away. I landed on my back, the wind knocked out of me. I could see darkness a the corners of my vision and felt the ground shake as it began moving closer to me. A shadow fell upon me as it towered over my body. Something inside of me felt broken and I struggled to lift my head. If I was going to die here, I would at least look death in the face. The giant golem raised both arms above its head preparing to finish me off. It was wreathed in purple light coming from behind it. That's right, I'd die here and Tempris would get away with whatever sinister plan he dragged me into. This was all my fault. I glared at Tempris who wasn't even paying me any attention anymore. I coughed and felt warm blood on my lips. At least I could get off one more shot at the bastard. I lifted one shaky hand not at the golem, but at Tempris who was still performing the ritual. I created a ball of fire and unleashed it right at him. The golem must have sensed what I was doing because it dove backwards and knocked the fireball off course. It crashed to the ground between Tempris and I.

Hmm, I saw Tempris' face change. That's right! The original golems surrounded Tempris, protecting him. It dawned on me that he must be vulnerable while he completes the spell. Without a second thought I summoned another fireball and blasted it towards Tempris. The golem rose up and spread its arms wide, protecting him. There was no clear shot at Tempris, but for the moment I was able to at least catch my breath. The more time that passed however, the closer Tempris got to completing his goal. On a whim I put both of my hands together and created an even larger fireball. It impacted the golem but this time I saw it stagger. Looking closer I saw that the area beneath the golems armpits was not completely covered by stone. Instead it was the same orange glow that came through the cracks covering its body. If I could pour enough magic into that thing maybe it will get through and destroy it. I breathed deep, thinking of all the training, all the attempts, and all the battles that lead to this moment. I poured magic into my palms, creating a ball of fire that grew bigger and bigger. My thoughts jumped back to when Tempris had me take my magic to its limits. I used that memory and the flames began to flicker and grow until the ball of flame I held was azure blue. "Hey Tempris! You wanted to make me powerful?! Well you got your wish!" I shouted, spit flying from my mouth with rage and excitement. I focused my will and sent the globe of fire flying. It collided with the golem. This time the golem wrapped its arms around it trying to contain the power. Its feet dug grooves in the ground as it was forced backwards closer to Tempris. For the first time, I could see worry on Tempris' face. The cracks in the golems stone skin began to fissure and crack, the orange turning blue as the fire magic made its way inside the creature. With a rumble and a whistling hiss, the golem blew apart in a shower of rock and flames.

I stood there, panting, the adrenaline ebbing away. "Not bad for a beginner, huh?" I said, spitting blood onto the ground. Tempris said nothing, but the purple orb behind him pulsed ominously, casting a sinister light on his pale face.

Victory was mine, but at a steep cost. I had used too much magic. A wave of dizziness washed over me, and I felt the familiar, dreaded sensation of my brain falling asleep. Pins and needles prickled at the edges of my consciousness, and my limbs felt just ran the Free Press Marathon.

"Not now," I muttered, trying to shake off the encroaching numbness. But it was no use. The more I tried to fight it, the worse it got. My vision blurred, and I sank to my knees, unable to move.

"Feeling a bit tired, Nolan?" Tempris's voice cut through the haze. "That's what happens when you overextend yourself. You should have learned your limits."

I lay there unable to move. Pins and needles stabbed into my mind repeatedly. It was more severe than the first time I'd experienced it. Each prick felt like it was barbed, my brain being picked apart hundreds of times a second. The crunching sound of gravel and snow filled my mind. Tempris was walking towards me. I tried raising my head off the cold dirt but the movement made me want to vomit. I could feel myself losing consciousness and could barely track Tempris walking around me in a circle, stalking me like wounded prey. The gleam of a revolver caught my attention as Tempris pulled it from his pocket. Think. Think! No! Don't think! I had to clear my mind. Clear my mind of the pain. Clear my mind of the thought of impending death. Clear my mind of Celeste, of the craziness of the past few months. Clear my mind of—wait. The thing Celeste sealed inside of me. What did her father say? It wasn't magic. Wasn't magic! If it wasn't magic, did that mean the same rules didn't apply? Could I reach for it, draw it forth, and use it in one last desperate attempt? Only one way to find out.

"Hey! Hey! Blue, misty, entity thing! Little help! I know you didn't ask for me to be some kind of vessel for you, and I'm sure you'd love to go back in your nice quiet wooden chest, but I can't make any of that happen if I'm killed and buried in a baseball field," I muttered, hoping against hope for a response.

I could see Tempris filling his revolver bullet by bullet while nothing happened on my end. Not even a "Sorry, I can't come to the consciousness right now but please leave a message after getting your head blown off." Tempris stood above me now, drawing the hammer back on the gun, the click somehow echoing in the vastness of Comerica Park. His grip tightened and his finger slid over the trigger. Then it happened.

Tempris pulled the trigger but recoiled as blue light burst forth from every part of my body. I heard the shot ring out and felt dirt spray my cheek. The bullet impacted an inch from my face. Energy coursed through my body, luminous and strong. My head began to clear ever so slightly, giving me the ability to at least rise to my feet. I stood on shaky legs, one arm holding up the other, palm facing Tempris.

"Surprise!" I managed to say with a strained voice.

All at once, the energy that had been surrounding me flowed into my arm and out of my hand directly at Tempris. I saw him throw up some kind of shield at the last moment before the entire baseball field was flooded with blinding light. There was no heat. There was no sensation. Even with my eyes pressed firmly shut, the light was finding its way in. I risked a glance so that I would see what was happening but all I could see was white and just like that it was gone.

Tempris was nowhere in sight. Relief and sadness washed over me simultaneously. I hated that it had come to this, that I had to destroy someone who had once been so close to me. But there was no time to dwell on that. A familiar laugh echoed through the stadium, sinister and mocking. I turned to see Tempris standing next to the now intensely glowing purple energy.

"Did you really think it would be that easy?" Tempris sneered, his voice dripping with contempt.

I glanced back at the spot where I thought I had blasted Tempris, only to see a large crater at home plate. It all clicked. Tempris could create illusions, mess with minds and memories. He had played me again. I was entirely spent, no magic left, no otherworldly entity to draw from, nothing. I exhaled and my legs gave out. I fell on my side, staring toward Tempris who was filling the air with laughter.

"You've fought valiantly, mate, but all of this...was always meant to tear down the veil once and for all," Tempris said, his voice full of triumph. "The magic realm and the mundane realm will become one."

I inched forward, dragging my body across the cold, hard ground. I thought about the city I loved so much, the life and memories I built here. Mornings at the Eastern Market, afternoons at the Detroit Institute of Arts, and cozy evenings at home with Celeste would all be gone. "You can't...you can't do this, Tempris. Think about the people. The worlds colliding...it'll kill so many."

"You can't make a new world order without a brand new world," Tempris replied coldly. "Sacrifices must be made."

Purple cracks began to form in the air around us, spreading like a spider's web. The fractures grew, pulsing with an ominous energy. I felt an overwhelming sense of failure. This couldn't be the end.

"Tempris, we were...we were friends once. You trained me. You saved me more than once. We were close," I pleaded, desperation in my voice. "You don't have to do this."

Tempris paused, a flicker of something—regret?—crossing his face. "We were close, Nolan. But everything I did was for this moment. Not just for me. For everyone's gain."

"But why? Why destroy everything?" I asked, trying to buy time, to find some way to stop him.

"Because the current world is flawed. It's broken. A new world, with me at the helm, will be stronger, better. The old world must be torn down for the new to rise."

"I don't know much about magic society or the veil, but I know this will bring nothing but death and destruction," I said, inching closer. "Please, Tempris. Stop this."

"You still don't get it," Tempris said, shaking his head. "This is beyond you, beyond any single person. This is about destiny."

The purple cracks were now spreading faster, the air around us shimmering with unstable energy. I could barely move, my strength almost completely gone. Tempris strode towards me and raised his gun again, aiming directly at me. "You've served your purpose, my friend. But now, you're too dangerous to be left alive," he said coldly.

The veil continued to shatter like stained glass around us, cracking and giving off a rainbow of different colors. It was as beautiful as it was saddening. I turned and looked at the barrel of Tempris' gun and shut my eyes resigned to my fate. The gunshot sounded much farther away that I figured it would.

"I wasn't expecting that," Tempris muttered, surprise evident in his voice. I opened my eyes just in time to see him clutching his chest, blood streaming between his fingers.

In the stillness, we both noticed the glint of a rifle scope in right field. Another shot broke through the silence, striking Tempris in the head. I had a horrible, sickening sight of Tempris' ruined face before he fell backward, crashing through the glass-like surface of the veil, disappearing from sight. The veil seemed to mend itself, leaving only faint traces of pale purple light from where it had shattered seconds before.

I laid there, trying to regain my strength and process what I had witnessed. The veil had begun to shatter, threatening to merge the magic realm with the mundane one. Tempris had pushed everything to the brink of chaos, and in those final moments, an unknown sniper had saved my life. As I thought about the strange turn of events, I realized that my journey with Tempris had led to this climactic confrontation. The bond we once shared had been twisted into something dark and dangerous, but now it was over.

Moments later, I heard footsteps approaching. Celeste appeared, cradling a Ruger Hawkeye in her arms. "Nolan, are you okay?" she asked, her voice a mix of concern and relief.

"I've been better," I replied, attempting a weak smile. "Nice shooting, by the way. You've got a hidden talent, it seems."

"Desperate times call for desperate measures," Celeste said, grinning back. "Besides, I couldn't let you have all the fun."

We shared a brief, humorous moment before Celeste looked over the damage Tempris had caused. "We might have stopped the ritual, but the damage is done," she said, her tone turning serious.

"You're a sealer, Celeste. Can't you seal it?" I asked, half-jokingly.

"That's not how my magic works, Nolan," she replied, shaking her head. "But we can't just leave it like this."

Summoning the last of my strength, I got to my feet. "Maybe I can try something," I said, determination surging through me. I moved to the center of the fracturing veil, the ground beneath my feet trembling as if the earth itself was in agony. I could feel the power of the entity inside me, a pulsing, thrumming presence just waiting to be unleashed. I took a deep breath and began to draw it forth, feeling its raw energy coursing through my veins.

My eyes glowed blue as I focused all my energy on the veil. The entity's power surged within me, a torrent of untamed force that I struggled to control. My skin prickled with electric intensity, and every hair on my body stood on end. I extended my arms towards the shattered veil, fingers splayed wide, and let the energy flow out of me.

Light erupted from my body, a brilliant blue radiance that spread outwards and filled in the cracks in the veil. The colors danced and shimmered, blending together in a mesmerizing display of luminescence. Each fracture in the veil drank in the light, the jagged edges smoothing and healing as the energy wove itself into the fabric of reality.

The veil resisted at first, its shattered fragments reluctant to mend. I pushed harder, drawing even deeper from the well of power within me. The light intensified, bathing the entire field in a surreal glow. The colors swirled and twisted, forming intricate patterns that pulsed with an otherworldly rhythm.

Slowly, the visible fractures began to vanish, the veil knitting itself back together with threads of pure light. The chaos that had threatened to tear apart our worlds was being driven back, replaced by a faint, serene glow where the destruction had been moments before. The air hummed with residual energy, the aftermath of the entity's power leaving an almost tangible stillness in its wake.

I dropped to one knee, the effort leaving me exhausted. My vision blurred, and for the umpteenth time in as many minutes I was incredibly dizzy. I took a deep breath, trying to steady myself, as the last remnants of the light faded away. The veil was whole again, its surface smooth and unbroken, a testament to the power that had saved it.

Celeste rushed to my side, her eyes wide with amazement. "Nolan, you did it," she said, her voice filled with a mix of awe and relief.

I managed a weak smile, feeling a sense of triumph despite my exhaustion. "Detroit, what!" I blurted out with as much enthusiasm as I could muster. Celeste shook her bear and laughed.

As I knelt there, exhausted, I couldn't help but think deeply about the events that had just unfolded. Tempris' death felt surreal, a sudden end to a complex and twisted chapter of my life. How had I known what kind of gun Celeste was using? I had recognized the Ruger Hawkeye in her hands with an instinctive certainty, as if some part of me had been aware of it all along. And how had I known that I could affect the veil? The knowledge had come to me in a moment of desperation, a deep, intuitive understanding that seemed to transcend my conscious thoughts. It was as if everything I had learned and experienced had culminated in this one moment, each step leading me inexorably to this point. What all had Tempris done to my brain? The entity inside me, the power I had drawn upon—it was more than just magic. It was a connection to something greater, something that had guided me through the chaos and uncertainty. The realization left me both awed and unsettled, as if I had merely glimpsed the edge of a vast and mysterious truth.

Suddenly, I became aware of Celeste talking to me, shaking me from my thoughts. "Where were you just now?" she asked, her voice gentle but curious.

"Nowhere, but I'm here with you now," I replied, offering a tired but sincere smile.

"We were able to open a small portal and I wasn't going to let you be here alone. Sorry I'm late," she said, a hint of relief in her voice. "I've worked with you for a while now. I'm used to you being late," I said with a smirk. Celeste put one small foot on me and nudged me as I knelt. I fell over, completely off balance and we both shared a deep laugh before locking eyes.

We shared a look of longing, of affection, of lies and truths ripped open. It was a moment filled with unspoken words, each of us understanding the weight of everything that had happened and the bond that had grown between us. Before either of us had a chance to speak, a shimmering blue light began to flicker in the air around us. Then, as if reality itself was tearing open, portals appeared one by one, swirling in a kaleidoscope of colors. They looked like ripples in a pond, but instead of water, it was space itself bending and distorting to reveal a glimpse of somewhere else. The air hummed with energy, and the portals cast an eerie glow on the snow-covered field, adding another layer of surrealness to an already unbelievable night. The snow, once pure, was now stained with the evidence of battle—dark streaks of blood, scorched patches of turf, and jagged cracks in the ground where Tempris had torn the veil between realms.

Commander Okoro stepped through first, his imposing figure framed by the swirling vortex behind him. He was flanked by Nash and Gravitas, both of whom looked on with expressions that mixed disbelief with determination. The team moved with precision, their military-like training evident as they fanned out to secure the area.

"Good work, Nolan. Celeste," Commander Okoro said, nodding to both of us. His voice, usually commanding, carried a slight edge of relief. "We need to secure the area and ensure there are no lingering threats."

I let out a breath I didn't realize I'd been holding. "Nice of you to join the party, Commander," I said, managing a wry smile despite my exhaustion. Every muscle in my body screamed with fatigue, and yet, I couldn't stop my mind from racing.

"We were monitoring the situation closely," Okoro replied, his tone serious. "We were just now able to break through the wards Tempris set up."

As his team spread out, the electric tension in the air began to settle, but I couldn't shake the feeling that something still lingered—something darker and unfinished. I turned and surveyed the field around me. Comerica Park, once a symbol of Detroit's sports pride, now looked like a war zone. The snow lay in uneven patches, where it wasn't melted or trampled, blood and soot had painted it. Ribbons of smoke still curled from spots where fire magic had scarred the ground, leaving blackened craters where the pristine grass used to be. It felt like I was standing in a nightmare, and yet it was all real.

In the center of the field, where Tempris had fallen, the ground was marked by the sickening sight of blood—his blood—pooling and staining the snow in dark, spreading blotches. The memory of the final moments came rushing back in vivid, horrifying detail. The gunshot, Tempris clutching his chest, the way his body crumpled as the sniper's bullet—Celeste's bullet struck his head. I watched it all, helpless to stop it.

I turned away, bile rising in my throat. My breath came in shaky gasps as I tried to block out the memories, but they came in relentless waves. I saw flashes of the cavern floor, where my ankle and ribs were broken, blood spilling from my body. The fierce battle with the entity that now resided within me, its power still thrumming beneath my skin. And then there was Tempris, the man who had once been my mentor, destroyed by the violence he brought into my life. It was too much—too much blood, too much chaos, too many curveballs thrown my way in a world I had barely begun to understand.

And then there was Celeste. My eyes flicked over to her, and I felt a new kind of pain—a gnawing ache that went deeper than the physical wounds. She had been my guardian angel in more ways than I could count, but she held as many mysteries as I did. There was something we were not saying to each other, something hanging between us like a cloud of secrets. I wanted to reach out to her, to find comfort in her presence, but I didn't know if I could anymore.

I could feel her watching me, trying to read the turmoil in my face. Her eyes were soft, full of unspoken concern, but I couldn't bring myself to meet her gaze fully.

"I just want to go home," I said in a flat, emotionless tone, trying to mask the whirlwind inside me.

Celeste's brow furrowed. She hadn't expected that. "I have to stay here, at least for a little while," she replied softly.

We looked at each other for a long time, the weight of everything we'd been through pressing down on us. I started to reach out to her, my hand hovering in the air, but I stopped myself. I remembered—I *couldn't touch her anymore.* Not after everything. Not after what we'd become—what I'd become. My hand dropped back to my side, heavy with the realization of all that was lost between us.

"I'll see you later, Celeste," I said, forcing a half-hearted smile. It was the best I could manage.

She nodded, her lips curving into a small, sad smile that didn't reach her eyes.

I gave her one last glance before turning away. The air felt colder as I walked past the groups of arriving mages, their voices a distant murmur in the background. Every step I took seemed to echo in the emptiness around me, each one pulling me farther away from the life I'd known, from Celeste, from the person I used to be.

As I stepped into the cold Detroit night, I felt a deep sense of dread settle into my bones. What was I becoming? What would tomorrow bring? I had no answers, just the relentless pull of a future that seemed darker than the one I had envisioned.

# Chapter 33

*A touching end.*

How do I say *not my problem* without saying *not my problem*? When someone escapes being killed or held captive, they don't just waltz right back into danger. I own a coffee shop. I love making coffee. I love my life. Sure, I wanted adventure. I wanted to peek behind the curtain and learn about magic—and I did. And that shit is *crazy*. Now, I've got to live the rest of my life with this weird thing inside me, and I'm leaving the rest of the magical nonsense to the professionals.

A week had passed since that day at Comerica Park. Somehow, my injuries healed faster than seemed possible—no lingering aches or stiffness. Physically, I was fine. But mentally, I couldn't shake the events. The news was calling the incident a "drone display gone wrong." I had to hand it to Commander Okoro's team. They knew how to control the narrative. There wasn't a single mention of magic or strange lights.

But the memories didn't fade as easily for me. They clung to me, sharp and jagged, piercing through my thoughts at the worst moments. The sight of Tempris, his chest splintered by bullets. The smell of burning ozone when I called down lightning. The cracks in reality splitting apart like an old cathedral window. And the moment —that moment—when I used the entity's power to mend the veil.

That memory haunted me the most. It was unlike anything I had ever experienced. It wasn't just magic; it was something more. It was like being plugged directly into the universe, every thread of existence laid bare in a dazzling web of connection. I felt time and space compress, wrapping me in their folds. In those moments, I could sense every person, every thought, every possibility—both mundane and magical—threaded together in perfect harmony. I could feel life pulsing through the cracks in the veil, desperate to return to its original shape.

It wasn't power I wielded; it was something ancient. Something infinite. And yet, when I touched it, it welcomed me. For a moment, I belonged—like I'd stumbled into the heart of the universe and found a piece of myself waiting there. It had been beautiful, terrifying, and utterly humbling.

And it scared the hell out of me.

Because now I had this thing inside me—this strange entity bound to my soul—and I had no idea what it meant. Or what it wanted. I kept replaying the battle in my head, especially the part where I recognized the rifle in Celeste's hands.

I don't know guns. I've never been interested in them, never even held one before. So how the hell did I know that rifle? The second I saw it, I knew the make, the model, and how it worked—like the knowledge had been stitched into my brain without my permission. And that was almost as unsettling as the power I'd wielded to mend the veil.

The cafe was quiet. Most people were off enjoying their long weekend, leaving me with just my thoughts and the occasional customer. And then, as if summoned by my longing, the door chimed.

And there she was: Celeste.

She walked in like a dream—cranberry-red peacoat, dark curls spilling down her shoulders, and that same effortless smile. She didn't slip behind the counter like she usually did. Instead, she lingered in front, studying the menu like a stranger.

"I'll take a Leftovers Latte," she said, her voice soft, playful.

I folded my arms, leaning against the espresso machine. "If you just needed caffeine, you could've gone to Starbucks," I said, my words sharper than I intended. "Where have you been, Celeste? Why haven't you returned my calls?"

Her smile faltered, but she didn't flinch. "Nolan... I'm sorry. It's just... it's been a lot to process." She sighed, brushing a strand of hair from her face. "If you haven't noticed, I kind of left the magic world behind. You dragged me back into it."

"To be fair," I countered, "it was the psychotic magician trying to tear apart reality who dragged us both into it. But I'll take my share of the blame too. I should've told you everything from the start."

I stepped around the counter, closing the distance between us.

Her gaze softened. "One thing you'll learn quickly about the magical world is that everything's connected—every thread, every thought, every action. It's not just spells and incantations. It's the entire universe, down to every magic atom." She stepped closer, and the air between us seemed to hum with unspoken emotions.

Her words stirred something deep inside me, bringing back the memory of that moment with the veil. The connectedness I'd felt...it was intoxicating, like glimpsing the architecture of the cosmos. And yet, it left me hollow. Because now I knew. I didn't want to live in that world—not full-time. I didn't want the complications or the danger.

"Celeste, I'm done with magic," I said softly. "I peeked behind the curtain, and all I found was that the Great and Powerful Oz is an asshole. I like this world. I like the life we could have here."

We stood in silence, the moment stretching between us like a bridge waiting to be crossed. The soft light inside the cafe wrapped around us, making it feel as though we were the only two people in the world.

"I'm not done," she whispered. "I thought I was. I tried to be. I built a life here in Detroit—a city full of more history and magic than most people will ever know. I made friends, built a home...I met you." Her gaze locked with mine. "But I'm being pulled back. There are things I left unfinished—things I can't ignore anymore. I have to walk in both worlds."

Both worlds. Her words felt like a punch to the gut. That world—the world she was choosing—was nothing but pain and danger. And I had no intention of returning to it.

"I'm not going back," I said firmly.

"I know," she whispered, her voice as soft as snowfall.

She stepped closer, and the space between us disappeared. Our hands brushed lightly, a spark igniting between us—not magic, but something just as powerful. We raised our hands, palms facing each other, and slowly pressed our fingertips together.

The sensation was electric—a rush of heat and longing that made my heart race. I closed my eyes, surrendering to the moment. Could I finally touch her? Could we finally be together?

Then she gasped, pulling away as if burned. Her face twisted in pain, tears welling in her eyes. I could see the effort it took for her to suppress whatever the entity inside me had stirred.

"I'm sorry," she whispered, her voice breaking.

Before I could say anything, she turned and walked briskly to the door. The bell chimed as she pushed it open, the sound echoing through the empty cafe.

I stood there, rooted in place, staring at the door as if willing her to come back. But she didn't.

With a heavy sigh, I turned to the counter and grabbed a scoop of medium-roast Arabica beans. The familiar motion was a small comfort, a reminder that some things in my life were still normal.

The door chimed again, and my heart leapt. For a split second, hope surged through me, foolish and electric. I whirled around, half-expecting—half-praying—to see Celeste standing there, her expression a mix of apology and resolve.

But it wasn't her.

It was Pen.

Mr. Motor City Magic strolled in like he owned the place, laptop in hand, his trademark smug grin plastered across his face. His hair was a little disheveled, and his jacket had the faint scent of familiar food, like he'd made a pit stop for coney dogs on his way over. He must have passed Celeste on her way out. For once, though, Pen didn't make any snide remarks or try to needle me with sarcasm. He just slid onto a stool at the counter, opened his laptop, and stared at the screen, the light from it reflecting faintly in his glasses.

I grabbed a second cup, poured him some coffee, and set it in front of him. Neither of us spoke. We didn't need to. The weight of everything that had happened hung between us, heavy and unspoken, like the rich scent of fresh espresso filling the air.

My thoughts churned like the cream swirling in my coffee. Should I run after Celeste? Should I return to the magical world, even though I had sworn it off? Could I ignore the power inside me—the thing that felt both foreign and a part of me at the same time? What about the knowledge I shouldn't have but somehow did, like an old book I'd read and forgotten until now?

The questions twisted and tangled in my mind, refusing to let me go. I gripped my mug tightly, the ceramic warm against my hands, grounding me. My gaze drifted to the window, where the first snow of the season was beginning to fall in soft, tentative flakes. Outside, the city moved on, oblivious to the battles fought and the secrets unearthed just beneath its surface.

I took a sip of coffee, letting the warmth spread through me. For the first time in what felt like ages, I allowed myself to breathe—really breathe. The chaos, the magic, the unanswered questions—they could all wait.

In the quiet, I found something I hadn't felt in a long time: stillness. It wasn't the absence of problems or the resolution of conflict. It was the eye of the storm, a fleeting moment of calm before this new world spun into motion once more. And in that stillness, I realized something.

The answers would come. Maybe not all at once, maybe not in the way I wanted, but they would come. And when they did, I would face them. Not because I had to, but because I wanted to. Because the world—magical or otherwise—was worth fighting for.

For now, though, the world outside could wait. Celeste, and my love for her, could wait. The entity inside me, the tangled threads of my past, even Tempris—whatever he was scheming—could all wait.

I glanced at Pen, who was sipping his coffee in silence, the faint hum of his laptop the only sound in the shop. He glanced up, catching my eye, and gave me a nod—not his usual smirk, but something softer, almost understanding.

In this quiet moment, I was exactly where I needed to be.

And for now, that was enough.

# About the Author

Donny Wilson was born and raised in the vibrant city of Detroit, MI, where the rich cultural landscape sparked his lifelong love of the arts. A storyteller at heart, Donny has explored writing, filmmaking, and theater as tools for connection, transformation, and truth.

A graduate of Wayne State University with a degree in Film Studies, he has spent years mentoring youth and championing creative expression in his community. Whether guiding young filmmakers or building stories of his own, Donny believes deeply in the power of narrative to inspire and empower.

Though screenwriting has long been his preferred medium, the story of Nolan West demanded to be told in novel form. *Motor City Magic* is the result—a blend of imagination, culture, and the soul of Detroit.

This is Donny's first novel, but it won't be his last. He invites you to join him as the adventure continues.

www.ingramcontent.com/pod-product-compliance
Lightning Source LLC
Chambersburg PA
CBHW051338020726
47501CB00007B/2151